**Also available from
Susan Andersen
and Harlequin HQN**

Susan Andersen

Some Like it Hot

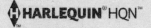
HARLEQUIN® HQN™

ISBN-13: 978-0-373-77776-1

SOME LIKE IT HOT

Printed in U.S.A.

www.Harlequin.com

Dear Reader,

I am so excited about this second book in my new Razor Bay series. You first met Max Bradshaw in *That Thing Called Love,* where he took his "man of few words" reputation to new heights when he caught sight of Harper Summerville. Max's tongue might get tied in a few knots around the sophisticated newcomer, but in a town the size of Razor Bay, he can't avoid her.

Many of you know the setting of fictional Razor Bay holds special meaning for me. I plunked it down on the precise spot on Hood Canal—a sixty-five-mile saltwater fjord in western Washington—where my folks built a little cabin when I was nine. Long before that, I'd spend two weeks every summer running wild with my brothers and cousins, swimming in icy, buoyant water until my fingers and toes were pruney, playing until the sun sank behind the soaring Olympic Mountains, roasting marshmallows and hot dogs over blazing bonfires. This, to me, is the most wonderful spot on earth.

I imbued Max with my love for this incredible corner of the world. Having spent too many years in war-torn countries, he has no plans to leave Razor Bay again. But he'll have his work cut out for him convincing Harper to share a life with him there....

~Susan

This is dedicated
with love
to
Jen and Margo
For always making me look way better than I would
without your priceless participation

And
to
the Mazama Crew:
Ken, Sue, Ron, Steve, Doug, Mimi, Martha & Gary
for the marvelous food, music, skiing,
snowshoeing and shopping.
And, oh, mama, for all the *laughter,* which is the glue
that glitters through everything else.

Love you all

~Susie

Some Like it Hot

CHAPTER ONE

OH, MY GOD. Is he coming here?

Before Harper Summerville glanced out her front window to see Max Bradshaw striding up the sun-dappled trail between the evergreens on the inn grounds, she'd been enjoying her day off. It was fun puttering around the little playhouse-size one-room-plus-loft cottage that was part of her employee compensation as the summer activities coordinator for The Brothers Inn. She loved, loved, loved the glimpses she could catch from up here of the fjord that was Hood Canal and the soaring Olympic mountains beyond it. The spectacular scenery was what brought people to the little resort town of Razor Bay, Washington.

Seeing a huge, unsmiling man bearing down on her, however, made that enjoyment falter. And her heartbeat inexplicably pick up its pace.

He looked different than he had during their previous two brief meetings. Plus, the first time she'd seen him, as well as on the handful of occasions when she'd glimpsed him around town, he'd been wearing his deputy sheriff's uniform. But there was just no mistaking a guy that big, that hard-looking, that intense and *contained* for anyone else.

She blinked as he suddenly left the path and disappeared from view, then shook her head at herself. *Oh, good show, Harper. Conceited much?* Because, despite her cottage being the only one up here before the trail wound into the woods, it apparently hadn't been Bradshaw's destination. Breathing a sigh of relief—right?—she plugged in her earbuds and turned back to the couple of boxes she'd put off unpacking.

Within moments, she'd revived her earlier enjoyment. She loved seeing new places, loved meeting new people and diving into a new job that was never quite like any other. Since she'd structured her life to do exactly that, she was generally a happy woman.

Harper sang along with Maroon 5 as they played through her earbuds. As she efficiently unpacked the boxes of odds and ends her mother had insisted on sending her, she swiveled her hips and bopped in time to the music.

Thoughts of her mother's hopes and expectations for her, however, elicited a sigh in the midst of crooning along with Adam Levine. Gina Summerville-Hardin refused to believe that Harper could live very contentedly without a permanent base or a host of belongings, since making a home had been *her* way of coping with the constant moving from place to place that had been part and parcel of her husband's work. Neither Gina nor Harper's brother, Kai, had loved the adventure of seeing new countries and meeting new people the way Harper and her dad had.

Still, Harper had to admit that she adored the throw pillows and candles her mom had sent. They added a homey touch to her minuscule cabin. Admitting as much certainly didn't take away from how she chose to live and honor her dad's memory.

All the same, when the song ran its course, she

thumbed through her playlist and pulled up her father's onetime theme song.

"'Papa was a rolling stone,'" she sang along with The Temptations as she focused on finding a place to put the other items her mother had sent, given that storage space was at a premium. "'Wherever he—'"

Something warm brushed her elbow. Her heart climbing her throat like a monkey riding a rocket, she jerked her chin downward. She stared at the rawboned, big-knuckled masculine hand touching her.

And screamed the house down.

"Shit!" Max Bradshaw's voice exclaimed as she ripped the earbuds from her ears and whirled to face him.

He was in the midst of taking a long-legged step away from her. His big hands were up, palms out, as if she had a howitzer aimed at his heart.

"Ms. Summerville—Harper—I'm sorry," he said in a low, rough voice. "I knocked several times and I heard you singing, so I knew you were here. But I shouldn't have let myself in." Slowly lowering his hands, he stuffed them into his shorts pockets and his massive shoulders hunched up. "I sure didn't mean to scare the sh—that is, stuffing out of you."

Even through the embarrassment of knowing he'd seen her shaking her butt and singing off-key, it struck her that these were probably the most words she'd ever heard him string together at one time in her presence. Drawing in a deep breath and dropping the hands she'd clasped to her heart like an overwrought silent film heroine confronted by the mustache-twirling villain, she pulled herself together. "Yes, well, intention or not, Deputy Bradshaw—"

"Max," he interjected.

"Max," she agreed, wishing she'd simply said that in the first place. After all, not only had they been introduced on the day she'd interviewed for her job at the inn but they'd attended the same barbecue just a couple weeks ago. "As I was saying—"

Her already open front door banged against the living room wall, and they both whirled to stare at the man barreling through it. From the corner of her eye, Harper saw Max reach for his right hip, where his gun no doubt usually resided.

The stranger's forward momentum carried him across the threshold and into the small room, the screen door slapping closed behind him. As he left the glare of sunlight flooding the porch, he coalesced into a tall, gangly man in his mid-thirties.

Then he was blocked from view as Max stepped in front of her. She leaned to peer around him.

"Are you okay, miss?" the man demanded, glancing about wildly. She assumed his eyes had adjusted to the dimmer interior lighting, for it was obvious from the way they suddenly widened that he'd gotten his first good look at Max. His prominent Adam's apple rode the column of his throat as he swallowed audibly.

For good reason. Max was six-four if he was an inch and probably weighed in the vicinity of two-twenty.

Every ounce of it solid muscle.

But Harper had to give the resort guest credit. He was clearly outmatched, yet while he looked as though he'd give a bundle to go back out the way he'd come in, he instead moved closer and ordered firmly, "Step away from her, sir."

"Oh, for God sake," she heard Max mutter, and hysterical laughter bubbled up Harper's throat. She swallowed it down as she watched Max do as directed.

Then she looked at the resort guest. "I'm okay," she said soothingly. "It's really not what you must think." She ran him through her mental database. "You're Mr. Wells, right? I believe your wife is in my sunset yoga class."

"Sean Wells," he agreed, shedding some of the tension that caused him to all but vibrate.

"This is Deputy Bradshaw," she said. "I screamed because I had my earbuds in and he startled me."

Sean relaxed a bit more, but he shot Max a skeptical look as he took in the bigger man's khaki cargo shorts, black muscle shirt and the tribal tattoos that swirled down his right upper arm from the muscular ball of his shoulder to the bottom of his hard biceps. "You don't look like a deputy."

The dark-eyed gaze Max fixed on him froze the other man in place. "It's my day off," he said with "Just the facts, ma'am" directness.

Harper had no idea why she found that so damn titillating.

"I just came by to ask Ms. Summerville to dinner," he added, and shock whipped her head around.

She gaped at him. "You did?" *Crap.* Was that her voice cracking on the last word? She hardly ever lost her poise. But in her own defense, during their previous encounters she'd gotten the impression Max viewed her as a mental lightweight. She would have sworn, too, that she hadn't even registered on his Attraction-O-Meter.

"Yes." Dull color climbed his angular face. "That

is, Jake sent me. Jenny's having a dinner party tonight and wants you to come." Glancing away, he leveled an are-you-still-here look on Sean Wells.

The man immediately mumbled an excuse and melted out the door.

"Thank you," Harper called after him, then quirked an eyebrow when the deputy turned back to her. "You sure know how to clear a room."

"Yeah." The shoulder with the tattoo lifted and dropped. "It's a talent of mine." He gave her a level look. "So, what do you want me to tell Jenny? You in or you out for tonight?"

"I'm in. What should I bring?"

"You're asking me? I'm the guy who usually shows up with a six-pack of beer."

She grinned at him. "I'll call Jenny."

He didn't smile back—yet something in his expression lightened, which might have been his version of one. Hard to tell, since his deep voice contained its usual crispness when he said, "Good idea. I'll leave it to you to let her know you're coming, then. So." He gave her the terse nod she remembered from their earlier encounters. "Sorry about scaring you. I guess I'll see you tonight." He turned for the door.

"I guess you will," she murmured to his already retreating back. She trailed in his wake as far as the screen door and watched through it as he strode down the path. She didn't turn away until he disappeared around a bend.

Wow. Nothing, not even the photograph she'd seen of him in the dossier the Sunday's Child's investigator had sent her, could adequately describe the sheer impact of the man in the flesh.

Then a small smile curved up the corners of her lips, and she shook her head. "At least this time he didn't call me ma'am."

MAX BANGED THROUGH the door to the upstairs room that his half brother, Jake, used as a workspace. Striding right up to the long desk where Jake sat, he stopped, slapped his hands down on its surface and leaned his weight on them. "She said yes. She'll come." He sternly ignored the way his heart rate continued to rev from those brief moments spent with Harper. "I still don't know why the hell you couldn't just invite her yourself—it's *your* fiancée's party."

"Like I told you, bro." Jake dragged his attention away from the computer monitor he'd been studying. "I've been home four lousy days, and they've got me on one of the tightest deadlines of my life."

"What's their big rush?" he demanded, all jazzed up and more than willing to take it out on his younger half brother. God knew that had been their mutual M.O. up until a few months ago. "Hell, you only lasted ten days of the three weeks you were supposed to be gone before you turned around and came home again. Shouldn't they have all kinds of extra time?" Pushing back, he folded his arms over his chest and gave Jake an assessing gaze. "For a guy who was in such a red-hot rush to get out of Razor Bay, you sure seem to have developed a taste for it."

"Yeah." Jake smiled. "You can blame Jenny and Austin for that."

"No fooling." Max's half brother had come back this spring to claim his newly orphaned, then-thirteen-year-old son Austin, whom he'd walked away from when he was just a teenager himself. His plan to haul the kid back to New York with him had hit the skids when he'd instead fallen head over heels in love not only with Austin but with the Inn's manager, Jenny Salazar, who had been a sister to his son in everything but blood.

Thinking about their relationship set off the "something's not adding up" instincts Max never ignored. "Why do you think Jenny decided on a dinner party when she knows your deadline?"

"Beats the hell outta me."

He found that hard to believe and simply fixed Jake in his best cop gaze.

And was tickled to see his half brother squirm.

"Okay," Jake said, giving the monitor a concentrated attention Max found suspicious, considering how rapidly he opened and closed the photo thumbnails, "I may not have stressed to her how short my deadline is."

"Seriously? Didn't stress or didn't mention it at all?"

"I might have forgotten to mention it." Jake essayed a negligent shrug, then gave up pretending to work. "Hey, if Jenny wants a party, then a party she gets." His smile was so fatuous Max was embarrassed for him.

"Okay. But getting back to your cut-short trip, what's *National Explorer's* hurry?"

"Unlike you, they never really expected it to take me the entire three weeks to do the job. And it was always understood I'd turn in the preliminary shots for them to choose from within a week of my return."

"So what you're saying is it isn't really the tightest deadline of your life."

Jake frowned up at him. "What the hell, Max—you gonna break out the hose and bright lights next?"

"Hey, I'm just trying to get things to add up. Like, if

you knew that seven-day deadline thing going in, why aren't you further along?"

"Uh, I might have spent most of it getting it on with Jenny."

"Jesus, do not *tell* me stuff like that!" Max involuntarily shuddered. "It makes me wanna scrub my brain with industrial-strength bleach to get the image out of my head." Until his half brother had come to town, he'd never once thought of Jenny as a sexual being.

Jake snorted. "Please. You're just jealous because you've got no women to roll around with."

Max's mind immediately went to the woman in the little cabin nestled just this side of the woods in the back acre of the resort. *Harper.* Of the beautiful creamy light brown skin. Of those big olive-green eyes and dark spiral curls. That smoky voice. He'd give his left *nut* to roll around—

With a rough, impatient jerk of his head to shake her image out of it, he said, "Hey, I could get a woman just…like…that!" He snapped his fingers under Jake's nose. Except he wasn't interested in any of the ones he could get. He was fascinated by Harper Summerville, and had been since he'd first clapped eyes on her when she'd shown up at Team Photo Day with Jenny.

He scowled at his half brother. "Next time find somebody else to run your errands. You're a dad, for God's sake. Why didn't you just order your kid to do it?"

"Would've if I could've, bro, but it's summer, he's fourteen and he's off in his boat somewhere with Nolan and Bailey, and bound to be gone all day. Besides—" Jake shot him a sideways glance "— didn't I carve some precious time outta my schedule to make coffee for you?"

"Big whoop."

"Hey, I showed you my *work*. Shared the genius of my very efficiently taken-in-ten-days photographs with you. I don't do that for just anyone, you know."

"And it was real special." He deliberately made his tone sardonic, but the truth was, getting to see his half brother's talent in a behind-the-scenes way…well, it really had been a treat. It wasn't every day a guy got to see hundreds of freshly downloaded photos taken in various locations throughout Africa by a well-known *National Explorer* magazine photographer.

He walked over to the open window of The Sand Dollar, the luxury cabin Jake had been renting on The Brothers Inn grounds since he'd come to town, and faked an interest in the eagle flying through the compound with a seagull and several crows hot on its tail. Watched as the summer breeze sent the heavy boughs to swaying in the evergreens that dotted the grounds.

Then he shoved his hands deep into his pockets and looked over his shoulder at his half brother.

Damned if even under deadline pressure, Jake didn't look like Mr. Upscale with his expensively cut sun-streaked brown hair and his pale green hundred-dollar silk T-shirt the exact same shade as his eyes.

Max still found it amazing that he and Jake were developing an honest-to-God relationship after almost an entire lifetime spent hating each other's guts. Who would have ever predicted that? Not him, that was for damn sure. Yet the fact that they were made it easier to turn around and admit, "It really was pretty awesome to see some of your process for winnowing down all those photos." His eyebrows drew together. "Doesn't mean you don't still owe me, though."

"Right," Jake said in a tone that was desert dry. "It being so tedious and all, having to talk to a pretty woman."

"She's not *pretty,* you idiot, she's beautiful. And have you *forgotten* the other two times you've seen me talk to her?" The way he'd lost all verbal skills when he'd found himself thrown in her company those times was nothing short of pathetic. He was a damn deputy sheriff— hell, a former *marine,* for God's sake. He could usually talk to anyone.

Except the silver-spoon girls.

"Oh." Jake sobered. "Yeah. You were really pitiful." He gave a decisive nod. "Okay. I do owe you."

"Damn straight," he muttered. "Although I will admit I didn't do as badly today. Which is a damn good thing," he said drily. "Embarrassing myself like that again doesn't bear thinking about. Not when I've got such ready access to an entire arsenal I could use to put myself out of my misery."

Jake raised skeptical brows. "Get real. You and I both know you're too much of a hard-ass pragmatist—never mind that law-and-order thing you're so wedded to—to ever choose such a permanent solution to a temporary problem." He shot Max a cheerful smile. "And look on the bright side, bro—you can only improve."

"Hell, yeah," Max said sarcastically, heading for the door. "How can I not, with faithful encouragement like that to prop me up? Get to work. I've got stuff to do, too—I can't hang around here all day. I'll see you at Jenny's at seven."

But as he loped down the staircase to the first floor, he thought, *From your lips to God's ear.* Because improvement couldn't come quickly enough to suit him.

He let himself out the front door of The Sand Dollar, allowing the screen door to bang shut behind him. Not nearly quickly enough.

For he was sure as hell tired of acting more tongue-tied than a horny thirteen-year-old with his first crush every time he stumbled across Harper Summerville.

CHAPTER TWO

MAX SLAMMED HIS car door and hotfooted it across the little parking lot to the back of Jenny's cottage. He took the stubby flight of stairs up to her mudroom in two big steps.

He hadn't deliberately been late for her dinner party. After leaving Jake's he'd gone out to Cedar Village, the group home for at-risk boys a few miles out of town. And he'd ended up staying longer than he'd planned.

Which was hardly a surprise, considering it was the same thing he did every time he went out there. At one time he'd been an angry teen himself. He knew what it was to get into his share of trouble, knew about having anger he didn't quite know how to manage. So he liked volunteering some of his free time to work with the kids. He understood where they were coming from.

But he'd let the time get away from him. The boys had roped him into a vigorous game of basketball, and the demand that he join them had been the first sign of softening he'd seen from a couple of the kids. If he'd blown off the opening they'd given him, he would've risked having them never give him another. That hadn't been an option.

He was already running late when he'd finally pulled himself away, but he'd had no choice but to go home for a quick shower and a change. Jenny, bless her heart, threw reasonably casual parties, but he was pretty sure she'd expect him to at least shave and throw on something a bit less scruffy than his day-off knock-around clothes. Especially when Jake, the love of her life, was one of those *GQ*-type dressers. And he didn't even want to think about what she'd have to say if he showed up smelling as ripe as only a guy who'd pounded up and down a court with boys who could run him into the ground could.

He smoothed his hand down the navy T-shirt he'd tucked tightly into his low-slung jeans to get the drawer wrinkles out. Straightened the button placket of the loose weave, sage-green short-sleeved shirt he'd worn open over it to dress things up a little. Shifting the six-pack of Fat Tire beer that Jake preferred to the Budweiser Max would have chosen were it just for him, he rapped on the mudroom door.

It whipped open, and the sound of dishes clattering and women laughing in the kitchen poured out at him. He looked down into the face of his nephew, Austin.

"Dude!" The fourteen-year-old, who was at that all shoulders, arms and legs stage, grinned at him. "Thank God—we *need* more guys here. Jenny invited way more chicks."

"Oh, way more, my butt." Jenny stuck her head into the room, her shiny brown hair catching the overhead light. "I invited a couple of women from work who didn't have plans. Hey, Max." She crossed the small space at the same time he stepped into the mudroom.

Having learned her ways, he obligingly bent so she could give him a hug. That was something new to him, and he always stood stiff as an oar in her embrace. Considering she kept *doing* it every time he arrived or left, however, Jenny apparently didn't mind.

And he had to admit, there was something nice about it—even if it did make him feel awkward as a working girl at a revival.

Jenny was a tiny woman who somehow failed to realize it, and she gave him a quick, fierce squeeze before stepping back. "The men are out on the front porch doing the barbecue thing," she said, patting his arm. "Why don't you take your beer out there—we put a cooler with ice and soft drinks to the right of the door."

She turned to Austin. "What are you doing this close to the kitchen if you're so uncomfortable with all the women?"

The kid puffed up. "I'm not *uncomfortable,*" he protested. "I'm just saying there's a bunch of 'em, and we guys are outnumbered. I only came out here 'cuz I'm lookin' for the croquet set. Dad said maybe we could play a game after dinner."

"Color me corrected." Reaching up, she ruffled his dark hair. "Set's in the shed."

Austin grinned at her and loped out the door.

Not all that certain he was ready to face a kitchen full of females himself, Max took a step back. "Well, I'll just head for the porch. Nice day, huh?"

She flashed him a smile he was pretty sure said, *Yeah, right, like you're fooling anyone.* But she truly was the nice woman he'd always considered her, because she simply rubbed his arm again and said, "You bet."

Jenny's best friend poked her strawberry-blond head in the room. "Jen, where can I find— Oh, hi, Max."

"Hey, Tasha. How's it going?"

"Pretty darn good." She eyed him where he stood

with one foot in the door and the other out on the stoop. "You coming in?"

"I was just gonna duck around to the front and say hi to the guys."

She raised an eyebrow. "Intimidated by the number of women in the kitchen, huh?"

"Completely—and that's without even knowing exactly how many that is." He got a sudden vision of how ludicrous he was being and smiled.

Tasha blinked. "Whoa," she said. "You really oughtta do that more often."

"What?"

"Smile," Jenny filled in for her friend. "You've got a great one, but you hardly ever use it."

"That's because I save 'em up for the prettiest girls," he said with rare flirtatiousness. "Annnd I really am going to the front now."

He heard them laugh as he strode down the stairs.

Climbing the front porch stairs a moment later, he spotted Jake and Mark, Austin's best bud's dad. "Whoa. This is it? Austin wasn't kidding when he said we were seriously outnumbered by chicks."

"Wendy Chapman brought her new boyfriend," Mark said, then shrugged. "But he's in that shit-faced-in-new-love stage, so he's hanging with the women in the kitchen."

They all shook their heads at the mystery of that.

Jake looked at the six-pack in Max's fist and laughed. "Hey, you brought the good stuff. There's some Bud in the cooler for you."

Refusing to acknowledge the blanket of warmth his half brother's thoughtfulness wrapped around his heart, Max made room in the cooler for the Fat Tire bottles, then fished out a Budweiser. He drank the beer, stuck his two cents in on how best to barbecue the steaks—because, really, what guy could keep his opinions to himself when fire, sharp utensils and red meat were involved?—and jawed with Jake and Mark.

He set up a long table when Jenny asked for a volunteer and Jake refused to relinquish the barbecue fork—then eyed a couple of the women as they decked it out with a tablecloth before dealing out festive plastic plates, silverware and napkins. They even plunked down a vase of flowers in the middle.

Then Harper carried out a big bowl of salad greens, and he was hard pressed to keep his gaze from following her every move.

Sometimes there was a stillness about her that made her look like a queen. Maybe it was the way she was put together: all exotic coloring, long lines and good bones. Or her posture, so proudly tall. Hell, maybe it was the solemnity of her full mouth in repose or the heavy-lidded eyes that gave her that appearance of aloof distance. Whatever it was, it reinforced the well-educated rich-girl image that never failed to tie his tongue in knots.

He didn't know where it had come from, this awkwardness he had around the silver-spoon girls. Surely it didn't go all the way back to the sixth grade crush he'd had on Heather Phillips. His mother had pointed out, with her usual I'm-unhappy-with-the-world surliness, that the girl was too damn rich for the likes of him.

Hell, it wasn't like he'd been bothered by Mom's flatly stated warning that he'd better not expect an invitation to any of *that* kid's parties anytime soon. She hadn't been wrong. And even if she had been, aside from the subject of his father, he'd mostly blown off Angie Bradshaw's negativity. If he'd allowed it to stop him from doing things or going after what he wanted, he would've been paralyzed a long time ago.

Because, face it, the woman bitched about *everything,* and had from the moment his dad had left them for Jake's mom.

But coming back to Harper, well, he oughtta cut himself some slack. He'd done all right earlier today. Besides, she hadn't been all that aloof when he'd caught her shaking her very nice butt and singing along with music only she could hear. She was also smiling and laughing with Tasha now as they carried out more salads, bread and a fruit platter and arranged them on the table. When she was like this, she radiated a friendliness, a charisma, that was electric.

"Meat's done," Jake said and piled steaks onto a platter.

Jenny carried out a pitcher of sangria damn near as big as she was, and Mark went around to the side of the cottage to call the kids who were setting up a croquet course there. For the next several moments pandemonium reigned as people took seats at the table.

Max sorted everyone out as the food was passed around. There were the teens Austin, Nolan and Austin's girlfriend, Bailey, plus Nolan's little brother. The unattached females consisted of Tasha, Harper and Sharon, the latter of whom he really didn't know all that well since she'd married a local who had graduated a good fifteen years ahead of him. They'd divorced a couple of years ago, and she had stayed to run the housekeeping department at the inn while the local had moved to Tacoma. Then there was him, Jake and Jenny, Mark and his wife, Rebecca, and Wendy, who owned Wacka Do's Salon on Harbor Street, and her new guy, Keith somebody or another.

The platters completed their circuit, and the laughter and chatter quieted down as everyone dug in.

A while later Tasha leaned forward to look down the table at Harper. "I saw the advertisement in the new brochures for the sunset yoga class you teach. I could use something like that. I'm not nearly bendy enough." She appraised Harper. "You, on the other hand, look real flexible."

Harper flashed the smile that changed her entire look. It was wide and heart-shaped and showcased not only bright teeth that looked as though someone had sunk a fortune into them, but a flash of the healthy gums in which they were anchored, as well. "You should drop in sometime," she said. "I doubt Jenny would mind that you're not an inn guest, since she told me you're her bestie."

"Oh, please." Jenny, who was sitting next to Tasha, grinned. "*Be* my guest."

Her friend gave her a friendly bump, but continued to address Harper. "You know, I'd definitely take you up on that—if it wasn't right in the middle of my busiest time."

"That's right. You're the owner of the pizza parlor in town, aren't you?"

"Yep. Bella T's."

"I haven't had a chance to try it yet, but I hear it's fabulous."

"Best pizza anywhere," Austin's friend Nolan said through a mouthful of corn on the cob.

Mark tousled his son's hair but smiled at Harper.

"The execution could have been more elegant, but the sentiment is dead-on."

"Then I'll definitely have to make the effort to get in there." She looked at Tasha. "Let's talk after dinner. We can probably come up with a time that'll work for both of us."

"What did you do before you came here?" Mark's wife, Rebecca, inquired.

"A little of everything—much to my mother's dismay. Since we came back to the States I've taken a number of temp jobs. I've worked at Nordstrom's, for a little college press and a remodeling company and did a stint as a contracts coordinator for a midsized construction company—"

Max didn't plan his interruption, but he couldn't help himself. "Why were you out of the States?" *And who is* we?

She tilted her head and looked into his eyes. "Would you like the long version or the short?"

"Long," all the women said in near perfect synchronicity.

"O-kay." Her olive-green eyes were mostly blocked from sight behind the dense lashes that formed little crescents when she laughed. "My folks met when they were in college and married within two months. Mom is Cuban, African-American and Welsh. My daddy was the only child of an old Winston-Salem family. It was no longer the South of the Sixties in those days, but his parents still weren't thrilled with his marriage. In fact, they went so far as to suggest he annul it."

She shook her head, a small, reminiscent smile curving up her lips. "You'd have to have known my dad to appreciate what a mistake that was. Grandma and

Grandpa did know better, but I guess they panicked, probably worried about what their friends would say." She made a wry face. "Anyhow, Dad's response was to pack his newly minted civil engineering degree and move Mom to Europe. We lived all over the world. I was born in Amsterdam and my brother, Kai, in Dubai."

"Wasn't that hard?" Jenny asked. "Constantly having to pick up and go?"

"No, it really wasn't. I was not only a daddy's girl but a chip off the old block. He and I loved getting to see new places and meet new people. Kai and Mom weren't as thrilled with the constant upheavals." A faint shadow flitted across her eyes. "I think that's why my mother's having trouble with the fact that I continue to travel. She and my brother were beyond happy to settle down after we moved back to the U.S. It bothers her that I haven't done the same."

Tasha planted her chin in her hand. "Did your folks ever reconcile with your grandparents?"

"Yes. Quite early on, actually. I don't personally remember the rift, just the stories about it. By my first memory, they'd come to love Mom almost as much as Dad did. And they were the greatest grandparents." Her smile lit up the room and made something in Max's chest ache.

Jake, who traveled extensively for his magazine, asked Harper about some of the places she'd been, and they compared their impressions from locations they'd both visited. Max sat silently listening...and working overtime not to give in to jealousy. God knew he'd spent far too many years doing exactly that—being resentful of his half brother—already.

But the sophistication of Harper's upbringing dredged

up old insecurities. It was a universe removed from the way he'd been raised, and chewing over the contrasts between their worlds, watching the ease with which Jake conversed with her, it was hard not to regress to feelings he'd thought safely in his rearview. He could feel them crowding in, however, demanding attention. He pushed them back, because damned if he'd allow the same tangled morass of twisted emotions he'd once had for his half brother to regain the purchase they'd claimed when he was a kid. He wasn't giving way to them now that he and Jake were finally in a good place.

Their mutual father had left Max and his mother when Max was just a toddler. If Charlie Bradshaw had simply left town as he had when he ultimately deserted Jake and his mother, as well, things might have been different. Or if Max had had a different kind of mother…

He gave an impatient twitch of his shoulders. Because neither of those things had happened. Charlie was one of those men who was all about the current family. In Max's case that had meant Jake and the second Mrs. Bradshaw. He'd seen the old man with them around town sometimes. It had been damn hard to miss, given the size of Razor Bay. So he'd witnessed Charlie acting the way Max assumed a dad should toward Jake, while *he* might as well have been the incredible Invisible Boy, so concealed had he appeared to be from his father's sight.

Even with his mind mired in the past, he was aware of Harper across the table, and he tracked her movements as she reached for the pitcher of sangria. The container was still fairly full, the distance wasn't optimum for her reach and he watched its weight immediately tip forward as she picked it up. Surging to his feet, he leaned across the table to steady the pitcher and slapped his free hand over hers on the handle to correct the forward momentum.

It was as if he'd grabbed the business end of a live wire. Heat streaked like lightning through his veins, and it wouldn't have surprised him in the least if someone started slapping at his head and yelling that his hair was smoking. He wondered if she felt it, too, or if this began and ended with him. She'd gone very still, and those big eyes were locked on him and rounded in the same O as her lips. But, hell, that could very well be due to the sheer speed of the events from her reach for the pitcher, to its tipping, to him leaping to the rescue like a tattooed, beefed up version of Dudley Do-Right.

The instant the pitcher touched the tabletop again— this time nearer her where its entire weight wouldn't be dangling from her hand with no arm muscle behind it for support—he yanked his hands clear. Thumped back into his chair.

He did his best to ignore the residual electricity zinging through him from the feel of her skin. Making a point of not looking at her again, he deliberately forced his thoughts back to the relative safety of his old animosity toward Jake.

His mom sure as hell hadn't helped the situation. Not that he'd seen that at the time; it wasn't until he was old enough and distanced enough to view the situation with an adult's perspective that he'd realized if Angie Bradshaw had been a different kind of woman, he probably wouldn't have suffered much damage from the desertion. Hell, he'd barely been two years old when Charlie had moved out. Most of the memories of actual time spent with his father had come through the home movies Charlie had left behind.

His mother, however, wasn't a big believer in letting things go. Rarely had a day gone by that she hadn't reminded him of what they'd lost. All he'd ever heard were acid-etched stories of the slut who'd stolen his father away, and of his little shit of a half brother who had gotten everything that should have been his.

It hadn't helped that in school his half bro had been a serious student and run with the kids of Razor Bay's movers and shakers, while *he* had pulled average grades, run with a wilder crowd and frequently gotten into trouble.

No wonder he was so fucked up when it came to the silver-spoon girls. They were simply the female version of Jake.

"Max?"

The sound of Harper's voice snatched him from his stroll down memory lane, and as his awareness raced to catch up with his inner musings, he realized his name hadn't been the first word she'd directed at him. Looking at her across the table, he felt the same crazy-ass clench of his heart he experienced every damn time he laid eyes on her.

And clearing his throat, he lied without compunction. "Sorry. I was thinking about work for a minute there. What did you say?"

"I was just asking what you did with the rest of your day off after I saw you."

Okay, this was something he actually *liked* talking about. "I went out to Cedar Village." He was surprised to see startled recognition in her eyes and raised his brows. "You're familiar with it?"

"I've heard it mentioned, although I can't remember where. It's a…boys' camp?"

Jake snorted, and Max gave her a one-sided smile. "Don't mind him, he thinks it's more like a reformatory. It's actually a group home for troubled kids—boys. And, yeah, most of them have been in trouble. But, so was I at their age and—"

"Look how well that turned out," Jake deadpanned.

He grinned at the sarcasm in his broth—*half* brother's voice. "I know, damn good, right? For instance, unlike Mr. Shutterbug here, instead of playing with cameras, I have a real job."

Harper was staring at him, and his smile faded, his self-consciousness resurfacing. But damned if he'd allow it to short-shrift his responsibility to the Cedar boys. He rolled his shoulders. "Anyhow, a lot of these kids come from dicked-up backgrounds—broken homes, substance-abusing mother or father or sometimes both. None of our boys' parents are physically abusive, but some are purposefully neglectful, while others simply have to work killer hours just to put food on the table or hang on to their house. A few of the boys actually come from warm, involved families—they just lost their way for a while or fell in with the wrong crowd. In every case, they need the attention, the *stability* that the counselors out there provide."

"Is that what you are—a counselor, as well as a deputy?"

"Me?" That startled another one-sided quirk of his lips from him. He shook his head. "Nah. I'm on the board of directors, but mostly I just hang out with the boys. But, *speaking* of my board position…"

Everyone except Mark's youngest son and the woman

named Sharon groaned, and Max laughed outright. "That's right, boys and girls. It's put-up-or-shut-up time. Our pancake breakfast fund-raiser is next Sunday. I know most of you have already bought tickets, but we also need volunteers to help man it. I just happen to have a sign-up sheet in my car."

"Can we be excused, Jenny?" Austin asked, hastily pushing back from the table. His friends Nolan and Bailey followed suit. "We have to finish setting up the croquet stuff."

"I'll take that as a yes," Max said. "You guys wanna be waitstaff or work in the kitchen?"

"Aw, *man!* Do we hafta?"

"We have several boys from the Village who'll be working the event, but we could really use more help." He looked his nephew in the eye. "These kids haven't had the advantages you've had. It's for a good cause."

Austin sighed but nodded. So did his sidekicks. Max turned his attention to the adults.

"Don't look at me," said Sharon. "Those boys scare the crap out of me."

"No, c'mon. They're just kids."

She shrugged. "Doesn't matter, they still scare me. I'll buy a ticket, though."

He knew better than to feel resentful on the kids' behalf, but it took a little effort to say mildly, "Thanks, that'll help. You want the eight or nine-thirty sitting?"

"I'll take the eight."

"You can sign me up to help," Harper said.

Max's head whipped around. *Oh, yeah, baby.* Sternly telling his libido it was out of line and to take a damn seat, he raised a brow. "Yeah?"

"Yes, sure. I have next Sunday off and it would be

a good way to see the town in action. I'll wait tables. I can get to know more people that way."

"Excellent. Thank you." He leaned back in his chair and looked around the table. "Now, that's what I'm talking about, people. Harper and the kids just gave us a decent start here. So, how 'bout the rest of you?" He gestured with uncharacteristic expansiveness. "Step right up, ladies and gents. The line forms to the left."

CHAPTER THREE

LAUGHTER, DEEP, LOUD and masculine, rolled out of the community center kitchen and across the counter where Harper had just picked up her industrial-sized platter of pancakes. She froze for an instant, and the chatter and clatter of crowded tables full of hungry pancake diners faded away as she searched the packed kitchen for the laugh's source.

Not that there was any doubt as to whose large chest *that* had come out of. She'd only heard it once before, and God knew it hadn't been directed at her. But no one who'd ever heard Max Bradshaw laugh would mistake it for anyone else's. Even someone as new to Razor Bay as she was grasped it was a rarity. Hell, a simple grin from him at Jenny's dinner party earlier this week had all but knocked her on her butt. His laugh was a steamroller that threatened to flatten her.

She needed to keep in mind that all this interest was one-sided. And, c'mon, how hard could it be to do so—she only had to remember Max's assistance at Jenny's when she'd tried to pick up the sangria pitcher from too far away and had nearly poured it all over the picnic table instead. His touch when he'd wrapped his hand around hers had all but electrified her—exactly the way it had the first time they'd met when she'd touched his bare forearm. It wasn't possible for a man's skin to be any hotter than anyone else's. So why did her mind insist it was?

She gave her head a subtle shake. The answer to that hardly mattered, so there was no sense even going there. Because if she'd been electrified, *he* had shaken free so fast you would've thought she was toxic waste, and he without his hazmat suit. Charm had always come easily to her, but either her ability abandoned her around the good deputy or he was immune. Either way, her mad skills were wasted on him.

She located him now over by the gargantuan stove, standing head—and in most cases shoulders, as well—above the boys around him. He looked like a Hell's Angel with those brown-ink tribal tattoos, his disreputably torn blue jeans and that brilliantly white, batter-splattered T-shirt that clung damply to his big shoulders and muscular chest. The faded blue bandanna tied around his dark hair only added to the image.

But his face was alight with whatever amusement had set him off, his teeth flashing a white bright enough to rival his T-shirt's, and most of the teens gaped at him as if he were a rock star. Given the absorption with which she was staring at him herself, she could hardly blame them. If their interactions with the guy were anything like her own admittedly limited exchanges, they, too, were likely more accustomed to seeing him sober and serious.

Forcing herself to get back to the business at hand, she turned away to carry her tray over to one of the long tables in her area. "Who's ready for more pancakes?" she demanded cheerfully.

And only glanced over her shoulder once to make

sure that Max was no longer visible from this vantage point.

A largely male-voiced roar of enthusiasm from the patrons greeted her question, and she laughed and chatted up people as she dished out fresh stacks to everyone who indicated an interest.

"How's the syrup holding up?" she inquired at one point and, being told that it was getting low, waved one of the teen volunteers over to exchange a full dispenser for the almost empty one. She summoned two other helpers as well to refill empty glasses from the pitchers of water and orange juice they manned.

"Megan, Joe, hello!" She forked pancakes onto the plates of two guests from the inn who had been in her guided kayak tour the day before. "I'm so glad you made it."

Joe grinned. "Seriously good pancakes. *We're* glad you told us about it."

She laughed. The pancakes were decent but nowhere close to seriously good. But they were plentiful, and the atmosphere in the hall was loud, cheerful and fun, all of which she suspected contributed to the food tasting better.

She ran out of pancakes halfway through the next table and almost mowed down Tasha on her way back to the kitchen for another refill. "Oh, hey, sorry." Reaching out, she steadied the other woman's tray, which unlike her own was loaded. "I wasn't looking where I was going—I was too busy marveling at the pancake-eating contest over there." She indicated a table on the stage at the end of the cavernous hall.

"I know, it's always kind of like watching jackals

taking down a gazelle. You really want to look away, but find you can't."

"So this isn't just an impulsive boys gone wild event? They've done this before?"

"Oh, yeah, it's an annual event." Tasha tipped her head toward the wiry little guy in the middle packing away an amazing quantity of pancakes. "Greg Larson will likely win. He almost always does. But every now and then, just often enough to keep things interesting, we have an upset." She shrugged and looked at Harper. "How are you holding up?"

"I'm doing great. Upbeat crowds like this give me oomph."

"Well, lucky you, Energizer Bunny." The strawberry blonde gave her a weary smile. "I had a long shift at Bella's last night that ran late, so I'm starting to wilt. And I'd sure like to know how the hell Jenny managed to weasel out of this detail."

Harper shrugged. "She said there was too much to do at the inn."

"Yeah, that's the story she fed me, too." Tasha raised her brows at Harper. "You buy that?"

"Not for a minute. Oh, not that the inn isn't really busy, because it's definitely jumping. But while I haven't been around forever like you natives, I get the impression that Jenny thrives on the summer madness." She looked askance at Tasha, who nodded her agreement.

Harper hitched a shoulder. "That being the case, and going by the fact that Jake's not here, either, my guess would be that they're sneaking some time together to make up for him being out of town."

"Yep. That'd be my take, too." Tasha really looked at Harper. "You know what? You and I should have a girls' night one of these days. Jenny can join us if we can pry her away from Lover Boy, but right now she's deep into that all-Jake-all-the-time stage, so I don't hold my breath over that happening. What do you say? You in?"

"Absolutely." One disadvantage to all of the traveling she'd done in her formative years was that she'd spent considerably more time with adults than people her own age. The upside, of course, was that it had resulted in far more sophisticated experiences than she likely would've received otherwise. But after the age of twelve she hadn't had what most women would consider real girlfriends. Watching Tasha and Jenny together made her feel she'd been missing out.

"Good." Tasha glanced down at her loaded tray. "I'd better pass these out while they're still lukewarm. I'll give you a call, okay? And this time I really mean it. I kind of let the yoga thing get away from me."

Harper executed the particularly French shrug she'd picked up during the eighteen months she and her family had lived in Clermont-Ferrand. "Believe me, I know how that goes."

They parted ways, Tasha plunging into the crowded room and Harper heading back to the food service counter that divided the hall from the kitchen.

She chatted up one of the boys on the other side while he refilled her tray with more pancakes. He'd just finished loading up when a horrendous crash of glass smashing to smithereens made them both jump as if someone had unexpectedly fired off a shotgun next to them. Her head swiveling in the direction of the sound, she focused in on two teenage boys standing in a quickly dissipating wreath of steam from the open door of a huge dishwasher. As she watched, one shoved the other.

"Look what you made me do, you dumb shit!" The shover gave the other, larger, teen another shot to the chest.

"Who the hell you callin' a dumb shit, ass cap?" The bigger boy pushed back, making the first kid stumble back several paces. Following up his advantage, Big Boy dogged the retreating boy's footsteps, thrusting his face into the other youth's. "*You're* the one who backed into me, you stupid fuc—"

"That's enough." Max's deep voice cut through the obscenity, and suddenly he was just *there,* reaching between the boys to separate them. "Sometimes accidents are just accidents. Jeremy, grab the broom."

"Why the hell do *I* have to sweep up his mess?" Big Boy demanded.

"Because we work as a team and I asked you to," Max replied evenly, giving the teen a level look that had Jeremy slouching away. The remaining boy snickered.

Max turned to him. "I wouldn't be too smug if I were you, because you're not off the hook. Go get a dustpan and the mop. After you pick up the glass Jeremy sweeps, you can mop the area."

"Hey!" The slighter boy adopted a belligerent stance. "*He* only hadda do *one* thing. How come I gotta do two?"

"Rules of the road, Owen." Max's voice was matter-of-fact yet somehow as calming as cool water poured over scorched earth. "Jeremy wasn't wrong, you know— you picked up a huge tray of glasses, then backed up without once looking behind you. And the guy going in reverse is always at fault."

"That sucks!"

Max reached out and squeezed the boy's shoulder. "Maybe so. But rules are rules, kid. Go grab the dustpan and mop."

The boy grumbled but did as he was told. Harper picked her tray up off the counter and turned away.

Great. Like it wasn't bad enough that she already harbored a fascination for this guy. Why did he have to go and be good with kids, as well?

She didn't understand this damn attraction; it was so not her general M.O. She'd never gone for the big, physical guys—she was usually drawn to older, more sophisticated men. But Max Bradshaw... Lord, whenever he was near she felt like a vampire trying to do the stay-on-the-straight-and-narrow-blood-bank thing.

All the while scenting a juicy vein.

And if that didn't make everything more complicated, she didn't know what did. Like things weren't convoluted enough already...considering the job with The Brothers Inn wasn't her sole reason for being in Razor Bay.

"You prob'ly better move, lady," the boy who had refilled her tray suddenly said, shaking her out of her reverie.

"What's that?" She blinked, then, following his gaze, glanced over her shoulder. Other volunteers, awaiting their turn, had begun stacking up behind her. "Oops." She flashed them her friendliest smile. "Sorry."

Picking up her tray, she threw herself back into dishing out pancakes.

When the last patron left, Harper nearly did, as well. She had wiped down her tables and straightened the chairs. And since she'd tucked her driver's license into her back pocket so she wouldn't have to deal with a purse, she was good to go.

But looking into the kitchen, she saw Max and his crew still hard at work cleaning up. She could see the boys had about reached their limit of volunteerism, and, with a quiet sigh, she rounded the end of the counter and crossed the kitchen to the teen who was about to carry a stack of plates on which he'd precariously balanced more glasses than was safe. He was the larger of the two boys Max had separated earlier, the one she'd privately labeled Big Boy.

"Let me give you a hand with that," she said, reaching to pluck the glasses off the plates and efficiently stacking them into two towers.

"Thanks, lady." The teen pulled an overhead cupboard open and shoved the plates in. He jerked his head to the cupboard next to his. "Glasses go in there."

"I'm Harper."

"Jeremy," he said in a voice that didn't encourage her to get chatty.

"Nice to meet you." Stepping alongside him, she reached up to set the glasses in her right hand on the shelf. Apparently she'd stacked them just a little too high, however, for the bottom of the uppermost cup bumped the edge of the cupboard and began to tilt back toward her.

Warmth radiated against her back, even though nothing actually touched it. At the same time a suntanned, white-cotton banded biceps came into her peripheral vision, and Max Bradshaw's deep voice said, "Hang on, let me take a couple cups off the top."

It only took him a second, but that moment stretched languorously as a cat after a long nap, her senses bombarded with his heat, with the salty, slightly musky scent of him mixed with that of pancake batter and laundry soap. She eyed the up-close view of the tail end of his tattoos undulating from beneath his sleeve hem with the movement of his arm, then transferred her attention to the muscles and tendons that flexed in his forearm, his rawboned wrist and long hand as he swiftly slid a couple of cups from the stack she still held aloft, dropped them onto the one in her left hand, then removed four or five of those and put them in the cupboard.

"There you go." He stepped back and Harper put the rest of the cups alongside the minitower he'd placed on the shelf.

Exhaling softly, she glanced at him over her shoulder. "Thank you. You seem to have a knack for rescuing me from glassware accidents-about-to-happen."

He stilled for a moment, and something hot and fierce flashed in his eyes. Or perhaps she only imagined it, because in the next instant he gave her a faint smile, polite nod and a murmured, "My pleasure."

Oh, trust me, it was mine, as well.

Probably a less than brilliant idea to go there, however, so she shook the thought aside and injected some starch in her spine. Then, seeing an opportunity and not shy about taking advantage of it, she turned to him fully. "Listen, I only work three-quarter time at the inn. I'd love to volunteer some of my free hours to Cedar Village."

"Yeah?" He studied her through shuttered dark eyes. "What do you have to offer?"

"I don't know. What do volunteers generally do? I'm pretty much a jack-of-all-trades. But what I really rock at is organizing activities. And fund-raising." When he continued to simply look at her with level, noncommittal eyes, she shrugged impatiently. People usually jumped at her fund-raising skills. "If that doesn't work for you, I could always just provide a woman's touch."

"I wouldn't mind a woman's touch," drawled a blond boy who was swabbing down the counter a few feet away, and his tone told Harper he wasn't thinking motherly thoughts.

"That's enough, Brandon," Max said, but it was the look that Harper aimed at the youth that made the boy squirm. It was a thousand-yard stare she'd perfected when she was twelve, a nonthreatening but cool gaze that made the recipient completely question the wisdom of uttering the words that had warranted it in the first place.

"Sorry," Brandon muttered.

"Not a problem." She gave him a slight smile that was warmer without encouraging him to repeat his blunder. Then she turned back to Max. "This won't help for today's event, but I could tell you how to make your next pancake breakfast more profitable. And while I can't promise anything until I talk to Jenny, maybe she'd let us offer the occasional supervised use of some of The Brothers' resources."

Max dug his wallet out of his back pocket, fished out a card and handed it to Harper. "Why don't you give me a call and we'll talk about it. But for now, you should go enjoy the rest of your day off."

Sliding the proffered card into her own back pocket, she nodded, recognizing a dismissal when she heard one. "I'll do that." She glanced at the teen still stacking dishes next to her. "It was nice meeting you, Jeremy." She nodded at the other boys who had stopped working to watch her.

Then she strode to the kitchen door and let herself out.

"Dude," she heard one of the boys say as the door closed behind her. "She's hot. Why'd you let her get away?" There was a beat of silence, then, "Oh, man. It's not because she's black, is it?"

Harper froze. Omigawd. *Was* it? That hadn't even occurred to her, maybe because she'd spent the majority of her life in Europe where race wasn't as big an issue—or at least didn't have the history that it had in the States. But for all she knew—

"*Hell,* no," Max's voice said emphatically. "Listen, kid, men don't hit on every hot woman they see." He was quiet for a moment, then said slowly, "Besides, did she strike you as the kind of woman who would *welcome* me hitting on her?"

Yes! Embarrassing as it was to admit, she definitely would welcome that.

"Nah, I guess not," the boy said.

"Oh, for c'ris—" Harper cut herself off, blew a pithy raspberry and stalked over to her car.

Her feet hurt from being on them all morning and she was cursing having worn her tallest wedged espadrilles as she blew through the front door of her cottage. Loggins and Messina played "Your Mama Don't Dance" on the cell phone she'd deliberately left behind, and she crossed the room and snatched it off the little coffee table.

"Hi, Mom." She kicked off her shoes and headed straight for the mini-fridge, where she pulled out a nice cold bottle of raspberry-green-tea-flavored artesian water. She rolled its cold plastic across her warm forehead.

"Hey, Baby Girl."

Ever since her dad had died—and that had been a few years ago now—she and her mother had been at odds more often than not. So, hearing the nickname gave her a rush of pleasure. Tucking the phone between her ear and shoulder, she twisted the cap off the bottle and drank half of it down in one large swallow.

"For heaven's sake, are you gulping something in my ear? Did your Grandma Hardin and I not teach you better manners than that?"

Harper tried not to feel resentful, she really did. She was thirty years old, for God's sake; long past the age to be either scolded like a child or react as if she were one.

She inhaled and blew out a quiet breath, and *still* a vestige of attitude she simply couldn't expunge colored her voice when she said, "Sorry. I just spent three-plus hours serving pancakes for a Cedar Village fund raiser, and I'm tired and thirsty."

There was an instant of silence. Then Gina Summerville-Hardin said softly, "How did that happen?"

Oh, God, it had been so easy, Harper still couldn't quite believe it. She'd almost fallen off the picnic bench at Jenny's dinner party when Max had presented the opportunity. "My boss's boyfriend's half brother is Max Bradshaw."

The sudden silence was so absolute that Harper began to wonder if they'd lost the connection. "Mom?"

"Yes, I'm still here. The same Max Bradshaw who's on the Cedar Village board?"

"Yes."

"I was quite impressed with his dossier, being both a deputy and a veteran and all. He sounds like a very responsible man. Still, I must say I'm stunned at the coincidence."

For a few seconds, her thoughts got hung up in that touch they'd shared over the sangria pitcher. Then she shrugged it off. "Well, Razor Bay is pretty small. It's tougher to maintain my anonymity in a one stoplight town, but the upside is it's easier to get to know the players, as there are just plain fewer of them. But, man. I thought I was lucky to get the job at The Brothers." A dry laugh escaped her. "I had no idea *how* lucky."

She'd taken the position because it was right up her alley, considering it was the kind of job she'd done before her dad's death had pulled her into the nonprofit charity her parents had started when her father retired his engineering degree. But primarily she'd taken it because ever since she *had* joined the fold, her year-round job had become assessing the worthiness of the less-established charities applying for grants from Sunday's Child. In this case Cedar Village had submitted a request to the family foundation for a grant that would enable them to hire an additional counselor, fill the gaps in their supplies and fix the roof on the classroom building where the boys kept up with their education even as they learned the skills they'd need to reenter society as fully functional young men.

Her dad was the one who had originated the policy of anonymous evaluations after his first few trips to meet grant applicants had resulted in lavish dog and pony shows presented strictly to impress him. He'd decided a better way to get the true measure of how a charity was run was to assess them anonymously in their day-to-day business.

"I still don't understand why you took that job at all," her mother said, pulling Harper from her reverie. "It doesn't take you thirteen weeks to make your assessment."

"Mom, I told you—the only other reason to be in a town this size would be to take a vacation, and who'd believe a single woman on vacay had a sudden yen to volunteer at a home for delinquent boys? How would she even hear of it? Besides, I kind of *needed* a vacation."

"So you took a job?"

Harper bit back a sigh, because they'd had this conversation before. "I took a *fun* job, and it's a break from lying to people. That *is* a vacation."

"Yet you're lying to these people, too, aren't you?"

Harper was suddenly so weary she could barely hold her head up. What the hell had happened to them that they were so far apart these days? "Yes, Mother. You're absolutely right. I'm a liar no matter what I do."

"Darling, I didn't mean it that way. I simply think if you're unhappy, you should let someone else do that job and come home."

"I'm *not* unhappy." Yes, she got tired of the subterfuge sometimes, but she genuinely got the reasoning behind it. And she loved the new places, new people aspect of it. Loved getting to help charities that made things easier for kids. But her mother, who wanted her to quit traveling and settle down, would never believe that.

And she really didn't feel up to justifying her choices yet again. "Whoops. There's the doorbell. I'll talk to you soon, Mom."

"Harper, wait—"

"Gotta go. Bye." She disconnected. Then, blowing out an unhappy breath, she tossed the phone on the table and flopped back on the couch.

This was the right way to do things, she assured herself. Her dad had done it so, and she still trusted his judgment unswervingly. As for the niggle of doubt her mother's words had created?

Taking a steady, calming breath, she flicked it away.

CHAPTER FOUR

MAX WAS ON his way to Harper's cottage the next evening when a movement in his peripheral vision caught his attention. Glancing left, he expected to see someone lounging in the inn's hot tub. Instead, the spa appeared empty. Then another tiny shift along the water's already bubbling surface drew his focus, and he saw a woman free-floating, only her neck and head supported by the edge of the tub.

Her warm, gorgeous coloring seized his attention, and it never even occurred to him to question her identity. He knew who she was by the hot jolt of electric pleasure that sparked through his veins. Veering off the path, he made a beeline for the little oasis of plantings where the tub resided just outside the inn's pool house. This made things both simpler and more difficult.

Simpler because he wouldn't have to be alone with Harper in her tiny bungalow. And harder because, well, hell—look at her. Close up, he could see the light brown skin of her breasts, framed by the deep V of her black-and-white patterned halter top, rising out of the bubbling water. The uppermost curve of her long, smooth thighs and her orange-tipped toes broke the waterline, as well.

He shook his head impatiently. He'd sworn to himself he would meet with her tonight and *not* think about sex.

Yeah, it was a stupid promise, but his word was his

word, dammit. "*How* could you have made the pancake breakfast more profitable?" he demanded as he stopped at the tub.

And watched her give a start and damn near go under before she righted herself. Her head came up, and her shoulders shot out of the water as her butt lowered to sit on the submerged seat. And he realized she hadn't merely been überrelaxed. "Aw, crap. Did I wake you?"

"What? No, of course not." She yawned widely, then dropped the dripping hand she'd raised out of the water to cover her mouth and gave him a tiny lopsided smile. "Well, maybe. What time is it?"

He consulted the big tank watch on his wrist. "Going on eight."

"It was around a quarter 'til when I climbed in the tub, so I guess I did drop off for a bit."

He couldn't help it; deputy was pretty much his default mode. "You know it's not safe to sleep in a hot tub, right?"

"Yes, Papa." She started to roll her eyes but apparently thought better of it, for she went all faux solemn-eyed on him and offered a polite smile instead. "Is there something I can do for you?"

A raft of dirty suggestions popped to mind, but since he wasn't a damn fourteen-year-old—even if that was the way he invariably felt around her—he wisely swallowed them. Particularly since he didn't know why he'd come to grill her in the first place. Hell, hadn't he given her his card so she could be the one to get in touch with him?

Whatever his reasons for showing up unannounced, here he was, so he might as well make the most of it. Hooking a hip on the corner of the tub, he braced his other foot against the grass and ignored the splashed water soaking into the seat of his jeans. "You said yesterday morning you could tell me how to make the next pancake breakfast more profitable. How would you do that?"

She merely looked up at him for a moment. Wreathed in steam, moisture beaded her face, and her hair, pulled atop her head in a high ponytail, curled wildly, crazy little corkscrews plastered damply to her temples and nape. "Buy me a Coke and I'll tell you."

Good idea. A nice cold drink might cool him down, help him quit thinking about licking the water drops sliding down her silky-smooth cleav—

He surged to his feet. "Be back in a sec." Fishing his wallet from his back pocket, he crossed to the vending machine in the ice machine room attached to the pool house.

Moments later he was back. He popped the tab on one icy can and handed it to Harper, then opened his own and knocked back half of it as he resumed his perch on the edge of the tub.

She took a long swallow herself and used the tip of her tongue to absorb a drop of soda from her upper lip as she lowered the can. Setting it aside on the little shelf that filled the gap between the back of the hot tub and the pool house's outer wall, she focused her attention on him.

"One way to make your breakfast more profitable," she said, "is to host a silent auction. That can be as elaborate or as simple as you want, but you have a captive audience in the people who come to eat, and everyone loves the idea of getting something at a bargain price."

Pushing against the foot planted on the ground, he straightened. "Is it hard to do?"

"Not really. It can be time-consuming, but that's where volunteers like me come in. You use us to solicit donations from local businesses and set up a table or two to accommodate the acquisitions. We can also help with things like deciding on a price to start the bidding for each item and at what increments to increase and make individual sheets for them—"

"Wait, wait. Explain what you mean. And pretend I don't have a clue."

She laughed. "Because you don't?"

"Yeah." His own mouth crooked up in a smile. "I'm a cop—and before that a marine. Stuff like this is way outside my experience."

"Okay." She scooted to the edge of her submerged seat. "Say Wendy at Wacka Do donates a haircut and she usually charges thirty-eight dollars. You'd make a sheet that says Haircut at Wacka Do's, value thirty-eight dollars. And since it's a service and not, say, a pretty gift basket that visually pops to catch a potential bidder's attention, you might want to add a photo of Wendy doing a haircut, or a styled wig on a wig stand. You with me so far?"

"Yep."

She took another sip of her pop. "Regardless of the visual, the sheet needs a starting bid, so say three-fifty or around ten percent of its value, with fifty-cent or one-dollar increases. Now, if your brother were to donate one of his photographs, on the other hand, you'd have a much higher value amount because he's well known in his field. That would make both the starting bid and the increments higher. See?"

"Yeah, I do." And he liked the idea. No one else in town was doing anything like it. "So you just flop the stuff down on a table and you're good to go?"

"God." Her mouth quirked up. "You're such a guy. The idea is to try to make the presentations as striking as possible to capture as much bidder interest as you can. You also need to give people enough time to both look at what's offered and to bid again if someone trumps them. And have a clear end time. Then you'd need someone responsible to collect the money, but that's pretty straightforward. The winner simply brings the sheet to the cashier and pays the final bid amount on it. And since it's for a charity, you don't have to deal with collecting sales tax—although I'd double-check that one in case Washington state differs in that respect."

"That's so cool. What else you got?"

She blinked those olive-green eyes at him. "'Scuse me?"

"You said 'for starters.' Does that mean you have even more ideas?"

"Oh, honey." Stretching her arms out along the tub's rim, she tipped her head back and let her torso float up to the surface again. Smooth skin stretched over toned thigh muscles and all that beautiful cleavage as her various curved parts cleared the roiling water. Raising her head again, she caught him dead to rights checking out the entire kick-ass package and sank back beneath the water. "I've got a million of 'em."

"Excellent." He grinned and settled in, feeling truly comfortable with her for perhaps the first time since they'd met. Hell, she had pointed it out herself; he was a guy. When guys were presented with tits and gorgeous legs, they looked. They sure as hell didn't apologize for it. "Let's hear 'em."

"Was the community center space donated?"

"Yeah. We had to put down a damage deposit, but we got it all back. Well, except for the cost of replacing some broken glasses."

She grinned at him. "Yes, I was having my tray re-filled when that happened. Did you solicit the food and the paper goods?"

"Huh?" That straightened him up. "No. We got a re-bate from the pancake manufacturer for fund-raising, but it never occurred to us to ask The General Store to donate it."

"Next year make a list of everything it takes to put on the fund-raiser, then try to get as much of it donated as possible. I'm guessing your boys are from places other than just here, right?"

He nodded. "We don't actually have any kids from Razor Bay—they're mostly from the Silverdale or Bremerton areas. But some come from as far away as Seattle or Olympia."

"From what you've said about some of the boys' home lives, parental involvement might be far differ-ent from the families I've worked with. But if any of the parents do actively engage in their kid's recovery—especially if they live in the nearby areas since the re-gional aspect works best—get them to hit up their local grocers, printers, party stores—anyplace that might contribute something you'd otherwise have to buy. The idea is to funnel as much profit back into the program as possible, right?"

"Absolutely." The timer for the jets clicked off, but for once his attention didn't go to her suddenly much more visible body. He gave her a puzzled look. "How do you know so much about this?"

"I've had a bazillion temporary jobs, and one of them was taking over an auction coordinator position for a private school when the one they had was put on bed rest during the final trimester of her pregnancy."

"And you just—what?—knew what to do?"

"No." She gave him a rueful smile. "Far from it. I didn't have the first notion how an auction was run. Luckily for me, several of the parents who'd spent their PIP hours working on the auction did, and they taught me."

"What the hell are PIP hours?"

"Oh, sorry. It stands for Parent Involvement Program. Most private schools designate a given number of hours parents are expected to volunteer at their kids' school." She stood up and water cascaded down her. "Hand me that towel, will you?"

Sweet Mother Mary. His good intentions went up in smoke, but screw it—he claimed the guy defense again. Fumbling for the towel folded near his feet, he handed it over, then simply stared as she patted herself dry. He'd assumed she had on a bikini, which until tonight he'd pretty much considered the gold standard of sexy beachwear.

The one-piece suit that molded faithfully in all the right places was hands-down sexier. The band beneath the black-and-white bra part tied around her neck and behind her back like a bikini top, but was attached to a solid black body that was cut in toward her waist, low on her back and high on her thighs. And its wet spandex clung to every luscious inch it covered.

"Hooyah," he breathed when she turned three-quarters away from him, propped a foot on the edge of the tub and bent to dry her lower leg. He had to physically restrain himself from reaching out to stroke the sweet, firm curve of her ass. He cleared his throat and sternly recalled the topic they'd been discussing before her rise like Venus from a fucking shell had blown it from his mind. "Why didn't one of those parents just take over?"

She glanced over her shoulder at him. "You're a logical thinker, aren't you? And hiring someone familiar with the program would make sense…if even one of them had been in the market for a short-term job that was about to transition from part-time to ten-hour days."

That got his mind back in the game. "I thought you said it wasn't that difficult!"

"The scenario I propose for Cedar Village isn't. But the kind of auction I did for the school was held in an Atlanta hotel, featured a sit-down meal and included enough items to fill a ballroom. It also employed an auctioneer at a live auction for the high ticket items. That's a much more time-consuming endeavor."

She climbed from the tub and balanced gracefully on one foot while raising the other to towel it dry. Upon finishing both feet, she turned, crossed her arms beneath her breasts and pinned him squarely in her sights. "So, have I demonstrated enough experience to volunteer at the Village?"

Luckily for him, it was dim out here, so the blood he felt surging up his throat and onto his face likely didn't show. He'd inferred that she might have nothing the home could use yesterday—or that the boys would make mincemeat of her, because he'd been rattled by the microsecond spent all but wrapped around her when he'd stepped in to help with the leaning tower of glasses. Rattled—and wanting nothing more than to avoid running into her at the one place he felt most like himself.

But he'd known when she'd made Brandon squirm with nothing more than a look that she could hold her own with the Cedar Village boys. "Yes," he said honestly. "And then some. Do you want a regular schedule—" which he'd prefer so he could arrange, for both their sakes, to be elsewhere "—or—"

"I'd rather come when I can, if that works for you. My hours at the inn change week to week and sometimes even day to day."

"Sure." He pulled out his wallet again and searched through it for a Village card. Locating the one he knew was in there somewhere, he pulled it out and extended it to Harper. "Sorry this's so battered, but the director Mary-Margaret's name and number are on it. She's the one to talk to, but I'll let her know about our conversation on Thursday, which will be the next time I'll be there, so she'll know who she's talking to when she gets your call."

"Thanks, Max." She pulled a vivid red cover-up over her suit and slid the card in its pocket, then gathered her room card and the still half-full can of pop from the little shelf. "I'll give her a call on Friday."

"Are you headed back to your place?"

She nodded. "Yeah. It's been a busy day I'm going to call it a night." She looked him over. "You have to be pretty whipped yourself. You slaved over a hot stove and rode herd over teenage boys for a good part of yesterday, and have obviously worked today." She indicated his department uniform and holstered gun.

He shrugged. "What can I say—I'm tough." One

hand hovering just above the small of her back, he gave her an *after you* sweep of his free fingers. "Come on. I'll see you to your place, then I'm gonna head home, myself. I've got a beer calling my name."

"You don't have to walk me home." She grinned up at him. "But you're going to anyway, aren't you, 'cause you're Mister Responsible." She turned in the direction he indicated and headed down the path that intersected with another that led to her cottage, getting ahead of his hand, which he dropped to his side.

"That's me," he agreed. "And for a woman I'd lay odds on being pretty damn independent, you're being suspiciously easy to steer."

"Never get between a man and his beer, I always say."

"No fooling?" Tucking his hands in his front pockets, he strolled a scant inch behind her. "I just might have to marry you."

He thought he saw her step falter, but maybe not, because he blinked and she was walking with hip-swinging ease. Not to mention the wry smile she shot him.

"You don't think you might have kind of low standards for a future wife?" she inquired.

"Hey, I'm pretty serious about my beer." And damn amazed that for this moment, at least, he felt downright at ease with her.

"Ah, well, then."

They arrived at her cottage, and she turned to face him. "Thanks, Max. You truly are a nice guy."

"No, I'm not!"

Her dark brows furrowed. "That's not an insult."

Except for the part where being a "nice" guy was usually the kiss of death when it came to getting laid.

He straightened. What the hell difference did *that* make? It wasn't as if a woman like Harper was going to sleep with a guy like him anyway.

"You're right," he said, giving her a stiff smile and falling back into the professionalism he'd used from day one as a shield against his attraction to her. "It was a very nice compliment—it's just been a long day, like you said. But I'm always glad to be of assistance." He tweaked the room card from her fingers and slid it into the slot, then turned away for her to punch in the code.

He twisted back when he heard the door open and gave her a crisp nod. "You enjoy the rest of your night, now."

"O...kay," she said faintly.

But he was already off her porch and halfway down the path.

CHAPTER FIVE

"I'M SO GLAD we finally managed to get together." Harper said as she slid into a chair across a small wooden table from Tasha at The Anchor bar Friday afternoon.

"No fooling—I'm happy you could get away during the day." The tall, attractive strawberry blonde gave her a rueful smile. "I'm afraid the downside to owning my own pizza joint is that my work is generally just kicking into high gear about the time everyone else's is winding down and they're getting ready to go home for the day."

"And erratic hours are rather the upside of my job. I guided a kayak group along the shoreline to town this morning, but Fridays are a big transition day—checkouts in the morning and even more ins during the late afternoon, so I don't have anything scheduled until my sunset yoga class this evening. So, good-oh for us, huh?"

"What's good-oh for you two?" A purse landed on the table next to Harper, and she looked up to see Jenny pulling out the chair beside hers. "Tell me I didn't miss anything good."

"Nah." Tasha shook her head at her friend. "We were just congratulating ourselves on finding some mutual time off."

"Yeah, too bad about you peons." Bouncing a fist off

her chest, Jenny flashed them a big smile. "It's good to be boss."

"Hey, I'm a boss, too," Tasha said. "I'm the boss of me."

"And yet you're always tied to Bella T's from late afternoon on. Hell, from lunch on most of the summer."

"Yeah, I should probably think about hiring more people to give me some flexibility." She slid them a sly smile. "Still, it could be worse. I could be the peon like Harper."

"Now, that's just cold!" But Harper laughed, enjoying herself immensely. She'd been sitting with the two women for less than five minutes and already it had occurred to her that she'd done herself a huge disservice when she'd failed to pursue more female friendships over the years.

Tasha grinned at her, and Harper determined then and there that she would actively work at having a relationship with her and Jenny. For once in her life she wasn't going to allow the length of time she spent in a given town to dictate the effort she put into getting to know people. This time she'd make friends on a deeper level than her usual enjoy-them-while-they-last-but-don't-get-too-involved way.

"I'm surprised you managed to pull yourself away from Lover Boy," Tasha said to Jenny as she raised a hand to catch a nearby waitress's attention.

"It wasn't easy," the small brunette agreed. "But it's been far too long since I've had any decent girl time. And much as I love Jake, the estrogen deprivation was starting to make me twitch."

Tasha gave her a solemn nod. "I totally get that.

Lovely as men can be, there's such a thing as testosterone overload."

"But, oh, what a way to go," Jenny murmured with a small, private smile.

All three women laughed. "Oh, sure, rub it in for those of us who haven't been as lucky lately," Harper said. She raised her brows at Tasha. "Or maybe that's just me."

"Nope. Much as I'd love to say it is, I'm part of the ain't-getting-any demographic myself."

A college-aged blonde stopped by their table to drop three coasters in front of them. "You ladies ready?"

After they placed their orders, they watched the blonde stride off. Then Jenny turned to Harper. Planting an elbow on the table, she propped her chin in her palm to study her. "I never would have pegged you as a beer drinker."

"What did you think I'd drink?"

"Martinis," Tasha said unhesitatingly, and Jenny nodded her agreement.

"Really?" She shifted her gaze between the two women. "Why?"

"Probably because you've got that whole—" Jenny rotated a hand "—sophisticated thang going for you."

This time Tasha nodded.

Then the petite brunette dismissively flapped the same hand. "That's not important, though," she said, focusing her attention on Harper. "I was wondering… how would you like to take on some added responsibility at the inn?"

"Well, I don't know." Harper was at once excited at the idea and uneasy. She always enjoyed the challenge of learning or conquering new skills. At the same time, the goal that had brought her here had nothing to do with her job at The Brothers. "You know I'm not looking for a full forty-hour week."

"Right now you're not even up to thirty hours." Jenny sat straighter in her chair. "What I have in mind will add maybe an extra five hours a week. And I think it's something you'd not merely enjoy but be really good at."

"Okay, now you've got me all curious."

"Me, too," Tasha said.

"Every year, from the Thursday before Labor Day through the holiday, the town holds its annual Razor Bay Days. Max told Jake, who of course told me, about your ideas to bump the Village's fund-raising efforts up a notch. That's exactly the kind of thinking we need for handling the inn's participation in the events."

Jenny must have seen her instinctive shake of the head, for she hurried to say, "You don't have to reinvent the wheel, sweetie. It's mostly a matter of handling the things we already have in place. For instance, we always buy a block of preferential seating for the Saturday parade and Sunday night fireworks in town, and you're in a perfect position to let people know they're available. The actual sales will be handled at the front desk. You'd set up an Adult Night with an appropriate theme and activities, as well as a coordinating Game Night for the kids. You're so damn inventive, this stuff oughtta be right up your alley."

"I'm surprised you're not doing it yourself," Harper said slowly. "You must have it down pat by now."

The cocktail waitress arrived then with their order, and the three women exchanged pleasantries with her as she placed their drinks on the table. When she walked away again, Jenny leaned forward.

"That's actually part of the problem. Razor Bay Days is the inn's single largest occupancy week, and it's routinely sold out as much as a year in advance—in many cases to people who come year after year. I feel we need some fresh eyes on this, fresh ideas."

A few ran through Harper's mind, and she couldn't help the excitement that coursed through her veins. She loved doing this sort of thing. "Okay, it sounds like fun. I'll do it."

"Excellent!" Jenny smiled hugely and leaned into her. "Let's get together at my office tomorrow and—"

"Everything was *fine* until you came along," a belligerent voice suddenly cut through their conversation, and Harper twisted in her seat in time to see a man take a swipe at the drink in front of another man sitting with a woman at the bar. The top-heavy glass tumbled over, and liquid spilled across the bar to waterfall over the side.

The woman leaped to her feet, brushing at her shorts and the waistband of her top, which were spotted with whatever had been in the glass.

"Crap. Wade's at it again." Jenny, who had turned toward the bar as well, swiveled back in unison with Harper to face center again.

"Who's Wade, and why on earth did he *do* that?"

"Wade Nelson." Tasha tipped her chin in the direction of the woman who'd jumped up. "He and Mindy were married once upon a time."

"But Wade has issues, and one day she finally had her fill of them and kicked him out," Jenny said, picking up the story. "Eventually she and Curt Neff started going out, and a year or so later they got married. Wade refuses to accept that it's over between him and his ex-wife."

The man was still loudly haranguing the ex-wife's husband. "You'd think they'd be furious, but I don't hear them saying anything to him in return." She wanted to turn around to see, but her manners-count upbringing deemed it best not to gawk at them again.

"They learned through hard experience that ignoring him is best all around," Jenny said. "I don't know if I could keep my mouth shut as well as they have, though. That has to be hard."

"Seriously hard. How long have they been doing it?"

"Seven years."

An incredulous laugh escaped her. "Are you bamming me? They've been apart seven years and he still thinks—what?—that she'll come back to him? When he acts like that?"

"She and Curt have been *married* seven years," the petite brunette corrected. "Mindy and Wade have been divorced damn near nine now. But you've got the basic idea right. He simply won't admit she's never coming back."

Sunlight flooded the front end of the bar for an instant as the door to the street opened; then the room regained its usual atmospheric dimness once again when it slowly closed behind the new arrival. A no-nonsense voice Harper would know anywhere said, "Let's go, Wade."

Like a compass needle seeking true north, she swung around to watch Max Bradshaw stride up to the bar. He wore his usual uniform of knotted-to-within-an-inch-of-its-life black tie over a khaki shirt with shoulder epaulets. A gold-toned badge was pinned to his chest, and gold, black and green shield-shaped patches, each sporting a spread-winged eagle and the Razor Bay Sheriff's

Office designation, decorated his shirt's sleeves above the hems that bisected the solid mounds of his biceps.

His jeans, soft and worn almost white at the seams, might have seemed incongruous with the crisp professionalism of his upper torso if not for the black web utility belt that bristled with the tools of his trade— including a deadly-serious-looking gun. Or perhaps it was his no-nonsense, you-don't-*even*-wanna-mess-with-me attitude that so efficiently negated any slacker-dude vibe the near-shabby jeans might have otherwise suggested.

She watched him put a big hand on Wade's shoulder— and shivered, remembering how crazy-aware she'd been of it hovering just above her own back when he'd escorted her to her cabin from the hot tub. "Let's go," he said again.

Wade shook him off so abruptly that he himself staggered—then glared at Max as if it were his fault. "Why the hell don't you take *him* in," he demanded, jutting a petulant chin in Curt's direction.

Max reached out to steady him before the other man lost his balance entirely and replied evenly, "Because the call I got said Mindy and Curt were just sitting here minding their own business when you showed up and made a scene. Since I've been called out dozens of times to deal with this exact same situation, I have no reason to question the information." He gave the other man a level look. "Now, you can come with me peaceably, or I can drag your ass out of here in cuffs. It's your choice, Wade."

"Fine." Tugging the neckline of his stained T-shirt away from his Adam's apple, Wade twisted his chin, stretching it first to the left, then to the right. "Whatever." And he shambled toward the door, with Max's hand planted between his shoulder blades to guide him whenever he hesitated.

At the door Max reached around Wade to pull it open. Sunshine splashed into the room again. Then the two men stepped out into the afternoon and disappeared from view as the door swung shut behind them.

Blowing out a quiet breath she hadn't even realized she'd been holding, Harper turned back to her companions. "I am simply amazed no one has snapped that man up."

"Who?" Jenny asked. She blinked then, and sat a little straighter. *"Max?"*

"Yeah. Oh, I know he's not the most sociable guy in the universe, but he's big, he's built, and God knows the man is competent at everything he does. I find that seriously sexy." Seeing her new friends gaping at her, she stilled. "Come on. I can't be the only woman in town who finds him attractive."

"Um...yeah, you kind of are," Tasha said. Then she shook her head. "That is, he *is* an attractive man. He's built like nobody's business."

"And he's got a killer smile," Jenny contributed. "But he's kind of stingy with it."

"And like you said," the strawberry blonde concluded, "he's not exactly Mister Social."

Jenny snorted agreement, and Tasha looked at Harper. "Max is just so sober and intense. Not to mention disinterested—and I guess between all of that, it scares women off. Because now that you mention it, I can't say I've seen him with a particular woman since he came back to town."

Harper planted her chin on her fist. "For some reason Max and Razor Bay are linked in my mind. Where did he come back from?" It was all she could do not to squirm in her seat. For the first time since she'd taken over the job of assessing grant applicants for Sunday's Child, she felt a hint of shame for pretending ignorance. God knows she'd thoroughly studied the foundation-generated dossiers on every Cedar Village board member.

Still, she had a job to do. And much as it bothered her to be duplicitous with Tasha and Jenny, her friends would likely find it odd if she *didn't* show an interest.

"He spent years in the Marines—mostly in war-torn countries." Tasha gave her head an impatient shake, her curls quivering with the motion. "But he's been back for years, and as I said, I can't think of a woman he's ever paid special attention to. Not that I don't see him talking to different ones occasionally, but it's usually more like they're talking to him and he's mostly just listening. I don't recall ever seeing him look as though he were *with* one of them, ya know?" She looked at Jenny. "Can you think of anyone?"

"Nope. I can't put him with anyone, either. Which is odd, when you think about it. Because I know he's kind of a lone wolf and all, but there's sure as hell nothing asexual about him."

"No shit," Harper murmured.

Jenny grinned at her. "Oh, good, you do swear."

She tilted her head slightly to study her friend. "And that's a good thing?"

"It's not good or bad—well, unless you're one of those high school boys who can't seem to string a sentence together without saying some variation of fuck every other word. It's just that most everybody does to some extent, but since we've met, you've just been so damn...perfect."

"I have not!"

"Yeah, you kind of have," Tasha said. "You have gorgeous manners, amazing posture—did you go through childhood balancing books on your head or something?—and you always dress exactly right for the occasion. Plus, you sound educated and—let's face it—rich girl when you speak."

"Yes," Jenny agreed. "For an American, your accent is not quite but very nearly British sounding."

She smiled. "Okay, I'll cop to that one. Because we moved so much as kids, my brother, Kai, and I often had tutors. And when we did stay in one place long enough to go to a local school, as with our tutors, the English spoken and taught there leaned heavily toward the Queen's version. I've been told I kind of retained the cadence, if not the actual accent." She took a swig of her beer, then shook her head. "I'm nobody's rich girl, though. My grandparents on my father's side are quite well-to-do, and my dad did okay for himself as well, although he didn't attain their income bracket. But me, personally? Not even close."

"Ah, but you're talking to a couple of girls from the wrong side of the tracks," Tasha said cheerfully. A man passing behind her bumped her chair, and she hopped it in a little closer to the table. "Well, Jenny actually started out on the right side, but circumstances dumped her in my part of town when she was sixteen." She flashed Harper an easy whatta-ya-gonna-do smile. "So we're easily impressed."

Her laid-back acceptance made Harper realize their assessment of her wasn't a you're-not-one-of-us judgment; it was simply a recitation of their impressions. She took a sip of her beer and leaned back in her chair. "I spent a good deal more time with adults than kids my own age growing up, so I suppose I don't sound quite like your average American thirty-year-old. But I can start swearing up a storm if you want."

They both flashed her unrepentant grins, and she grinned right back.

Then she sobered and gave them a curious look. "Razor Bay is small, and I haven't seen an overabundance of hot guys our age in the short time I've been here. So, weren't either of you ever even a little tempted by Max? I thought teenage girls were fascinated by the broody Heathcliff/Vampire Edward type."

"He wasn't around when Tash and I were in high school, and when he did come home we were both way more interested in improving our futures. So the idea of him as potential dating material never even occurred to us in our impressionable years. Besides, I like guys who make me laugh," Jenny said.

Tasha nodded. "Same here. And Max just isn't my type."

Harper studied her. "What is?"

The strawberry blonde grinned. "I like 'em tall, charming and fun," she said slowly. The words had no sooner left her lips, however, than her gray-blue eyes darkened as if a thick cloud had suddenly blown across the sun. And her mouth, with its exotically fuller-than-its-counterpart upper lip, tightened. She made an erasing motion. "No, I take that back—I've sworn off a type. I have awful taste in men."

"No, you don't," Jenny said firmly. "You had awful taste once. One time, Tash."

"Well, considering that one time landed my ass in a Bahamian jail," Tasha retorted coolly, "I think it's probably enough, don't you?"

Hello! Harper straightened. *That* sounded wildly intriguing. But one look at the rigid set of Tasha's shoulders—not to mention the other woman's blind-eyed attention to the wineglass in her hand—and Harper knew better than to pursue the conversational bomb that had just rolled onto the table between them. Not even the crystal green and blue waters of the canal at low tide were clearer than the vibe Tasha was putting out that she'd spoken unthinkingly—and this was *not* a subject she cared to discuss.

So Harper gave the other woman a cocky smile to lighten the mood. "I guess this means my Hunky Deputy and The Handcuffs fantasy is all mine, then, yeah?"

Her new friends laughed, and the tension that had hovered like a noxious mist over their table for a moment dissipated. "Oh, yeah." Tasha gave her a lopsided smile. "Which is not to say I don't wish you the best with it."

"Absolutely," Jenny agreed. "And should it ever come true for you…well. We expect details."

"Lots and lots of details," Tasha said. "Because Jenny's right. Max is far from asexual, and I for one would love to know if he's one of those tell-a-girl-exactly-what-he-wants-from-her-in-bed kind of guys."

Harper stilled. Oh, hell. Like her imagination wasn't active enough.

That was the *last* image she needed planted in her brain.

CHAPTER SIX

MAX STOOD IN front of the open refrigerator Saturday morning, absentmindedly scratching his stomach above the cutoffs he'd pulled on when he'd rolled out of bed. When it came to breakfast choices, there wasn't a lot to select from. The fridge was empty except for a few cans of Coke, fewer bottles of Bud, a lonely, nearly gone quart of milk that might or might not still be drinkable and an assortment of condiments that ran heavily on the mustard and pepper sauce side.

He could always throw on a shirt and some flip-flops and go to the Sunset Café to get himself a big plate of the Fisherman's special, he supposed. And in truth, bacon and eggs and hash browns, with a side of toast and jam sounded awfully damn good right about now.

But if he scrounged something up here, he could get an earlier start on the home improvement project he'd been planning for his next day off.

Which was today.

"Screw it." He reached for the milk carton, inverted the fold to the pour position and sniffed. What the hell. It didn't smell sour, exactly, so he kicked the fridge door shut and grabbed a bowl, a spoon and a box of Froot Loops from the cupboard. He carried everything over to the table, where he shoved aside a stack of unopened mail with the bottom of the milk carton, then unloaded the rest of his haul onto the tabletop. He turned back to give the coffeemaker, sitting cold and silent on the counter, a considering look. Then with a shrug, he returned to the fridge to grab himself a can of Coke. "Breakfast of champions."

He popped the tab on his way back to the table. As he took a long gulp, he hooked a bare foot beneath the stretcher separating the chair's back legs to tow it away from the table. Taking his seat, he poured cereal in the bowl, topped it off with milk, then picked up his spoon and dug in.

He ate fast, and as soon as he scraped up a lone Froot Loop and the last of the milk from his bowl, he climbed to his feet again. Taking everything back to the kitchen, he poured the little bit of milk still left in the carton down the drain and dumped the empty container, along with his bowl, spoon and can, into the sink to deal with later. Then he located an old pair of beat-up running shoes, shoved his feet into them and went out to the garage to gather his ladder and tools. He didn't want to spend his entire day off working, so the sooner he got started, the sooner he could get in a little beach time.

He worked steadily and had just finished applying a peroxide-based cleaner to the last of the cedar shakes on the north side of his house and was up on the ladder scraping mildew out of the grooves of the affected shingles when he heard car tires crunching up the drive. Curious, he tossed the scraper onto the ladder's shelf, jumped to the ground and strode toward the corner nearest the driveway. He didn't get much in the way of company.

Or, okay, *any* as a rule.

Rounding the corner, he was in time to see his half

brother climbing out of his fancy-ass Benz BlueTEC. Pleasure splintered through him, a recent sensation that caught him by surprise every time he saw Jake.

He gave himself a shake. It was hardly an oddity that he was not yet accustomed to the new direction their relationship had taken. God knew they'd spent a helluva lot more time being enemies than friends.

"Hey," he said. "I didn't expect to see you here."

"I figured the only way I'd ever get to see your place was to invite myself." Pulling his sunglasses down his nose, Jake gave him an unhurried once-over. "You've sure as shit never issued one."

"Yeah." Max rolled his shoulders guiltily. "Sorry about that. Most of the group I used to run with were either gone or on the wrong side of the law when I got back to town, so I guess I'm out of the habit of inviting people to drop by."

"Jesus, dude, don't you have any friends?"

"I have friends," he said defensively. "Most of them are marines, though, so we're scattered all over the place. But I have a couple of guys I shoot pool with at The Anchor or share an occasional beer with around town." But, okay, didn't really see otherwise.

Then he went on the offensive, since everyone knew that was the best defense. "And what the hell, Jake—you're one to talk. I haven't exactly seen you overrun with buddies, yourself."

Jake grunted and shoved his shades back up. "Gotta point." He turned away to check out Max's place.

Max would've sworn he wasn't a jumpy kind of guy. But when Jake took his sweet time surveying the house and its surrounding land, he found himself damn near twitching by the time his brother finally turned back.

Jake gave him an imperturbable look. "This is moderately cool."

"It's *hella* cool," Max corrected but then grinned. Because given the way they insulted each other on a regular basis, in Jake-speak "moderately cool" was a downright endorsement. It was pretty lame to be so thrilled by his brother's approval, but even in his wildest, what-kinda-trouble-can-I-get-into-now days, he'd never tried to lie to himself.

And that meant he had to acknowledge he pretty much was…well, maybe not *thrilled,* exactly, since that was for little kids and chicks. But pleased.

It struck him that he no longer thought of Jake as his half sibling—the guy was finally, simply, his brother in his mind. And, yeah, he was pleased that Jake liked his place. So sue him.

He'd stick a needle in his eye before he'd admit as much out loud—especially to Jake—but what he'd long wanted more than anything else in the world was a guy version of the white-picket-fence life. Right down to a loving wife who would put him first. Because *that*… well. That was something he could only imagine.

He'd never come first in anyone's life.

And he'd like kids, too, one day. He would *never* do what his father had—he'd sacrifice his right testicle before he'd cheat on his wife or abandon any kid of his.

Not that his lofty principles were of immediate concern, he acknowledged wryly, seeing as he was nowhere near attaining that dream—and didn't know if he ever would. A guy had to actually put himself out there to meet women. But he had this house. It was a first step. And, hell, maybe he'd take that second step one of these days as well, and head into Silverdale some Saturday night to spend a couple of hours at The Voodoo Lounge. He liked to dance, and it was a decent place to meet like-minded women.

And even if he didn't meet The One, at worst he might get laid. He sure as hell wouldn't mind that.

It had been a while.

He merely shrugged now, however, and got his head back in the conversation. They'd been talking about his house, not his less-than-titillating sex life. "I've been working on it. The place was a train wreck when I bought it, but she's got excellent bones and someday I think she'll be a beauty."

"Yeah, I can visualize it. How much land have you got here?"

"Four and a half acres."

Hands stuffed in his pockets, Jake rocked back on his heels and looked at the large yard Max had platted by removing some of the trees that surrounded it on three sides. "I like the privacy." He shot Max a crooked smile. "We're so gonna have to have the next barbecue here."

The idea of hosting *anything* sent a blip of panic racing through him. It wasn't that he was against the idea—and for sure he'd been to enough dos put on by Jake and Jenny that he likely needed to reciprocate. He simply didn't have any idea how to go about pulling together anything more complicated than putting out beer and chips. Swallowing his discomfort at the mere thought, however, he said, "Yeah. Maybe."

Jake snorted and shot him a fist to the shoulder, along with a knowing smile, as if he could somehow look right into his mind. But before Max could respond—or even decide how he should—his brother turned to look at the house again. "What were you doing when I got here?"

And just like that, Max's discomfort disappeared. He loved his place and, unlike a lot of other subjects, could always discuss it without having to dig for conversation. "This is the original stain job," he said. "Or at least the one that was on the house when I bought it. I've been waiting for both a spate of nice weather like we've been having and time off to spruce it up. Today I'm washing the shakes and scrubbing out mildew on the north side, getting it ready to restain."

"Handy guy. Need a hand?"

Max laughed and eyeballed Jake's designer T-shirt and shorts. "Yeah, right. And screw up your *GQ* look?" He indicated the muck splattering his own chin and neck and shoulders, smeared in the hair on his chest and down his abs and spackling his cutoffs. "Your duds probably cost more than my mortgage payment."

"Please." Jake made a rude noise. "That's an easy fix." Reaching over his back, he pulled his T-shirt over his head and tossed it aside. Then he unzipped his shorts and let them drop to the ground, stepping out of them and kicking them toward the discarded shirt. He turned back to Max wearing nothing but a tan, a pair of boxers and his Tevas. "I'm good to go."

"Jesus." Max shook his head. "You must be wicked bored."

"Yeah." Jake gave him a sheepish smile. "Jenny's at work, and Austin went out on his boat with Nolan and Bailey. I've cleaned up all my photo files and have been a fucking Suzie Spotless around my place. I need man work."

Max laughed and led his brother around the corner of the house where he showed him how to scour the shakes.

Once Jake started attacking the siding, Max went to the garage to scrounge up another scraper.

With two people working, they finished the north wall in record time. Max found sharing the chore and jawing with his brother a nice change to his usual solitary dig-in-and-just-get-it-done routine. So, after cleaning the brushes and putting them away along with the ladder, he invited Jake into his house to clean up. Then he showed him around, pointing out the improvements he'd made in his spare time over the past couple of years.

"This is really going to be something when you're done," Jake said with clear appreciation as they came back downstairs after viewing the still unfinished bedrooms. "Jenny and I have to start looking for something that's big enough for the three of us and an office and darkroom. I'm tired of living in separate houses."

"I bet. You gave her the ring—you got any concrete plans on tying the knot?"

Before Jake could answer, the phone rang. Max unearthed his cell from beneath a short stack of *Law Officer* magazines on the coffee table in the living room and checked the readout. Seeing the caller's name, he felt his usual combination of enjoyment and tension.

He looked over at Jake. "I've gotta get this. There's beer in the fridge and some chips in the cupboard above it."

When his brother walked into the kitchen, Max hit the talk button. "Hey, Ma. How's London?"

"Rainy," she said, and Max exhaled softly.

So it was going to be one of those calls. Ignoring the discontentment of her tone, he said cheerfully, "We've had a pretty good run of weather here for the past couple weeks. I look at it as our reward for the crappy wet winter."

"Well, I suppose we did have a pretty nice spring here," his mother allowed.

"There you go. How's Nigel?" he asked, naming his stepfather.

"He's doing great." Her voice perked up, and Max smiled to himself.

He'd been shocked to come home after mustering out of the Marines to discover his mother had packed up and moved to London to marry the man. She hadn't given him so much as a heads-up.

But Nigel Shevington had turned out to be the best thing that ever happened to Angie Bradshaw. She'd met him while waiting tables at the restaurant in The Brothers Inn. Nigel had proven himself a fast worker, sweeping Angie off her feet and getting her to agree to move halfway across the globe with him practically before she'd even presented him with the check for dinner. Nigel thought she hung the moon, and since meeting him, Angie was probably the happiest she'd ever been.

Happier than *he'd* ever seen her, at any rate.

Old habits were hard to break, however, and sometimes when they talked she fell back into her old churlish ways. He was content to have diverted her now.

"So what are you doing with yourself in the nice weather?" she asked him. "Are you working today?"

"No, I have a rare Saturday off. I spent some time scraping the shingles on my house to get it ready to stain and thought I might hit the beach in a bit."

"You and that canal," she said, her voice half indulgent, half exasperated. "Never in my life have I met anyone else so drawn to the beach and the water as you. I'm surprised you didn't buy yourself a house on the canal."

"The sheriff's department pays a pretty decent salary. But not that decent."

"I bet that little shit Jake—"

"Ma," he said with flat-toned warning.

"All right, all right." She was silent for a heartbeat, then asked, "So, what color are you going to paint your place?"

"I haven't quite made up my mind yet. I thought I'd ask—" *Shit*. Jake, he'd almost said, because his brother had a much more artistic eye than he did. And wouldn't *that* go over like a fart in church? "—a friend I know who's good with that sorta thing."

"Well, I'm sure it will look very nice. We've enjoyed the pictures you've sent. You've made a lot of progress with the place."

"Yeah. I have." He shoved down the memory of her demanding why the hell he was sinking good money after bad into such a dump. "It's coming along pretty good."

"Jesus, bro," Jake called from the kitchen. "You've got the diet of a twelve-year-old." He walked into the living room with a beer in one hand and a bag of Doritos in the other. "Oh, sorry," he said, stopping just this side of the doorway. "I didn't realize you were still on the phone."

"Who's that?" Angie demanded. *"Bro?* Who the hell calls you— Oh. My. *Gawd.*" Her voice rose in both pitch and volume with each word. "Is that *Jake Bradshaw?*"

As much as he wanted to say no, if only to avoid the inevitable temper tantrum about to rain shit on his head, he not only didn't lie to himself, he tried to make truth-telling an all-around general policy. Well, unless a woman asked him if something made her butt look big, that is. Because if it did, he'd lie like a rug with no compunction at all. He wasn't a complete idiot.

Okay, maybe that was debatable. Because, given the long history of bad blood between Charlie Bradshaw's first and second families, a smart man would probably lie his ass off. But not him, boy. Oh, no. He said, "Yes." Then braced himself.

His mother was nothing if not predictable, and it didn't take her any time at all to go off. "What the *hell* is he doing at your house?" she demanded. "And bro— he calls you *bro?* Aren't *you* all cozy with the enemy."

"He's not my enemy, Ma, he's my half brother. We're trying to get past our old relationship to build a new one. It's what grown-ups do."

A slight, ironic smile tugged at Jake's mouth, and he turned to go back into the kitchen. A second later Max heard the back door open and close and wasn't sure if Jake had just gone outside to give him some privacy or, reminded of the toxic treatment Max had subjected him to in the old days, had lit out for home instead.

"How can you *say* such a thing?" The fury in his mother's voice redirected his attention back to her. "He stole every damn thing that rightfully should have been yours."

He'd had a lifetime of practice letting her anger roll off his back. But wondering if his exchange with her had driven Jake to leave dredged up an ice-edged anger of his own. "No, Ma," he said with a cold finality. "He didn't. Dear old Dad did that all by himself. And your constant anger over it sure as hell didn't help. But Jake didn't ask for the situation any more than I did. Jesus, we were boys—just a couple of little kids caught in the crossfire of an adult war. But I'm not that teen who was angry because my mother thought I should be anymore. I'm through with that crap, and I'm getting to know my brother. Deal with it."

"Well, I never!"

"Yeah—and that was part of the problem. You never let me forget how badly we were wronged. Never let me just be a kid."

Jesus, Bradshaw. He had no intention of giving in on this, but he dealt with worked-up people on a regular basis and knew better than most how casting blame and putting them on the defensive benefited no one. So, with more effort than he liked to admit, he expunged the attitude from his tone. "Listen, Ma, I'm sorry—I'm not blaming you. But this *is* the new reality. I have a half brother that I'm getting to know, and I don't think that's an unreasonable thing. So give it some thought and call me back when you decide you can live with it."

"Don't hold your breath," she snapped.

"That's up to you. But you might want to keep in mind that I don't plan to change mine. So if you want us to have a relationship, you're the one who has to make adjustments this time."

They disconnected after an exchange of stiff goodbyes, and he took off for the kitchen. Once there he paused only long enough to grab a beer out of the fridge before barreling through the back door.

He spotted Jake leaning against the trunk of an evergreen, calmly sipping his brew and taking in the yard and the woods around him. Max blew out a breath as he felt the tension leave his shoulders.

Looking up, Jake pushed away from the tree. "Your mother still hates my guts, huh?"

"Yeah. But I don't." And hearing himself say as much out loud, he realized he truly had let go of the old baggage concerning his brother once and for all.

Jake grinned. "I loved the 'It's what grown-ups do' comment."

"'Course you did. You were the one who acted like an adult first."

Jake laughed. "Yeah, I did, didn't I? Am I a fucking genius or what?"

"A fucking something," he agreed.

"God, you're a hard case." Jake shook his head. "Probably due to your lousy diet. Christ, Max, there's nothing but junk food in your cupboards."

"What are you talking about? I had cereal for breakfast."

"With *Coke*. Don't try to tell me otherwise, the can was next to your bowl in the sink. Besides, *oatmeal* is cereal. Honey Smacks and Froot Loops are boxes of enriched candy."

"*Enriched* being the operative word."

"No, idiot—*candy* being the operative word. I wouldn't let my kid eat that shit."

He shrugged. It was what he'd grown up on. "Hey, the stomach likes what the stomach likes."

"If you need sweet cereal, I can recommend some healthier options. They still have sugar, but at least you get a decent amount of fiber to go with it."

Max stared at him. "Boy, you *must* be bored, if you're sitting around reading cereal box nutrition labels."

A trace of color climbed Jake's cheeks, but he merely said, "Jenny educated me when I came back into Austin's life. Dude, my fourteen-year-old has better eating habits than you. And that's not saying much."

Max gave him a look and Jake shot him a cheerfully unconcerned smile. "Okay, okay, I'm changing the subject now. Just…maybe think about it a little, okay?"

"Sure thing, Dad." His gaze dropped to the bag of Doritos in his brother's hand. "I'll do as you say, not as you do."

"Shit." He shook his head—then dug out a handful of chips. "Shut up and drink your beer."

Max laughed. "Now, there's fatherly advice I can get behind. What do you say we finish these up, then head down to the access to watch the idiots launch their boats?"

"Sounds like a plan to me." Jake gave him a sidelong look. "Let's go in your cruiser so I can work the siren."

CHAPTER SEVEN

THE FOLLOWING TUESDAY Harper parked her newly rented car in the Cedar Village parking lot. This was the first opportunity she'd had to check the place out since arriving in town, and the prospect of making her initial assessment of the nonprofit boys' home had a little frisson of excitement slithering up her spine. She locked the car and strode across the pavement to the archway in the black-stained wood fence that formed the grounds' front perimeter. Gazing out across the property, she noted that its other borders were made up of woods comprised of cedar and alder trees.

On the other side of the archway three paths veered off in separate directions. A post at their confluence bristled with wooden hand-shaped signs pointing toward the various buildings to be found down each one. As she started along the path indicated by a thrusting finger that read Administration, she looked around.

The homey, sprawling collection of one-storied buttercream-colored, black-trimmed buildings took her by surprise, even though she hadn't consciously envisioned the setting ahead of time. Somewhere in her psyche, however, she must have had a more formal configuration in mind. These structures, while immaculately maintained, looked as though they'd been shaken in a giant dice cup and tossed willy-nilly across the emerald landscape. It lent the place a friendly vibe—and made the "village" in Cedar Village seem particularly apt.

An outdoor basketball court slanted between her destination building and another that was set at an angle just this side of it. It rang with the shouts and grunts of a game of Shirts and Skins. Sneakers squeaked, a leather ball thumped, and, giving the constantly moving game a closer, but hopefully inconspicuous, examination, she saw it was made up largely of teenage boys with a few men she assumed were counselors or teachers thrown in.

Even as she watched, the boy currently in command of the ball, a tall, good-looking black kid with yard-long dreads pulled back in a thick ponytail, stopped dead and tucked the ball beneath his arm. When another teen tried to knock it from his hold, he twisted away, ramming his free elbow in the boy's side.

The kid on the receiving end swore roundly.

The black youth didn't take his gaze from her. "Dawg," he said by way of explanation to the other boy, jutting his chin in her direction, "we got us a woman come visiting." He subjected her to a slow, appreciative up and down appraisal. "A *hawt* woman."

Good God. Males were the same no matter what their age, apparently. Finding herself the sudden cynosure of an entire basketball court full of males, she simply gave them a cool glance and continued toward the admin building.

Until a voice she knew said quietly, "That's enough, Malcolm," even as another adult said, "Remember what we discussed about appropriate conversation?"

She whipped around and zeroed in on Max, who—Lord have mercy, didn't it just figure?—was on the

Skins team. How on earth had she missed him the first time around? The guy was half a head taller than anyone else there.

He was just an immense, strapping male, period. Hell, when he was *clothed* she found that chest, those shoulders and long, muscular arms infinitely sexy.

Seeing the whole package dressed in nothing but a glaze of perspiration, tattoos and dark body hair that feathered his forearms, fanned across his pecs and ran in a narrow path down his abs to disappear in his low waistband drove every drop of moisture from her mouth. And, dear God. Was that a *nipple* ring she saw glinting through his chest hair?

It felt like a millennium that she stood there staring, but in actuality it was likely only a second or two before the kid named Malcolm mercifully broke her single-minded focus.

"Hey," he said with a shrug, "is it really inappropriate if it's true? I mean, you can't honestly tell me she *ain't* hawt, right?" His teeth flashed white. "And she's a sister, too—at least partly. That's something you gotta admit is in seriously short supply in this white bread burg. Hey, baby, wanna date?" he called, then turned back to the men. "Now *that's* inappropriate. But only to demonstrate the difference, ya dig?"

She had to swallow a smile at his smart-ass insouciance. Knowing better than to engage him, however, she turned away and headed with new purpose—one that *didn't* involve gawking at Deputy Bradshaw's very fine body—toward the administration building. She heard the game start up again as she reached it.

A sign on the door invited her to come in, and, opening it, she poked her head in.

There was a small reception area with a desk facing the door, but no one manned it, and of the two doors she could see at first glance, one was closed and the other all but. Feeling a little like an interloper, she stepped inside.

The deserted room was clean and cheerful, with walls painted a few shades brighter than the exterior hue and hung with colorful framed posters of classic hot rods. She liked the way that, even in the management section, it was geared toward boys' interests. "Ms. Schultz?" she called softly.

"Yeah, hang on a sec," replied a female voice from behind the door that was just barely cracked open, and Harper heard the sound of a chair being pushed back. A moment later a middle-aged woman appeared in the doorway.

Unlike her cheery surroundings, she was quite grim-looking, with her thin lips that tugged severely downward at the corners, drab clothing and heavy peppering of gray that dulled her dark hair. "Call me Mary-Margaret," she commanded brusquely and strode out into the reception area. Stopping in front of her, the director thrust out a hand. "You must be Harper."

"I am." She shook the proffered hand and smiled appreciatively at Mary-Margaret's firm, no nonsense grip. "Thank you for carving some time out of your schedule to see me. I'm sure you must be busy."

"Thank you for asking about volunteering at the Village," the other woman said, smooth and somehow easy despite that grim mouth. She stepped back, waving Harper into an office cluttered with paperwork and an accumulation of boys' personal effects. She swept a baseball mitt, a school-type backpack and one large running shoe off the chair facing her desk, tossed them into an oversize box next to it and waved her hand at the cleared chair. "Have a seat."

Harper sat, crossed her legs and regarded the director across the desk. "I wasn't sure if you accepted the help of unlicensed volunteers. I imagine the boys you help here come with a wide range of problems, some or many of which I'm sure I have no experience with. But I like kids and I know Deputy Bradshaw gives a lot of time to the organization. So I thought you might find something for me to do."

Mary-Margaret's lipstick-free lips turned up in a fond smile that turned her naturally dour appearance unexpectedly sweet. "Max is great with the boys. He had a rough childhood himself, so he gets them." Her smile turned dry. "Believe me, they know and respond to that."

Max'd had a rough childhood? Harper would have loved to follow up that tidbit, to dig for more information and get the details. Instead, she stored away the stingy teaser to mull over later, for the director was still talking.

"What most of these boys need more than anything," Mary-Margaret said, "is simple old-fashioned, one-on-one positive attention. Max offers that in spades."

Harper nodded. "Yes, that was very apparent at the pancake breakfast. He's got the touch."

Mary-Margaret studied Harper with a cool, calm thoroughness. "You, for the moment, are an unknown quantity. I'd have to see you with the boys in a supervised environment before I could turn you loose with them. But I like that you volunteered at the breakfast, and Max did say you demonstrated an amazingly ef-

fective deflection of one of our boy's inappropriate re-
marks without even opening your mouth."

The older woman grinned suddenly, once again softening her stern features, and Harper began to believe
that *this* was the real Mary-Margaret, and the older
woman's naturally downturned lips likely just a prod-
uct of the musculature surrounding them.

"He also told me about your ideas for improving our
fund-raising," the director continued, "and I'd love to
talk to you about that in more depth. Working on that
here with me might be just the place for you."

Harper knew she shouldn't feel disappointed. Working with Mary-Margaret was a logical use of her abilities and would suit her purposes just fine, since it would
keep her close to ground zero at the heart of this charity. And if she had kind of hoped to work with the boys
one on one?

Well, perhaps it wasn't a great idea, anyhow. She'd
already received two separate come-ons, because these
were hormonal teen boys. That wasn't exactly the usual
demographic she worked with.

"On the other hand," Mary-Margaret said, "Max
mentioned you might be able to offer some of The
Brothers Inn resources for the boys?"

"Yes, I talked to Jenny Salazar, and we brainstormed
a few things that might work for the boys without dis-
rupting the inn's paying guests."

"It would sure be nice if they could get some time
around the water," Mary-Margaret said wistfully. "Other
than taking them down to the public beach at the state
park occasionally, that's one experience we can't offer
them—even though our liability insurance covers off-
campus excursions."

Harper uncrossed her legs and sat a bit straighter in her seat. "If we can coordinate their schedule with the inn's least busy hours, we can offer some tubing behind a boat, kayaking and a tide pool exploration. I can make the latter two both fun and educational. The tubing, I'm afraid, is just…tubing."

The director laughed.

"We're considering letting the boys swim from the dock as well, but that would depend on your assessment of their behavior, since the swimming area is a lot more difficult to segregate from the guests. And I do understand your concern over my ability to handle them. Ordinarily, I'd tell you I can, since as a general rule I'm quite good with people. But I appreciate that these aren't run-of-the-mill kids. I tend not to jump into situations I can't control—and without some idea of the depth of these boys' problems I have no way of judging if my abilities are up to the challenge."

The other woman leaned forward. "I like you. You're not one of those starry-eyed do-gooders—you've clearly given this a great deal of thought. So let's do this. Let's introduce you to the boys in a couple of controlled situations where I or one of the counselors can assess your abilities. If those go well, we'll turn you loose with a hand-picked group of boys. The truth is, for the sort of treats you and the inn are offering, we tend to reward the kids who've made appreciable inroads on their issues anyhow. Regardless, we never just send them off with nonprofessionals. If they go off site, we'll send along someone from here to lend expertise, muscle and additional support."

Harper nodded, pleased with the proposal. "That sounds perfect. I wish I could promise you consistent hours, but mine change almost daily depending on the inn's occupancy and who's signed up for what activities. But I could likely give you twenty-four hours' notice."

"Would you be willing to take a child-safety class?"

"Absolutely."

"Then your schedule will work just fine. It's pretty much the same thing Max does. Well, he generally knows his schedule a week in advance, but things still regularly come up to throw spanners in the works." Mary-Margaret rose to her feet. "Can you spare an hour right now?"

"Sure." Harper rose, as well.

"Excellent. Let's check out the game room. We'll see how you do with the boys."

A FEW DAYS later, Max walked into Mary-Margaret's office. "Hey," he said when the older woman looked up from the work she was poring over on her computer screen. He bent to pick up the Lost and Found box from the floor next to her desk and started tossing the odds and ends littering the seat of the visitor chair into it. He usually eased into his volunteer time here by tracking down who belonged to what misplaced item.

"Hey, yourself." Mary-Margaret, who always looked pleased to see him, stared at him with even more delight than usual. "I don't remember seeing your name on the schedule for today. But, Lordy, am I ever glad to see you!"

"Yeah, I was supposed to work today." He rubbed his aching head. "You hear about the accident up on the highway last night?"

"Oh, hell." Her expression turned serious. "I did. One

teen killed and three more in the hospital? From Chico, right? You caught that?"

"Yeah. I was first responder and was on it until three this morning." And watching those kids being scraped up had pushed far too many of his buttons, had edged him too damn close to that old snake pit of emotions he'd worked so hard to leave behind on the war-torn roads and urban landscapes of the Middle East. "Damn kids must have downed two and a half cases of beer between 'em. The driver tried to take that curve by the Olmstead place at close to eighty miles an hour, and his car took down two trees when it went off the bank." He shook the raw meat visions of the dead boy out of his head. "Sheriff Neward sent me home, but—" He clenched his jaw, unwilling to admit, *I'm not ready to be alone.*

"I'm sorry that you had to deal with that—I can only imagine how awful it must have been. But your availability turns out to be a godsend for us. Jim either ate something that didn't agree with him or caught himself a case of the flu. Either way, he was supposed to take a group over to the inn to go tubing with Harper. The boys are all pumped about it, and I've been dreading having to tell them we have to cancel. Still." She looked at him with concern. "Are you up for it?"

His headache receded a bit. *Well, let me see.* Which would he prefer, having the images of mangled teenagers running through his head or the opportunity to see Harper in a bathing suit again? But he merely said, "Sure," and returned the Lost and Found box to the floor. "I'll have to make a quick stop at my place to grab my board shorts. I've never tubed, myself, so I have no idea if I'll be needed in the water."

"Take the van. You've got Malcolm, Brandon, Jeremy and Owen."

He nodded his approval. "Good choices for her maiden voyage."

"Yeah. They're not all the way there yet, but of the current crop they've come the farthest."

Twenty minutes later, Max pulled the van into the lot behind The Brothers Inn. He turned off the ignition and twisted around to look at his passengers. "This is the first time we've been given an opportunity to use the inn's resources," he said, giving the teens his best listen-up look. "Keep that in mind, because if you screw the pooch, there won't be a second time."

They gave him solemn nods, then poured out of the van with let-out-of-school whoops and raced for the beach. Max snorted, but couldn't help but grin as he picked up his pace behind them.

The Olympics were out in their full glory, rising layer upon green layer of mountains out of the canal until their tallest rugged peaks, etched white with the last remaining snow, scraped the cerulean sky. A lone lenticular cloud floated its cap above the double peaks of The Brothers.

They found Harper on the dock, stooped next to a sleek little runabout. Checking her out, he blinked. Well, hell, no bathing suit.

Okay, thinking about it from a purely practical standpoint, he had to agree that Harper in that sexy black-and-white suit he'd seen her wear The Day of the Hot Tub, as he'd privately dubbed it, probably wasn't the best scenario around a bunch of teenage boys who had sex on the brain 24/7. The turquoise-and-black neoprene wet suit she had on was sexy enough, and *that* covered her from her neck to just above her elbows and knees. It also hugged her body like spray paint and showcased her toned arms and legs. And, Sweet Mother Mary, that high, round ass.

He blew out a breath, shook out his hands, then got his head back in the game. "Hey," he said, walking up to her. "Isn't that Austin's boat?"

"Well, hello, there. I was surprised when Mary-Margaret said you were coming And, yes. Austin donated it to the cause…with a stern caveat that only you drive it." She grinned up at him. "I don't know whether to be offended or not."

"Have you ever driven a boat?"

"A couple of times, although I will admit to being more at home in kayaks and the like."

"There you go."

"I could so drive it!" Owen, the smallest of the four boys, stepped between them, his narrow chest puffed out.

"No, Sport," Max said easily. "You can't. If the owner stipulates only me in order for us to use the boat, then only me it's going to be."

"Besides." Harper smiled at the teen. "You get to do something way cooler. You get to ride the Gladiator Rage."

"What's that?" Owen demanded, but his gaze had already followed the sweep of her hand and he stilled. "Oh, man!"

The rest of the boys looked where he was staring, and suddenly there was a stampede to the huge blue, gold and black towable U-tube that stretched across the end of the dock. They whooped and clustered around it, checking it out.

"Holy shit." Jeremy, who tied Malcolm as the largest of the teens, nodded at the four red sets of handles across the top of it. "This thing'll take all of us at once? That's *monster* epic!"

"I call the outside," Malcolm said. "That's the position that makes you bounce the highest."

"I call the other one," claimed Brandon.

"Aw, man!" Jeremy groused.

Max noticed that Owen didn't say anything.

So, apparently, did Harper. "You all *do* know how to swim, right?" she asked.

Jeremy, Brandon and Malcolm all agreed they did with varying degrees of scorn. Owen looked at the dock.

Max slid his arm around the smaller boy's shoulders. "Buddy?"

Owen looked up at him. "I can swim a little," he said. "But I'm not whatcha might call a strong swimmer."

"Everyone's going to wear a life vest," Harper assured him. "That keeps you buoyant even if you do go in the water."

"Hey, I'm a great swimmer," Brandon protested. "I was on swim team for four years. I don't need no stinkin' life vest."

"And yet you get to wear one, anyhow," Harper said with an easy smile. "The inn has rules, and this one goes, no vest, no ride." She turned back to Owen. "So, as I said, you'll have a vest to keep you safe. But is this something you want to do? Because, if it makes you uncomfortable, you can always ride in the boat with us."

"It's not quite as bouncy in the middle," Malcolm said. "And whoever's next to you can try to lean in on the jumps to keep you in place." The other boys nodded their agreement, whether out of solidarity or a fear that Owen's reluctance might somehow tank their afternoon, Max couldn't say.

But Owen nodded. "That'd prob'ly work."

"Then, put these on," Harper said, handing out the life vests. Once the boys each had one, she tossed a larger model to Max, then pulled on her own. She looked at the three bigger boys. "Start out with Malcolm and Brandon on either end, then take turns switching off with Jeremy, so everyone who wants a shot at that position gets one. Can you live with those terms?"

"You bet!"

"Yes!"

"Hell, yeah!"

"All right then." She grinned at them. "Let's have some fun."

Max handed her into the boat, then found himself rubbing his hand against his board shorts in an attempt to eradicate the feel of her smooth skin from his fingertips. He turned back to supervise the teens as they put the tube in the water. Even as he got the kids situated on the tube, he eyed her covertly, using an inspection of the tow rope she was feeding out as his excuse.

"Let me know when the rope is taut," he said to her as he slowly maneuvered the boat away from the dock a moment later, then added, "That was smooth."

She glanced at him over her shoulder. "What was?"

"The way you handled Brandon not wanting to wear a vest."

"Hey, rules are rules." She grinned at him. "Until you mean to break them, anyway." She turned back to gauge the rope. "It's tight."

Max half lifted out of the driver's seat. "You guys ready?" he called.

The boys yelled an affirmative. And he thrust the throttle forward, surging away from the dock.

They spent the next hour speeding up and down the canal, towing the Gladiator behind them. When it whipped out over the wake, the bounce lifted the teens, who were connected only by their grips on the red handles, up off the tube before dropping them back down again to bounce at whatever angle the Gladiator left them.

It turned out there was no way to lean in on Owen and keep him from raising off the tube. In fact, as the lightest of the boys, he bounced the highest. But by the end of the first run it was clear he was loving it, even going so far as to insist on taking a turn on the outside.

Max found himself smiling almost nonstop. Seagulls swooped and cried overhead, the sun beat down on his shoulders and the sound of unbridled laughter from boys who didn't always have a lot to laugh about filled the air.

Then there was Harper. Acting as their spotter, she mostly kept her eyes on the boys to ensure that if anyone lost their grip and bounced off the tube they could promptly circle around to pick him up. That meant when he glanced around his view was of her long back, longer legs and that wanna-fill-my-hands-with-it ass.

There was a sight he had no complaints with.

To his surprise, however, even better than the visual feast of Harper's body were the moments when one of the boys laughed with pure joy and the two of them glanced over their shoulders at each other to grin in mutual appreciation.

The smartest thing he'd done today was go to the Village. Because a day on the water, a hot woman who shared his pleasure in providing a fun day in the sun to boys who didn't get an abundance of them?

Well, that beat the hell out of skulking around his house, trying not to brood about an accident whose outcome he'd had no way of changing.

CHAPTER EIGHT

MAX JINGLED THE change in his pocket as he waited in line at the Stop and Go outside of town. Friday night was finally here, he had just gassed up his rig, and if Conner, the cashier, and Woody Boyd, who was paying for his half rack of Heineken, ever quit their damn jawing, he'd be on his way to Silverdale for that night on the town he'd been thinking about for dog years.

Even better, if things went the way he hoped—and Chatty and Chattier put a cork in it—by the end of the night he might well have reason to use the box of condoms he was waiting to purchase.

It had been too damn long since the last time *that* occasion had presented itself.

Shifting sideways to let Woody by a moment later, he finally stepped up to take his place at the register. Vaguely, he heard the tinny sound of the little bell over the door. He paid it only scant attention until he heard, "Hey, look, there's Uncle Max!"

Then he turned to see Austin barreling through the door with Jake ambling in his wake. He watched his nephew head his way, the kid's mouth stretched in a big, toothy grin—then turned back long enough to slide a twenty across the counter to Conner Priest.

He'd given the clerk a warning just last week after pulling him over for doing fifty on Orilla Road. Anyone who'd lived here longer than a month knew it was posted at thirty-five—and Conner was a Razor Bay native. Still, the kid hadn't begged special consideration. He had, in fact, given Max zero attitude—handing over his license with a respectful maturity Max saw in damn few adults in the same situation. Fifteen over the limit generally guaranteed the offender a ticket, but Max had cut the young man some slack.

It was just too rare that he didn't have to listen to a load of bullshit at traffic stops.

Austin muscled his way past the postmistress in line behind Max. "Sorry, Ms. Verkins," he said. "I'm not trying to cut—I just wanna say hi to my uncle."

Conner repaid Max now by quietly sliding the condoms into a paper bag before counting out his change. Max gave him an appreciative nod before turning to his nephew. "Hey, buddy. What are you guys up to?" He steered the boy out of the line.

"I'm spending the night at Nolan's, and Dad brought me here to get some Flamin' Hot Cheetos to take. They don't carry 'em at the General Store."

Max shook his head. "That's criminal."

"Tell me about it. You oughtta go arrest 'em."

"Max isn't wearing his Deputy Dawg suit," Jake said, "so that probably won't happen tonight. And it's Friday, bud—everyone and their brother's getting their weekend supplies. You better make sure they haven't sold out of the Flamin' Hots here."

"Better not have!" Austin hustled toward the chip aisle.

Jake turned to Max. "Got yourself a cool hat—" he gave Max's Brixton classic fedora a nod of approval "—and a big box of Trojan Supras. Hot date?"

"Jesus, you must have eyes like a raptor. How the hell could you tell what brand I bought from the door?"

"Recognize the box." Jake grinned at him. "Who you going out with?"

"No one, yet. But I'm heading over to The Voodoo Lounge, hoping to change my luck." A quick visual of Harper slammed through him, but he firmly shut it down before it could etch itself into his brain like acid. One fun day out on the water with her hardly stepped him up into her league.

Jake looked at him in surprise. "You like to dance?"

"Sure. Don't you?"

"I like slow dancing. I'm not too crazy about the fast shit, though."

"Yeah." Max nodded. "It's guys like you who leave the field wide open for me. Ladies just love them a man who likes to dance." He gave his brother a cocky smile. "Not that you'd be any competition even if you could dance."

"Hey, I can dance!" His response sounded like the knee-jerk defensiveness of their enemy days. But then Jake shot Max a crooked smile. "Okay, not well, but I can dance."

"Dad!" Austin ran up, a bag of his favored chips in his hand and a look on his face as if the world were ending. "I told Nolan I'd bring my new video game and I forgot it at home!"

"Not a problem," Jake said easily. "It's not like we have to go miles out of our way to swing by the house." Reaching out, he hooked his elbow around his son's neck, hauled him in and gave him a noogy. "Let's get in line and pay for your grub."

Max suffered a fierce stab of wanting what Jake had

with his son. He cleared the lump of envy from his throat. "I'll see you two later," he said. "Have fun at Nolan's, kid."

Austin grinned. "I'm gonna."

"You have a good time, yourself," Jake said. He tipped his chin at the bag in Max's hand. "Happy hunting."

The teen looked Max over. "You're going hunting? In your good clothes?" He shook his head. "Man. If it was me doing that, Jenny'd have something to say about it."

Max laughed. "Your dad was being funny. I'm going to a club in Silverdale to dance."

"And no one's making ya?"

"Nope. I like to dance."

"Huh. I thought guys only pretended they did." He hitched a narrow shoulder. "But happy hunting."

Max felt his mouth tug up in an off-kilter smile. "Thanks, kid. And a little tip? Girls love guys who like to dance."

With a wave as Jake and Austin crossed to the now-nearly-free-of-customers counter to pay for Austin's snack, he headed out to his SUV. Twenty minutes later he was pulling into The Voodoo Lounge parking lot.

Pushing through the big teak door, he felt his energy jack up as he was hit by the wall of voices talking and laughing over and under the blast of DJ music. The throng on the crowded dance floor moved almost as one in time to a Rihanna song, but he ignored them to check out the tables he wound between on his way to the bar in the back, homing in on the ones that were filled with women he hoped were looking for a good time.

He grinned inside. Because, helpful guy that he was,

he was willing to help them with that. He lived to serve, after all.

Once he'd made his way through the three-deep crowd at the bar, he ordered a beer on tap, then found a space away from the bartender where the ranks thinned enough for him to lean back against the black ironwood bar as he sipped his brew and broadened his search beyond the tables he'd passed.

He loved this place. The DJ was good, the beer was decent and the women invariably outnumbered the men two to one. He had his eye on a tall brunette when a petite blonde stopped in front of him.

"Hey, there!" She raised her voice to be heard, and still he had to bend down to catch everything. "Want to dance?"

"Sure." He looked at the beer in his hand.

"You can leave that at my table, if you want."

He nodded his agreement and followed her to a table nearer the dance floor. She turned to him.

"These are my friends," she yelled without introducing anyone. "Your beer's safe with them."

He set it on the table, then followed the swing of his new partner's hips, which moved to the beat a little more emphatically with every step that brought them closer to the dance floor.

Reaching it, they carved out a couple square feet for themselves and began to dance. She was good, which he appreciated, and he was just truly getting into it when the song came to an end.

The blonde laughed and stepped aside to let by some of the dancers deserting the floor. More continued to mill around, waiting for the next song to begin, and she leaned into him. "Bad timing. I'm Kim, by the way."

"Max."

"Nice to meet you, Max. Care to try another dance?"

"Sure. You're good, you know."

Her face lit up. "Why, thank you! So are you."

The next forty-five minutes flew by. He danced with Kim and talked with her and her friends when they weren't dancing. She was pretty, she had a good job as the office manager of a multi-physician clinic, she was nice—and she'd made it clear she was into him. Pretty much perfect, in other words.

So he wasn't sure why he wasn't more interested in her than he was.

Maybe it was because she was petite. He generally went for taller girls, having discovered the hard way that he'd end the night with a backache from having to perpetually hunch. Or maybe it was—

"There you are, Max!"

He knew that voice, and he whipped his head around to search the area where it had come from. He watched incredulously as Jenny made her way toward him through the crowded, insufficiently spaced tables. Looking beyond her, he saw not only Jake, but Tasha and Harper as well, following in her wake.

What the hell? He rose to his feet, aware of all of them, but his gaze locked on Harper. Her lips were creamy red, she'd done something to her eyes that made them all smoky, and she was shrink-wrapped from collarbone to midthigh in a flaming-red dress.

All the women were dressed in hot clubwear, he noticed when he dragged his gaze away, and Jenny strode right up to him on what looked like five-inch heels and gave him one of her ubiquitous hugs. When she cut him loose and twisted to see if her friends were coming, he turned to his half brother. "What the fuck, man?" he demanded beneath the new song starting up.

"I'm sorry, bro. This wasn't my idea, I swear." Jake took a step closer to Max but away from his fiancée. "Austin spilled the beans when we stopped at the house to pick up his video game. And before I could pull Jenny aside to tell her you were on the hunt for more than an opportunity to boogie, she'd decided she just had to go dancing, too, and was on the horn to Tash and Harper."

Jenny muscled Jake aside to grin up at Max. "You have to dance with me!" she yelled over the music. "Austin tells me you actually *like* dancing. In my experience, a guy who doesn't merely tolerate it is a rare, rare animal. It's not every day a girl gets a shot at one."

"Uh…" He looked helplessly between her and Kim, and Jenny followed his gaze.

"Hi!" She leaned around him to offer Kim her hand. "I'm Jenny, Max's brother's fiancée. You don't mind if I borrow him for a dance, do you?"

"I…guess not." But she didn't look thrilled about it.

Jenny either didn't see it or didn't care. "Great!" She wrapped her hand around his wrist and tugged. With a helpless shrug at Kim, he followed in her wake. Speaking of little women, Jenny almost made Kim look statuesque.

But as first his brother, then he had learned, she had a will that was gigantic.

He was feeling ambushed and a little pissed off, but he let the negative feelings go as soon as they hit the dance floor. He really didn't get why more guys didn't like to dance. It just felt so good to move to the music, and women really did dig the hell out of it. Shooting

Jenny a grin, he yanked her into him and executed a dirty dancing move.

Oh. My. God, she mouthed, sliding free one of the hands she'd grasped his shoulders with when he'd dipped her back over his arm. She used it to pat a rapid heartbeat against the satin covering her left breast.

Then she performed a grinding sort of dirty dance move of her own.

He laughed and threw himself into the remainder of the dance.

"Omigawd, Omigawd," she said, bouncing on her tall heels when the song ended. "You. Are. So. Good! How could I have not known that?" She shot him a rueful smile. "I don't suppose you'd give me one more before we head back? Seeing as how this wasn't a whole song and all?"

"Uh, you sort of dragged me away from a decent prospect of getting lucky tonight."

She reached up and patted his cheek. "Ah, Max. You consistently underrate yourself, you know that? You're gainfully employed, you're good-looking, you're *built—and* you dance. Don't you know you could pretty much snap your fingers at any woman here and get her to go home with you?"

Heat crawled up his face. "No, I couldn't."

"Yeah. Yeah, you really could." Standing on her tiptoes, she gave him another hug. "But I'll let you get back to your decent prospect. I expect one more dance tonight, though. And you definitely have to share the thrill and dance at least once with Tash and Harper."

He grunted noncommittally and escorted her to Jake, who was still standing by Kim's table.

"Harper staked us out a place over there," he said, indicating a spot five tables away.

"Neat trick," Max said. "How'd she manage that after ten on a Friday night?"

"Apparently she heard some women in the ladies' talking about taking off to go hit the One Ten in Poulsbo." He grinned. "She accompanied them back to their table so she'd get first claim on it."

"Enterprising," Max said drily.

"*Really* enterprising," Jenny agreed. "I swear, that girl can do any damn thing she puts her mind to."

Didn't he know it. He'd been watching her for a week since they'd taken the Cedar Village boys out tubing.

She'd been great with the boys that day—and had shown up at Cedar Village three times since then, somehow volunteering at the same time he was. Not that he thought for a minute she had arranged it that way. For this week, at least, their down times had simply meshed. Bottom line was: he'd been there and she had been there.

Not watching her hadn't been an option.

He rolled his shoulders impatiently. So he was attracted to her—big deal. It wasn't exactly breaking news, and he was a big boy. He knew how to compartmentalize unwanted feelings, knew how to shove them down and forget them while he took care of the stuff in real need of his attention.

Besides, his attraction to her aside, she was damn good with the kids, beautifully low-key and easy with them. It was a gift not everyone possessed. No matter how much an adult might like children—or thought they should anyhow—not all of them were comfortable with the species. That was especially true when you threw teenage boys who'd clearly had their share of trouble into the mix.

"Max?"

Something touched his arm, and he looked down to see Kim's hand on his forearm. Dragging his attention back to the here and now, he smiled down at her. "Hey there. I'm sorry for the interruption. My brother's fiancée is a force of nature. You want to dance?"

She gave him a delighted "yes," and he steered her toward the floor with a light hand on the small of her back. But his glance went over her head to the table where Harper sat laughing with Jake, Jenny and Tasha. As he watched, a man bent over her and said something. Smiling up at him, she rose to her feet and strolled ahead of him to the dance floor.

Where she stopped not three feet away from Max.

Ignoring an inexplicable prickle of irritation, he angled his body away from the new pair. Yet when the music segued from fast to slow a few minutes later, he couldn't seem to stop himself from glancing over as Harper's partner pulled her into his arms.

A low growl sounded in Max's chest.

"What?" Kim tipped her head back to look up at him.

Realizing he'd forgotten about her for a moment, he blinked down into her eyes. "Huh?"

"Did you say something?"

"No. It was nothing." Stepping forward, he wrapped his arms around her and started to move. "Nothing at all," he repeated grimly.

The moment she tucked her head against his chest, however, his gaze went back to Harper.

Which was how he saw the guy's hands slide down over the curve of her short, snug red dress to grasp that beautiful round ass. Being taller than most people had its advantages.

Having a bird's eye view of *that,* however, was not one of them, and he stiffened.

Then he relaxed and nodded approval when Harper promptly reached behind her, wrapped her fingers around the guy's wrists and moved his damn hands to the more appropriate area of her hips.

Not one minute later they crept back.

Max stopped dead. Yet even as he did so, Harper froze, as well. Her immobility didn't last, however. The hands she'd rested on the guy's shoulders slid to his chest, and she gave an emphatic shove, taking a large step back as he stumbled in reverse. She whirled and stalked away.

His lips curving up, Max picked up the rhythm again. He must have thought he'd been standing there longer than was actually the case, for Kim was just now lifting her head to see what the problem was. His renewed movement had her resting her cheek back against his chest almost in the same motion that she'd used to raise it.

His brows drew together when Harper didn't go back to the table but instead picked her way through the close-packed tables to let herself out through the big teak door. Then he gave a mental shrug, because what did he know about how she felt? It wasn't as if anyone had ever pawed him the way she'd just been; maybe she needed a minute to gather her composure before she rejoined her group.

None of whom were at the table, he saw when he glanced that way. He looked around the dance floor and spotted Jake and Jenny swaying in place and, after a second, Tasha dancing with a guy who made Max look like a shrimp. He glanced back at the door.

Just in time to see Mr. Handsie passing through it.

"Sonofabitch!" He stepped back, catching Kim by the shoulders when she staggered and blinked up at him. "I'm sorry," he said. "Something's come up—I've gotta go."

"What? *Now?*"

Not waiting to reply, he turned on his heel and strode for the door. He caught it before it could close behind a noisy group of twentysomethings who had just entered the Voodoo. As the thick teak door closed behind him, his ears rang in the sudden quiet.

The silence wasn't complete, however. Tuning in midconversation, he heard an angry male voice snarl from not too far away, "Can't just shove me and walk away!" Max turned to follow the sound.

"Be careful who you call a bitch," he heard Harper reply with her cool, near-British diction. "And I certainly can walk away when you put your hands all over my butt and refuse to get a clue when I remove them."

"If you didn't want hands on your ass, you wouldn't wear that tight skirt to bring it to everyone's attention!"

"Tell me you did *not* just say that. 'It wasn't my fault, judge,'" she said in a surprisingly good imitation of his voice. "'Sure, she removed my hands from her butt in no uncertain terms. But you could tell by the way she dressed that she wanted it.'" Her voice went back to normal. "The classic rapist's defense."

"What?" The guy sounded genuinely shocked. "I'm not a rapist!"

Max finally located them in the shadows cast by the corner of the building, and he lengthened his stride.

"Everything okay here?" he asked in his sternest cop voice as he walked up.

The man's head snapped around. "Yeah. Jesus. Who the hell are you?"

"Everything is fine, Deputy Bradshaw," Harper said calmly. "My friend here was just leaving."

"Yeah. Right. Deputy," the idiot scoffed, giving Max's club clothes a skeptical once-over. "You don't look like a deputy to me."

Max pulled his shield out of his back pocket, flipped open the leather holder he kept it in when it wasn't on his uniform and held it up. "The lady said you were just leaving. Hit the road."

"Fine, I'm going." He turned to Harper. "But I'm no rapist."

"No, you're not. But when you put your hands where they don't belong, refuse to take responsibility for your actions, then follow your victim when she walks away?" Harper said in the hardest tone Max had ever heard from her. "You're the next best thing."

"Shit," the guy muttered. But he looked shaken as he walked off, so maybe he'd actually give what she said some thought.

Max moved in closer to Harper. "You okay?"

"Yes. I'm more pissed than anything."

He looked her over, trying to assess the truth of that. Then took a deep breath. "You, uh, need a hug or anything?"

"No." She gave him a faint smile. "But thank you." Her shoulders squared. "I'm damned if I'll let him ruin my good time—it's been forever since I've been dancing." She gave him a comprehensive look. "You certainly are a good dancer. Maybe you could give me a spin about the floor."

"Absolutely. I'll even keep my hands off your butt."

As he'd hoped, she laughed. The sound shot straight to his dick, and he knew one thing for sure as he escorted her back into The Voodoo Lounge.

He wouldn't be using his new condoms tonight.

CHAPTER NINE

WHAT THE HELL am I doing here?

Tapping a finger against the steering wheel, Harper braked on a road outside of Razor Bay as her headlights picked out BRADSHAW in neat black stencil on a utilitarian gray mailbox.

It had been a week since she'd seen Max but *this* was a bad idea. If she had a lick of sense she'd head home and call it a night.

Yet still she found herself turning into the driveway and slowly making her way up its long lane. Woods crowded in on either side, the forest floor covered in lush ferns stippled almost silver wherever the moonlight managed to filter through the foliage. Then she drove clear of the trees, her headlights illuminating a large sweep of lawn, and—

Stomping on the brakes, she looked at the dark, clearly unoccupied house.

Okay, that was likely a good thing. Right? She'd been pretty damn ambivalent about her presence here to begin with. And if she felt perhaps the slightest bit disappointed?

Well, she could just blame that on the wine.

Forty-five minutes earlier

HARPER POURED HERSELF a glass of sauvignon blanc and carried it out to the porch where she settled into one of the two old bentwood rockers. Relaxing into her seat, she soaked in her surroundings. Although she could make out faint snippets of conversations and the occasional burst of laughter from guests passing by on the main path below, up here on the edge of the woods what she heard most were the more soothing sounds of nature. A playful breeze soughed through the alders and firs behind her cottage, setting needles and leaves to softly rustling, while crickets chirped in multipart harmony, the raucous song of their wings rising to a crescendo, then going abruptly silent when something disturbed them.

The moon had risen above the trees at her back to spotlight the canal, its reflected light shimmering a path across the water's slightly rippled surface like a silver brick road to the Olympics. They in turn soared to majestic heights above the water, forming rugged silhouettes against a midnight-blue sky.

It was beautiful, a sight to inspire not only awe but a sense of peace. Yet serene was the last thing Harper felt at the moment. She took a sip of her wine.

Then a swallow.

Then a gulp so big she nearly drained the goblet as she finally admitted to herself the cause of her anxiety.

She was enjoying her stay in Razor Bay way too much.

Setting aside the wineglass, she thumped her feet flat on the porch deck. *Too much? Really?*

That was ludicrous—why shouldn't she enjoy herself? It wasn't as if she was doing something wrong. Sunday's Child forged long-term relationships, and she simply needed to be sure its dollars went to the best of the best.

And just because it was nice to rise from the same bed every morning for a change, it didn't mean she was looking for permanence or anything. The differences she discovered in the new places she visited were precisely what she adored. They were what turned new locations into an adventure. She gained fresh experiences and met fun, interesting people. She had a network of friendly acquaintances all over globe.

And yet…she hadn't had a serious, Capital G Girlfriend since she'd had to leave Anke Biermann behind in München when she was twelve.

Oh, she understood the why of it. As grand as it was to meet new people, it was considerably less so having to say goodbye. And perhaps, just perhaps, since that wrenching, long-ago parting with Anke, she might have subtly discouraged true intimacy even as she'd had those grand times with her global playmates.

But if that were true, it sure wasn't working on Jenny and Tasha.

They had stormed her defenses like Attila stormed the Gauls, except with a better end result. She credited that to their choice of weapons: irreverent humor and an easy, taken-for-granted inclusion in their lives. They hadn't asked if she wanted to be sucked into their orbit. From the very first day she'd come to Razor Bay to interview for The Brothers Inn gig, they had simply been the moon to her tide, drawing her in with irresistible force.

And she was seriously loving it. It felt like a very big deal.

Yet it was small spuds compared to her attraction to Max.

Ever since he'd rescued her from the guy with the

roaming hands at the dance club last weekend, she'd been forced to admit that if suddenly having real girlfriends was big, her fascination with Max was *huge*.

It would be easy, she thought, setting the rocker in motion, to attribute her growing attraction to seeing him out of uniform. He'd looked just plain hot with that skinny-brim fedora tipped down over one inky eyebrow, the retro shirt hugging the breadth of his shoulders and the granite curve of his biceps, and those charcoal slacks that did the same thing for his most excellent butt.

But to her surprise, it wasn't his very fine body that had gotten to her the most. *That* had been the light in his dark eyes and the grin he'd worn practically the entire night, a startling contrast to his usually stone-serious demeanor. His obvious pleasure at being out on the town and getting to dance had been altogether unexpected and totally charming. She'd just wanted to be with him all night long.

This single-minded preoccupation with him was confusing. And utterly unlike her. She'd *always* gone for suave, cerebral men. Older men.

Yet all of a sudden she couldn't say why. Not when Max was so big. So earthy. So...

Sexual.

A frisson of defensiveness shivered through her. Her previous lovers had been sexual. They'd left her perfectly satisfied.

But remembering his moves on the dance floor, not only with her but with the other women she'd watched him dance with, she was pretty sure Max would take satisfaction to an entirely new level. And that he wouldn't go about it half as politely as her previous lovers had.

Just the idea had her literally burning to discover what that would be like.

"So why don't you?" she whispered.

Harper rose to her feet so abruptly she set the bent-wood chair to madly rocking. Excellent question. Why didn't she?

Because there's no chance of it lasting?

But it didn't have to be a forever thing. God knew this attraction she felt was to-infinity-and-beyond enormous. And while she couldn't say so with complete certainty, she was pretty sure Max wasn't entirely indifferent to her, either. So what did she have to lose?

"He could reject you," she muttered.

And that would bite, no two ways about it. Not to mention make future encounters rather awkward.

But what if he didn't? The idea pulled her to her feet.

So HERE SHE was in Max's yard, feeling idiotic beyond belief as she stared across the yard at his house, which was pitch-dark except for a single light on over his garage. Beautiful. Could she be any worse at this if she tried? He wasn't even home.

With a sigh, she put the car in gear to turn it around.

She'd barely pointed it in the right direction when light filled the tunnel through the trees that led to the road. Even through her closed window, she could hear the growl of a vehicle coming up the lane with a lot more speed than she'd used. She shut down her engine and climbed out.

A second later his rig shot into the opening, then came to a halt so abrupt, the SUV rocked on its shocks. The door swung open, and Max got out, tension clear in the set of his jaw as he looked unsmilingly at her across its top. "Harper? Is something wrong?"

Okay, not exactly a *Hey, glad to see ya,* but Harper had to admit it was a valid question. What *was* she doing here? Because what had seemed like such a great and adventuresome idea on her porch now seemed really stupid.

"Oh, no. Everyone's fine. I, um—" *Think, girl!* "—just wanted to thank you again. I haven't been able to get Friday night out of my mind." *Okay, good—that's good. The truth always plays better.* He didn't need to know it was him rather than Grabby Guy that she'd been dwelling on. "But listen. This was a dumb idea and probably a lousy time to come calling. I know it's late—I don't know what I was thinking. So I'll just be off. Get out of your hair." *You can shut up any time now.* Tossing her purse through the open door, she concentrated on watching it land on the passenger seat to avoid looking at him again, then reached for the door handle.

"Wait." Rubbing at a furrow between his brows, he started toward her. As if his movement were a signal, a sliver of moon cleared the cloud it had been lingering behind. "I'm sorry. I had a crappy shift. But I shouldn't be taking it out on you."

She could see the weariness on his face. And instead of his usual pristine uniform, he'd unbuttoned the top of his shirt and had clearly given the knot of his tie a big yank. It draped in a canted ellipse across his chest, the ends pointing sideways. "What happened?"

He blew out a breath. "I could use a beer. You wanna come in?"

"Are you kidding me? Jake's been lording it over Jenny and Tasha all week because he's seen your house and they haven't." She grinned at him. "Of course I want to come in."

He shook his head, his expression lightening as he walked up to her. "I don't get what the big deal is." Resting his hand lightly on the small of her back, he escorted her to his front door where he reached around her to open it. The heat of his chest pressed against her back for a moment as he worked his hand along the interior wall. Then a light inside sprang to life, and he straightened. Cool air rushed in to fill the space that warm muscle had touched. "But I guess I'd better invite them over. Jenny's reasonably mellow, but Tasha will cut off my pizza privileges in a New York minute."

She was already looking around as he moved through the room, turning on a trio of table lights. "Wow. This is really nice." Even in the pale moonlight coming through the windows at the dim end of the room, that was plain to see.

"Yeah, I'm pretty happy with the way it's shaping up." He motioned her into the large open Great room. "The space was all chopped up when I bought it, so I took out some walls to open it up."

"By yourself?" She looked at him in admiration. "Weren't you afraid everything would cave in?"

"No." His teeth flashed white in the here-and-gone smile he crooked at her. "You can learn to do just about anything on YouTube, so whenever I had to remove a load-bearing wall, I replaced it with a support beam in the ceiling. Ignore the kitchen," he said, waving a hand at the breakfast bar's bare plywood counter and the ancient cupboards beyond it. "That's top of my list after I finish staining the exterior. And that's not gonna happen until Jake helps me pick out a color." He gave her a sheepish look. "I figure, him being a photographer and all, he'll have a better eye for what'll look good." Shrugging, he moved into the kitchen and turned on an under-counter light. "You want a beer?"

"Sure." She crossed to the lamp by the leather couch and turned it on, then walked over to admire the tile work on the fireplace surround and hearth. "This is gorgeous," she said as he joined her, beers in one hand and a bowl of potato chips in the other. She relieved him of one of the bottles and took the seat he indicated on the leather couch. "I don't think you have a thing to worry about if you chose these colors." She indicated the creamy gold of the walls and the tiles of rich browns and deeper, earthier golds.

He shrugged and flopped down next to her. "I stole both it and the idea for the fir surround on top of the tile one from a picture I found online."

"Whatever works, right?" She'd been admiring his work, but turning to look at him more closely, she did a double take. He hadn't simply unbuttoned his collar and loosened his tie. His usually sharp uniform was completely mussed up, half of his shirttail pulled free of his jeans and hanging down, the placket's top two buttons missing. Something damp and rusty-looking smeared the khaki fabric along the edge of his now-opened collar. "My God, Max. What happened to you?"

"You don't want to know."

Pulling a knee up, Harper shifted around to face him. "Yes. I really do. I'd love to know what the heck did that to a uniform that's always very spiff."

"That would be from starting and ending my shift with a D and D."

"What's that?"

"Sorry, drunk and disorderly. The usual Razor Bay drunks know me, and, except on rare occasions, they tend not to get out-of-bounds obnoxious, because it *will* land them in jail if they give me too much shit. Even temporarily impaired, they mostly understand this—it's one of the advantages of small-town life. But with the summer trade, I run into people who just don't know when to quit testing my limits."

"And you had one of those tonight?"

He blew out a tired breath. "I had three—*three* frigging drunks. I'd only been on maybe forty minutes when The Anchor called me in to deal with a drunk-on-his ass, shit-for-brains peckerwood tourist who'd been pissing people off right and left. When I refused to let him get behind the wheel, he slopped beer on my shoes and bad-mouthed my intelligence, my parentage and the size of my—" He cut himself off, and his gaze turned inward as though he were recalling the encounter. Then he shook his head. "The guy was about as much fun as a raging case of—uh—acne, but at least he was all talk. The call I got out to Low Harry's—that was something else again."

"Low Harry's?" Harper's brow furrowed. "Where's that? I've never heard of it."

"Honey, no one you hang out with would be caught dead there. It's about five miles out of town, and the place is a cesspool, peopled by every lowlife within a thirty-mile radius." His big shoulders suddenly rolled as if trying to shake something off. "Damn," he said. "I was *this* close to not having to take that call. I should have been turning the shift over to Blackwell, the other deputy, but he was late getting to the station."

"What did you mean when you said that call was something else again?"

"It was ten times—no, make that a hundred times—worse."

"Why?"

"Because these drunks were women. Women on a *tear*. And you do *not* want to get between two women going at it the way those two were." His long fingers rose, as if of their own volition, to touch that damp rusty patch on his shirt.

Suddenly suspicious, Harper leaned forward. "Oh, my God—is that—?" It was; it was drying blood. Gently, she fingered the shirt away from the side of his throat and saw a taped-down gauze four-by-four, dotted with blood, from where the pad of his shoulder began to rise away from the curve of his neck to just beneath his collarbone. Another, smaller bandage was taped to the side of his neck above the first one. Ragged tails of a couple welts, shiny with what she assumed was anti-biotic ointment, stuck out beyond the edge of the bandage nearest her.

"Good God," she breathed, raising her gaze to his face as she sat back. "I'm glad you at least got medical attention."

"Yeah, the clientele at Low Harry's isn't exactly known for their hygiene, and that catfight was already bloody when I got there. God knows what diseases those two crazy-ass women might have."

"Did you at least crack their heads together?"

"I'm a trained professional, Summerville," he said sternly. "We arrest—we don't crack heads." But a slow smile split his face. "I have to admit that's a pretty cool fantasy, though."

He looked so boyishly wistful that her heart just melted. That smile. Oh, Lord, that much-too-rarely-seen smile. It got to her, and without thought, she leaned into him and whispered a kiss across his lips.

They were both soft and firm at the same time, and opening her own she touched them with her tongue.

And promptly felt as if she'd grabbed the business end of a live wire at the damp contact with the seam of his lips. She jerked back and, pretending her knees weren't shaking, rose to her feet. Better to concentrate on that lie than to admit that a simple kiss—not even a let's-let-our-tongues-go-crazy soul kiss at that—had totally wrecked her. "Omigawd. That was so presumptuous. I'm— I should go." She headed for the door.

Before she could take more than a couple of steps, he was moving. She felt his heat again as one hard-skinned hand slipped around her waist and splayed across her stomach to pull her back against him, easily holding her in place.

"Yeah," he murmured, his breath brushing her ear. "That was *very* presumptuous. I might have to arrest you for assaulting an officer." He turned her in his arms. "Or…" His dark-eyed gaze locked on her mouth. "I could just do this."

And his lips came down on hers, hot and demanding.

Head swimming with the abundance of sensation, she opened for him. His tongue took immediate advantage, exploring every sensitive inch of her mouth as if it were property he'd just acquired. Helplessly, she wound her arms around his neck to cling tightly.

He didn't say a word, didn't even flinch. But feeling the brush of gauze against her inner arm, she remembered his injuries and pulled back. "Sorry. I forgot."

Hands running down her arms, causing goose bumps to crop up in their rough-skinned wake, he leaned back, putting a few inches of space between them. "Don't apologize," he said authoritatively, "relocate." And grasping her wrists, he pulled them around his sides.

She slid them up his back, and, holding her shoulders in a light grip, he gave her an approving nod. "There you go. Look, Ma, no wounds to worry about."

Then the smile faded, and he stared at her, bringing a hand up to brush a curl away from her eyes. "God, you're pretty," he said, and lowered his head.

This time the kiss was an ode to gentleness, his lips slow and firm as they rubbed hers apart, his tongue a benediction as it stroked hers. Harper found herself rising onto her toes to feel as much of his hard body against hers as she possibly could.

And just like that, the kiss leaped out of control again. Max pulled her in tighter, bending his knees until his hard sex nudged the soft, rapidly dampening notch between her legs. For a second they both froze, hissing in simultaneous breaths. Harper had a second to wonder if he was as aware as she that the thin layers of their clothing were all that separated them. Then Max's mouth grew rougher, more demanding, all teeth and tongue and I'm-in-charge sexuality. Never having experienced anything remotely comparable, Harper found herself on the verge of stimulation overload.

His hands framing her face, he lifted his head for a moment to come at her from a different angle. She responded mindlessly when his lips closed over hers again with firm suction, and a gritty rumble of satisfaction sounded deep in his throat. He palmed her left breast and oscillated his hips.

Oh, God. It was so good, so hot, and wanting, need-ing, a connection that was even closer—preferably hori-zontal and naked—Harper anchored her fingernails in his back and stropped her inner thigh up the outside of Max's, giving herself a great deal of pleasure when the movement caused his rigid sex to drag against her sweet spot.

Then abruptly all that pleasure went away as his hands gripped her arms and held her in place while he took a large step away from her. "God," he panted. "We've gotta slow down here."

"What—?" Her skin rapidly cooled as she blinked up at him. "Why?"

"Because…" He looked baffled for a moment, as though he didn't know himself. Then his firm jaw squared. "Because jumping your bones the first time I kiss you is way too high school. And I respect you too much to act like a seventeen-year-old."

"Oh, don't," she said urgently. "I respect myself enough for both of us." Okay, that wasn't exactly PC. But she *wanted* him to jump her bones. More than she'd ever desired anything, she wanted that. "Besides," she added, "I never had that particular high school experi-ence, so I'm probably owed it, don't you think?"

"You never made out in high school?" he asked in-credulously. "No hot kisses under the bleachers, no backseat petting?"

She shook her head. "I moved around too much and mostly went to all-girls schools."

"Yeah?" He gazed down at her with those intense dark eyes. "Did you wear a uniform?"

"Yes."

"Hot." He looked her over as if visualizing it. "You want the high school experience?"

"Oh, absolutely." She nodded emphatically. "Let's have sex."

"Man, I'd love to." The fervency in his voice sounded genuine. Then he shook his head. "But…no. I'm saving myself for marriage."

He was putting too much effort into appearing virtuous, and Harper smacked his arm. "You are not. You're a guy—everyone knows guys think about sex, like, every twenty-five seconds."

"Sounds about right," he said. "But on the twenty-sixth—or, okay, maybe the twenty-seventh, twenty-eighth—I shove those thoughts down. I have standards." He wrapped one of her curls around the forefinger of his free hand. "And if you want to work your way up to *maybe* making me relax them and have premarital sex with you, you'll have to play by my rules."

It sounded pretty one-sided, but she'd never seen Max playful. And she wanted more.

A lot more. So she nodded. "Fine, we'll play by your rules. Because I like you like this and I want to see if you can sustain it or revert back to Brooding Bradshaw."

Then she leveled a stern look on him. "For *now,* that is. I wouldn't get too used to it, though, if I were you. I'm nobody's pushover."

"Yeah," he agreed. "I pretty much know that already."

"Good. Then know this, too. I'll be coming up with a few rules of my own."

CHAPTER TEN

MAX SPOTTED HARPER passing through the archway to the Cedar Village paths as he parked his SUV. He shut down the engine and swung open his door. "Hey, Harper! Hold up!"

She glanced over her shoulder, and he gave her a c'mere wave. "Can you give me a hand?" He'd already been feeling pretty damn good over his big score. Knowing she was here to see it just made the day seem that much brighter. Okay, he knew wanting to show off his find was Mikey Middle School. He just didn't give a rip.

She strolled over, looking fresh in a pair of sky-blue capris and a white T-shirt with matching blue baseball-type sleeves. Although his expression didn't outwardly change, he smiled inside. Because, really: appropriate, those.

"I have to ask myself what big, strong Deputy Bradshaw can't handle on his own."

"Come see." He reached out to give one of the curls exploding from her high, short ponytail a tug, then went around to the back of his SUV and opened the hatch.

Having followed, she leaned around him to peer in—then gave him a delighted smile. "Where did you *get* all this?"

"Isn't it great?" He grinned at her and leaned into the cargo hold to pull out the stack of three bases and a home plate, which he handed to her. "Little League's not using the baseball gear today, so I talked them into lending it to me, then hit up the parks department for the bases and all these mitts, which apparently they've collected in their Lost and Found over the years. They said we could keep those, since not one of them's been claimed in the past year. The rest we have to have back by four-thirty, but I called ahead to let Mary-Margaret know, and she said she'd gather up all the kids who aren't currently in trouble over an infraction. Let's haul this out to the field."

"If we had another duffel, we could do this in one trip," she said, eying the one stuffed full of bats and balls, then the bazillion and one mitts scattered all over the back of the cargo hatch. Her good-natured tone, however, said she didn't really care how many trips it took.

"Not an issue as it turns out." He glanced past her. "Looks like help's on the way." Two counselors and four teens were striding up the path. The instant they made eye contact, the boys broke into a run, whooping loudly.

Within minutes all the equipment was on its way to the big mown field behind the cottages—where every teenage resident appeared to be waiting.

It took the kids no time at all to set up. Then, without their usual wrangling, they chose Malcolm and Jeremy as team captains and Mary-Margaret as ump. Malcolm won the coin toss for first pick.

He immediately crooked a finger at Harper.

Laughing, she joined the young man. "You should've chosen Max," she said cheerfully. "I've heard he was quite good back in the day, while I've never even been to a baseball game, let alone played in one."

"We'll grab him in the next draft," Malcolm said, but it was obvious to the object of their conversation that the youth was happy merely having Harper on his team. And Max doubted that it was strictly due to her pretty femininity or the fact that she, like Malcolm, was of mixed race. No, he was confident it was her charm, humor and the ease with which she interacted with the boys that was rapidly turning her into a Village favorite.

A good thing, since Jeremy chose Max as his first pick. Observing the cheer with which the kids quickly filled out the rest of their teams, it quickly became evident that they just wanted to play ball. And as had been the case with Harper, they seemed to select more with an eye toward the counselors and other boys they liked than toward any athletic ability.

It must be the nature of nonleague baseball, a sentiment Mary-Margaret bore out when he eased over to her as the kids hammered out some final details before the bat toss to determine whose team would be first up. "Is it my imagination," he murmured to her, "or is every kid in the Village here? Aren't any of the usual Anger Management kids on hiatus from group activities until they complete their course?"

"You know perfectly well that Nathan and Harry should be," she said with a shrug. "But it's baseball. I warned them this is a one-off furlough and if they screwed it up I'd cancel it so fast Wile E. Coyote's Roadrunner would look like a sloth by comparison." Once again her shoulders hitched. But then her naturally downturned lips curled up. "But as I said, Max, it's baseball. Every boy oughtta be given the chance to play."

"Amen to that, my sistah."

They smiled at each other in perfect understanding.

Jeremy won the toss, and Max met up with his team at the dugout while Malcolm's took the field. To his amazement, they put Harper at second base. He'd thought for sure she'd be relegated to left field.

Then Jeremy started laying down some of the plays he had in mind, and Max pulled his attention back to the matter at hand. He had to consciously relax his brows when they threatened to meet over his nose. Most of Jeremy's plays were crazy ambitious, but manfully Max kept his opinions to himself. *It's about playing, not so much the winning—isn't that what you were just thinking? Let it go, dude.*

But being a guy who'd been a serious competitor back in the day, as Harper had termed it, he had to keep silently replaying the let-it-go mantra in his head. Then the first inning began, and Max got sucked in by the same simple joy of the game that was infecting the boys.

Their first batter hit a ground ball right to Harper. She squatted, gingerly scooped it up in her mitt, then rose to her feet. "What do I do with it?" she called to the batter. "Brandon, what do I *do* with it?"

The boys thought that was hilarious. "Put it in your pocket," Owen, on Max's team, called out, while Brandon yelled, "Throw it to Edward, Harper!"

Wisely taking her teammate's advice, she tossed it toward the boy covering first base. She threw like a girl, however, and the ball landed in the grass a good yard shy of its goal. The batter had already attained first base by this point anyhow, and he divided a speculative glance between the ball and Harper, clearly tempted to go for second. She gave him the stink-eye, and, grinning, he settled with his heel against the edge of the base and the rest of him stretched out and prepared to run as the first baseman picked up the ball and winged it to Brandon.

Next up was Nathan, and he, too, deliberately hit toward Harper. But Harry, her team's shortstop, had clearly anticipated it, for he raced over, whipped up the ball and gently lobbed it to her. "Step on the base, Ms. Summerville," he directed when she caught it.

She did so, forcing out the man on first, and when Harry explained the way that worked, she whooped and did a little victory dance. "All *riiiight!*" she crowed. "*That's* what I'm talking about." She located the teen returning to the dugout and called, "That's *karma,* baby. I might be the weakest link, but Harry and I put you *out!*" She raced over to give the shortstop a quick, fierce hug, then stepped back. "Okay, it was mostly you, but still!"

He laughed at her exuberance, and they exchanged high fives.

Max was up to bat next, and he glanced at Harper as Brandon wound up on the makeshift mound. She was wearing sunglasses, so he wasn't a hundred percent certain she was looking at him as well, but as he watched, she leaned forward intently and wet her lips with her tongue.

Brandon's first pitch whizzed right past him.

He narrowed his eyes at her—which, okay, she likely couldn't see since he was wearing his own shades. Then he made himself ignore her as he choked up on the bat. Keeping his eye firmly on the ball, he was paying attention this time when the teen let fly with a decent fastball.

It came screaming over the plate, and the crack of leather against hickory and the zing in his wrists as his bat connected was a bullet train back to a few of the perfect moments in a childhood not particularly riddled with them. He knew without following his ball that he'd hit it out of the park, and, vaguely aware of the kids on his team screaming like maniacs, he saw Nathan take off for second base as he slung the bat aside and took off for his victory lap around the bases.

Edward, on first, was bent double laughing so hard he gasped for breath as Max nudged the base with his toe. Likely feeling his shadow, the boy raised his head to look up at him and lifted the hand he'd had braced against his knee to point down the baseline. And howled.

Following his gaze, Max felt his own mouth jerk up in an idiot grin.

Crouching and leaping, dodging from side to side, Harper danced between Nathan and second base, waving her arms like Michael Jordan preventing Magic Johnson from taking a shot at the hoop.

The sight made Max relinquish any remaining princess vibes he may have been hanging on to regarding her. Laughing out loud, he jogged over, circled his teammate and waded in. Snatching her up in his arms, he was conscious of the heat of the side of her breast against his pec and her clean, soapy scent as he jerked his chin at Nathan, who'd been gaping at her antics in stunned bafflement, to get him moving again.

"I didn't want to hurt her," the youth muttered. "Or make her hurt herself."

"I know," he agreed "But go run your bases now. You earned it."

"Hey!" Leaning back, Harper slid her sunglasses down her nose to glare up at him. She blew a loosened curl out of one of those olive-green eyes. "Hands, buddy, *hands!* Ump!" she called. "This can't be legal."

"It isn't, precisely," Mary-Margaret agreed, walking

up to them. "But neither is guarding à la basketball in a baseball game."

"Oh."

Mary-Margaret laughed. "I'm afraid I have to rule for the deputy on this one."

"Sure." Harper nodded her understanding as Max set her down next to second base, and bent to straighten the hem of her T-shirt, which had ridden up, and gently push her shades back up her nose. "I get that. He has the power to write you a ticket and I don't."

Mary-Margaret shrugged. "There is that. But don't underestimate your own powers. Max doesn't have anything approaching your fund-raising skills."

Harper's lush mouth curved up. "That's true. Shall we play some more ball?"

"I believe we should," the director concurred. She looked at Max. "That was an obvious home run, but I'm penalizing you two bases for unauthorized handling."

Max nodded. He didn't mind being on Harper's base—although he could have lived without all the razzing from Malcolm's team.

"Nathan's run stands," Mary-Margaret added decisively, and Max acknowledged something he'd understood in high school but had clearly forgotten as an adult. Catcalling wasn't nearly as obnoxious when it was your own team dishing it out.

Then Mary-Margaret gave a loud clap. "All right, people!" she called out so everyone could hear. "Let's play ball!"

And the game resumed.

THE KIDS WERE beside themselves after the game. They relived it play by play, and Harper's lack of baseball knowledge was a favorite topic. Call it adrenaline or call it endorphins, they were buzzing with an overload of it. Max knew it could turn to flat-out wired in an instant—and would if he and Harper didn't do something to bring down the over-the-top energy level in the activity room where most of the teens had congregated. So he scrounged up graph paper and pencils and set the boys to drawing small-scale race cars based on the stack of pictures he'd set out, with the promise of actually building their designs another day.

Several of the kids were enthralled simply with the dreaming/drawing aspect, but more weren't, and he knew it wouldn't be long before they became disruptive. Harper got up and left the room.

"Seriously?" he muttered. *The going gets a little rough after the fun afternoon, and she just walks away?*

But the thought had scarcely crossed his mind when she strolled back in carrying a copy of *The Hunger Games*. She flopped down in an easy chair, opened the book, and began to read aloud.

"Really?" Owen demanded. "Kiddie hour in the reading room—*that's* what we're down to?"

"Shut up, dude." Harry crossed over to sit in a chair near Harper. "I love this series."

A couple of the other boys scoffed along with Owen, but Max took note as one by one, they were drawn in by the story and soon formed a ragged semicircle around her. He didn't know if it was the power of the words or Harper's posh voice reading to them that was the biggest draw. Hell, probably both.

Even Trevor, who had ADHD, joined them. He was a poor listener, however, and was soon sidetracked by a long string poking through the seam of Nathan's shorts. He reached out to tug on it.

Nathan knocked his hand away. "Hands off, 'tard!"

The almost primal hum of awareness that raced through teenage boys when a fight was in the offing pulled more of the kids' attention away from Harper's story.

But Trevor diffused it when he rose to his feet with no apparent knowledge that he was expected to fight. "I'm not a 'tard," he muttered and ambled over to the foosball table where he spun a pole and watched the three strikers attached to it go 'round and around.

Harper hadn't paused in her reading, and with the potential brawl off the table, the kids settled back into listening.

Moments later, Edward, the Malcolm team's first basemen, stuck his head into the room. He started to withdraw, then slowly stepped inside. "Is that *The Hunger Games?* I've never heard it read out loud." He walked over and collapsed on the floor.

Except for Harper's voice and the occasional comment or question from the boys working on their car plans, the room was quiet for the next twenty minutes. Eventually Jim, one of the Village's counselors, came in.

"Hey," he said easily. "So, this is where everybody disappeared to, huh? Aren't the lot of you due for counseling and/or chores?"

"Dude, do you mind?" Owen protested. "We're in the middle of a book here!"

Harper closed it and smiled at the teen. "We'll pick up where we left off next time I come."

The boys grumbled, but the room cleared. On his own way out, the counselor stopped by the table where

Max had begun cleaning up. "We were thinking of ordering pizza from Bella T's to kinda keep the baseball high going. You in?"

"You bet." He pulled out his wallet, fished out a ten and forked it over. "I'm on duty tonight, but put this toward it."

Jim gave an ironic shake of his head. "Well, I guess that answers my second question, which was are you available to pick the pizzas up if we come up with the scratch." He turned a hopeful look on Harper as she walked up.

"Sorry," she said. "I'm scheduled to take the inn guests kayaking, then I have my sunset yoga class. I'm happy to kick in some money, though."

"Appreciate it. No donation goes to waste."

"Speaking of which—does the pizza parlor give us any kind of discount?"

He made a hell-if-I-know face. "Doubtful, but I can't say for sure."

"I'll ask Mary-Margaret. If they don't, I'd be happy to give Tasha a call and see if she's open to knocking a little off the total in the name of a good cause."

"That would *rock*."

"No guarantees, of course. My purse is in Mary-Margaret's office," she added. "I'm going to be taking off here in a few minutes, so is it okay by you if I leave my money with her when I go?"

"You betcha." He glanced at his watch and cursed. "Speaking of having to go—I've got a counseling session in about two minutes. Thanks for the donations, the bodda yas."

He left the room, but Max heard him call out, "Hey, Ryan! Wanna kick in on pizza for the boys?"

"You do that often, don't you?"

Max looked at Harper. "Do what?"

"Go the extra mile for the Village. This isn't the first time I've seen you all digging into your own pockets for something for these kids."

He shrugged. "It's a small nonprofit, and getting ends to meet is tough sometimes. We help out where we can." He gave her a level look. "I didn't see you turning Jim down. In fact, you asked if Tasha gave us a discount."

"So?"

"It's the first time you've included yourself. Just yesterday you would have asked if Tash gave *you*— meaning Jim or Mary-Margaret or any of us who put in time here—a discount."

She gave him a startled look as a flush washed roses atop the toasty brown of her cheeks. Then she smiled sheepishly. "Gotta admit the kids are hard to resist."

"That they are." He watched her busy herself gathering together the few materials he hadn't yet organized and leaned his weight on the hands he'd pressed against the tabletop. When hers came within touching range, he spread his fingers and nudged his pinky against hers.

They both stilled. Then Max raised his little finger and outlined hers with its tip. "I should get that equipment back to the parks department."

"Mmm-hmm." The agreement came out in a sultry little hum, and Harper cleared her throat. "That is—I need to get going myself."

But neither of them moved as both their gazes locked on his hand sliding over hers. It looked so primitive, so big-knuckled and banged up against the unmarred elegance of Harper's, that Max's first impulse was to yank it back and apologize.

No, who was he kidding? Not that doing so wasn't a genuine impulse, but it sure as hell hadn't been his first...and probably not even his second. He laced his fingers with hers.

"Soft," he murmured and had to swallow a self-deprecating laugh. *There* was a fucking understatement if he ever heard one—the skin of her inner fingers was downright silky. It made him wonder what the places a guy normally considered soft on a woman would feel like.

She was silent for a heartbeat, then nodded. "Isn't it?" she murmured back. "It comes from bathing regularly in fairy tears."

"Yeah? You have to make an appointment for one of those? It must take those little suckers a long time to fill up a tub."

"They cry really big tears." But she laughed as she slipped her hand out from under his and stepped back. "I really do have to get going."

"Sure." He let her almost reach the door before he said, "We make a pretty good team, you and I."

She turned back and met his gaze. "Yeah?"

"With the kids, you know? We work well together with them."

She nodded. "Yes. We do, don't we. See you later, Bradshaw."

"Right. See you." Max watched her disappear through the doorway, then thunked his fist against his forehead three times before dropping his hand back to brace against the table once again. He hung his head.

"What the hell, dawg," he said to the tabletop. He was standing here because he had a damn hard-on you could drive nails through concrete with, and trying to walk would likely cripple him.

Ever since he'd severed the sexual potential with Harper the night she'd shown up at his house, he'd been kicking himself. So he'd had a headache and a set of scratches that had throbbed like a bitch in heat—it sure as hell hadn't been *those* that had stopped him. The sad truth was, a momentary case of she's-too-good-for-me had pulled him back. One minute his only thought had been how *right* she felt in his arms. Then out of the blue he'd started questioning what made him good enough to put his hands all over her. Weren't these the same hands he'd dirtied over and over again picking fights with his brother and pulling far more triggers than he liked to think about?

So, instead of moving them to his bedroom where they'd so clearly been heading, he'd made a big joke of his refusal.

Okay, that had actually been kind of fun, since he wasn't generally a joking kind of guy. But it was also dicked up, given the hit to his self-respect and all the cold showers he'd had to endure since then. And how wrong was it that he'd allowed a decision he'd known was whack even as he'd made it to mess up the one thing he wanted more than his next breath—to make love to Harper?

Annnd reduced himself now to a guy with a hard-on from touching her *fingers,* for Christ's sake.

He shook his head. Jesus. He hadn't been this pitiful with the ladies when he was twelve.

He didn't even want to think how long it would take to get his mobility back if he let his mind envision Harper naked in her bath.

CHAPTER ELEVEN

"So, BASICALLY WHAT you're telling me," Tasha said beneath the conversations and clatter of Bella T's, "is that Deputy Dawg diddled your fingers and got you all orgasmic?"

"I know." Harper nodded emphatically. "It's ridiculous. Juvenile. Heck, it's—"

"Clearly true," the strawberry blonde interrupted. "I mean, look at you, all flushy cheeked and pointy-nippled."

She could *feel* the heat in her cheeks, but she nearly gave herself whiplash checking out the second assertion. And, oh, God, it was a stone-cold fact; her nipples could have been carved from tungsten, so solid did they look poking out the stretchy cotton of her T-shirt, even through the additional layer of her bra.

"I'm completely jealous, if you wanna know the truth," Tasha said, once again reclaiming Harper's attention. She sighed. "I wish I had someone who could do something as simple as play with my fingers and have me all primed to jump his bones. It's been way too long, let me tell you."

"I know what you mean. I wouldn't mind getting more than a little finger job, myself." Harper gave a startled laugh. "Okay, *that* came out sounding way dirtier than I meant."

Tasha gave her a solemn smile. "Especially when you know there'd be nothing little about it. Max's fingers are like the rest of him—nice and big."

"You are so bad. You know I meant having *my* fingers diddled, not being diddled by Max's—" This wasn't helping to cool her down, and her sudden urge to tell Tasha every last detail about that crazy-hot kiss she and Max had shared just cranked the heat up that much higher. Every time she thought about it—and God knows she'd done that far too often—it jacked her temperature into the stratosphere.

She stepped away from the counter. "Shutting up now. In fact, I should get to the inn before I'm late for my kayak tour. So can I tell the Cedar Village director that Bella T's will give them a fifteen percent discount on their orders from now on?"

"Wasn't that the agreement, Ms. Silver Tongue?"

She grinned. "Yes, it was." No one had ever given her a nickname. Well, her mother called her Baby Girl sometimes, but no one her own age had ever called her anything but her name, and Harper had to admit she enjoyed Tasha's teasing. "And thank you again. It is so appreciated. I'll make sure Mary-Margaret knows to send you a monthly receipt for the discount, since it's definitely a charitable write-off."

"Then it's a win-win all the way around."

"Um, sorry to interrupt," a male voice said, and Harper turned to look at the man who'd come up behind them without her hearing.

He was average height, average weight, average coloring, which made him a forgettable-looking sort of guy. He shot her an apologetic glance before turning an even more apologetic one on Tasha.

"Hey, Will," her friend said cheerfully. "What's up?"

"I'm really sorry to do this to you on such short notice," he said, "But I got a really great job offer in Seattle that I can't refuse."

"You're moving out?" She turned to Harper. "Will rents my extra studio apartment upstairs," she explained, then turned back to the man. "That's excellent news on the job, but I'm going to miss having you next door. You've been a great renter. When do you have to go?"

He shifted uneasily. "The first of the month."

"Of *September*?"

"Yeah. I'm really sorry it's such short notice," he repeated. "But you can keep the last month's rent I paid up front."

The strawberry blonde blew out a breath. "I guess we all have to grab our opportunities when we can. Good luck to you, Will."

As if she'd just lifted the weight of the world off of them, his stiff shoulders relaxed. "Thanks. Meanwhile, I'll ask around to see if anyone's looking for a new place."

"I'd appreciate that," she said, but her own shoulders slumped when he walked away. "Crap."

"You okay?" Harper reached across the counter to touch the back of her friend's hand, which was braced against the top with so much force it had driven all the blood from her fingertips.

"I've come to count on the studio for makeup revenue during the winter months. I can get by without it, but it makes my profit margin leaner."

"You want me to stick around for a while?" She had a feeling Jenny would understand if she blew off one tour.

"No." Tasha reached for a knife and pulled a bowl of big waxy green peppers toward herself. "I'm fine."

She didn't look fine. She looked a little shell-shocked. But before Harper could say anything else, Tash gave a wave of her knife.

"Go. Shoo," she said. "Lead your tour. I've got work to do."

Still not knowing if leaving Tasha alone was the right thing, she rose onto her toes and leaned across the counter to plant a kiss on her friend's cheek. The other woman gave her a little smile, and they bid each other goodbye.

She called Jenny to fill her in on her way to the inn, then called Mary-Margaret to give her the news about the discount and discuss the paperwork involved in the type of contribution Tasha would be giving the Village. As she parked behind her cabin moments later and dashed in to change into her wet suit, she gave herself a lecture on the need to put everything—Tasha, the Village and Max—out of her mind for a few hours. It was time to focus on giving the guests who had signed up for this evening's kayaking excursion the best tour she could.

THAT WAS EASIER said than done. Oh, she didn't give a half-assed tour; she worked diligently to make sure that didn't happen. But in between pointing out landmarks, or eagles who often had an entourage of crows and seagulls in their wakes, or the occasional osprey diving for fish from high in the sky, there were plenty of quiet moments. And not even the guests' delight in the way the osprey dive-bombed the canal, shot out of the water and soared high back into the sky moments later with its catch in its talons, only to plummet a good ten feet while shaking salt water from its feathers, prevented her mind from wandering back to Max and the boys at the Village outside of town.

It was during one of the quiet moments, as gentle waves from the wake of a passing boat lapped the side of her kayak and water rolled down the raised end of her paddle to drip like diamonds back into the canal, that she came to a decision. There was no reason to put off calling her mother to green-light Cedar Village's grant application. She'd had longer than usual already to decide this was precisely the kind of charity Sunday's Child loved to support.

After the tour ended and the paddles and boats had been stowed in their proper places, she had just enough time to run back up to her cottage to peel out of her wet suit and pull on yoga pants and a Prana Leyla tank before heading back down to the big patch of lawn bordering the beach. She set out mats and greeted the students she knew by name as they trickled in, learning the names of three new inn guests and memorizing small details about each that would help her remember them when they met again.

Wendy, the owner of Wacka Do's hair salon, whom Harper knew from the party at Jenny's, ran down from the parking lot at the last minute, her yoga bag banging off her thigh. Harper's class was gaining popularity with several of the local women, so much so that Jenny had set up a special rate for them, the only stipulation being that they provide their own mats.

At the end of the class, she bid her sister yogis *Namaste*. The moment the last woman left, she put the big tote of rolled mats away and headed straight up to her cottage for the night. She changed for the final time into a cami tank and pajama bottoms, then made a beeline to the tiny kitchen area to pour herself a glass of wine. Grabbing her cell phone out of her purse, she carried it and her drink onto the porch where she took a seat on one of the bentwood rockers. For a few peaceful moments she simply rocked and sipped her Walla Walla Valley Northstar merlot. Finally, blowing out a soft breath, she set her glass down on the deck, picked up the phone and called her mother, who answered on the fourth ring.

"Hey, Mom. I hope I'm not calling too late. I forgot the time difference."

"Not a problem, darling, I'm just reading in bed." Gina Summerville-Hardin's voice traveled warmly down the line. "It's good to hear from you. How are you?"

"I'm really good. It's astoundingly gorgeous here—I'm simply spellbound by how much. Which is ridiculous, right? Because how many places have we seen in all our travels?"

"A million," Gina said drily.

"It feels like it sometimes, doesn't it? Which is why it amazes me that a little speck of a town in Washington State can speak so loudly to me. Did you get the photos I emailed?"

"Yes, it truly is quite spectacular, isn't it? One doesn't usually hear the word *canal* and think of mountains like that rising out of it."

"People who've lived here forever tell me it's actually a fjord." She shrugged, even though her mother couldn't see. "Whatever you call it, it's not only stunning, it's *peaceful*."

Dead air ruled the line for a moment. Then Gina said, "*Peaceful?* That's…not a word I generally associate with you, Harper."

She laughed a little uneasily. "I know. Yet…it is." And she realized that for maybe the first time in, oh, say, *ever* she wasn't experiencing her usual fidgety urge to move on. Ordinarily, by this point in a project, she would have started to feel restlessness building along her nerve endings like an unscratchable itch. But, nope—she did a quick assessment. Not even a trace.

How odd.

And a little disconcerting, so she shook the thought from her mind and said, "Still, that's neither here nor there. One of the reasons I'm calling is to give you the go-ahead on Cedar Village." She could hear her own enthusiasm as she added, "They're fabulous, Mom—exactly the kind of charity we're always looking for."

"Excellent," Gina said crisply. "I'll get it in the works and see that their acceptance letter is in the mail by the end of the week. Does that mean you're finally coming home?"

Denial hit like a wreck on the highway, and she jerked as if she'd been in the car that had been hit. "No!"

Then she pulled herself together and said in a more moderate tone, "I can't, Mom. You know I'm contracted at the inn until after Labor Day."

"Surely they can find someone else."

She didn't question her resistance to the suggestion, she simply replied, without any idea if she spoke the truth or not, "In the middle of their high season? I don't think so. And I'm not a quitter, Mom—I don't just stroll away from my commitments."

"I wish you felt the same way about your family. Kai

and I see you less often than all those many acquaintances you love to make."

Harper blew out a breath. "Do we have to do this again? I don't fault you for disliking travel, Mom. Why can't you extend me the same courtesy for my love of it?"

"But *do* you love it, Harper? Is that truly what you adore above all else? Or is all your traveling simply a way to honor your daddy's memory?"

"Of course not!" But even as she said the words, something suspiciously like recognition shuddered through her.

She promptly pressed her feet against the porch deck to stop the rocker and sat up straight. Of course that wasn't the reason. She adored traveling. Maybe occasionally she got a little weary of mostly living out of a suitcase, but after a brief respite—like this job—she was always raring to go again.

"Fine, then," her mother said. "I'll say no more. But it would be nice if you'd carve a little time out of your schedule to visit Kai and me. And I know your grandparents would appreciate seeing you, as well."

"I will, Mama. I promise. I know my trip to see Kai graduate university was way too rushed because this job was scheduled to begin. But I'll spend a couple weeks with you when it wraps up—I promise."

"We'd all like that."

"I doubt Kai cares one way or the other."

"Of course he does!"

Harper let her silence speak for her. Gina held out for an instant, then laughed. "All right, he's a little wrapped up in himself, his job at the foundation and his ever-changing string of pretty girls."

"In that order, I bet."

"He's a twenty-two-year-old male, darling—that's typical of the species. Well, except for your father," Gina added in a warm, God-you-had-to-love-the-guy tone. "He was the least self-absorbed twenty-two-year-old I ever knew." Then her voice turned brisk. "But back to Kai, his self-absorption doesn't mean he doesn't love the stuffing out of you."

"Oh, I know that. I just won't hold my breath for him to kill the fatted calf when I visit."

"Your grandma and grandpa and I will see to that." As if putting a period to that portion of their conversation, Gina suddenly said, "We haven't really talked about anything except our obligatory disagreement and Cedar Village. Have you done anything in Razor Bay just for fun, Baby Girl? Something aside from your jobs?"

The warmth in her mother's voice and the feel-the-love family nickname loosened the slight reserve with which Harper had been dealing with Gina in recent years, and she found herself talking about Jenny and Tasha and Jake and Austin. Max's name might have popped up a little more often than her other friends, as well, but that was only because of his connection with Cedar Village.

Without mentioning Mr. Handsy, she related her night out at The Voodoo Lounge and told her mother about both the fun jobs she performed for the inn and the added responsibility that Jenny had asked of her. Her enthusiasm was such that she'd sipped her way through the remainder of her wine and talked herself dry before she finally came up for a breath.

"I'm sorry, Mom, I didn't mean to go on so."

"Don't apologize," Gina said. "You sound like you really like it there—that you like those people."

"I *do*." But a little surge of guilt that her affection for Razor Bay and the friends she'd made was somehow disloyal to the critical job of vetting the foundation's charities that her father had felt so strongly about made her rush to add, "Not that I plan on staying here past Labor Day. Still, it's really fun for now."

Gina sighed. "You always have fun. And heaven forbid that you should stay anywhere a moment longer than necessary."

Gritting her teeth, Harper sighed, as well. Hadn't her mom just been urging her to find someone else to do her job so she could come home for a visit? "Maybe we should call it a night."

"Yes, I suddenly find myself quite tired," Gina agreed. "We'll talk again soon, though. I love you, darling."

"I know you do, Mama. I love you, too."

They said their goodbyes and disconnected. Harper sat in the darkness on her porch for a long time afterward, just rocking and rocking.

And wondering how they'd come to grow so far apart.

CHAPTER TWELVE

Tasha called early the next morning. "What's your schedule like? We need to coordinate," she said, sounding much more cheerful than when Harper had left Bella T's yesterday. "You, me and Jenny are going to Max's house."

"Yeah?" Harper didn't question the happy little burst of energy that buzzed through her. She simply smiled into the phone. "He finally broke down and invited us, huh?"

"Ah, not exactly." Tasha laughed. "You may have breeched the walls, but according to Jake, if Jen and I wait for an invitation, we're all going to be plucking our chin hairs in the nursing home without ever having seen it. So we decided to invite ourselves. Here's the deal, though, kiddo—it needs to be this morning. Jenny called Amy Alvarez, the dispatcher at the sheriff's office, and found out Max's shift starts at noon."

"It's Friday, that shouldn't be a problem." Harper climbed up to the loft. "I'll check to be sure, but I don't usually have anything in the morning because people are getting ready to check out—and check-in for the weekend people isn't until three." She crossed to the dresser and picked up her schedule. "Yes, nothing until five."

"Great, that's what Jenny thought, too, so we'll pick

you up at nine. Jake said we should take Max some oatmeal and a carton of milk. He wouldn't say why, and he's probably just messing with us, but we thought we'd stop at the General Store to pick some up anyhow. See you in an hour."

Clouds had rolled in by the time Jenny pounded on her front door. "Hey, you ready?" the petite brunette demanded when Harper opened it. "You might want to bring your stuff in," she said, waving at the notebook, whose pages were riffling on the seat of one of the rockers. "The wind's picking up." She gave it a closer look as Harper retrieved it. "Hey, is that Razor Days stuff?"

"Yeah, but nothing noteworthy. I was trying to brainstorm some ideas last night but was too upset over a call from my mom to really concentrate."

"Is everyone okay?"

"Yes. That is, nobody's sick or anything. Mom and I just have differing philosophies about how I should run my life, and it's been getting in our way more and more often the past couple of years." Since her dad died.

"Families can be a bitch," Jenny said solemnly.

"They absolutely can." She waved it away. "But let's not talk about that. Let's go horn in on Max's morning."

Jenny laughed. "Yes, let's do that. I'm so excited."

Harper shot Jenny a curious look as she grabbed her purse and locked the door. "Haven't you known Max most of your life?"

"We've been acquainted since he left the Marines and took the deputy job," Jenny said as they headed down to the lot where Tasha had parked between Jenny and Jake's cottages. "But to me he was just this big, unsmiling, not very talkative guy. I didn't bother looking deeper until Jake came back to town. Now I'm getting to know Max as an adult, and I've discovered I like him way more than I ever would have dreamed. I always thought he was kind of humorless, but he's not. He might not be the chattiest guy in town, but he can be funny as hell when he and Jake get to insulting each other. And I really, really want to see his place."

The drive to Max's house didn't take long now that Harper knew where it was, and after a quickie stop at the store they drove straight there. Pulling up to the end of Max's drive, they sat in the car for a moment looking at the darkened house.

"Not at home, you think?" Tasha said.

"His SUV's here," Harper pointed out.

"Only one way to find out for sure." Jenny opened her door. "Grab the bag, Tash."

They all climbed from the car and walked up onto his porch. Jenny knocked on the door.

There was no answer, and she knocked again with more emphasis.

Something crashed on the other side of the door, and Harper heard Max's voice swearing. A second later, the door swung open.

"Omigawwwd," one of them breathed, although Harper couldn't have said for sure who.

Max filled the doorway, bleary-eyed and sullen-mouthed, his hair flattened on one side and sticking up on the other, his jaw shadowed with stubble. He was all brooding angles, from his sharp cheekbones to the rawboned massiveness of his shoulders, wrists and big-knuckled hands.

But that wasn't what had her and her friends gaping at him. No, that would be the fact that the only thing saving him from total nudity was a pair of black boxers.

The man was built, there was simply no two ways about it. His shoulders barely cleared the door's lintels and he was hard-bodied and so damn *male,* with solid curving muscles, soft standing veins snaking down his inner arms and dark body hair on his calves, forearms and chest and in a stripe that arrowed from the latter to bisect his muscular abs, then disappear beneath those low-slung boxers. The welts the nasty drunk had carved on his neck the evening he'd broken up the roadhouse catfight had faded to the faintest of pink lines.

But they flashed Harper straight back to Max's kiss. That. Hot. Perfect. Kiss.

"Dear Lord," she murmured, "I think I'm having heart palpitations." Which surely weren't brought on by the mere memory of the kiss they'd exchanged that night. It had to be Max's body. Sure, she had seen him half-naked the day she'd caught some of the Skins and Shirts game at the Village. But his size, the pure, stunning impact of his masculinity, was even more potent up close.

"What time is it?" he demanded, then turned up his wrist to peer at the silver tank watch strapped to it. "Oh. Guess it's not as early as I thought. I need coffee." He turned and shambled toward his kitchen, leaving the front door open.

The women looked at each other. Tasha fanned herself, and they all grinned, then followed Max into his house.

They found him in the kitchen opening and slamming cupboard doors. "Coffee, coffee, where the hell did I put the coffee?"

Jenny unscrewed a lid, then the stopper from a thermos Harper hadn't even noticed the little brunette had.

Striding up to Max, who was still pawing through the cupboards, she waved its opening beneath his nose. "I've got coffee." She looked over at Harper. "Find him a mug. I have a feeling this little cap/cup thingie isn't going do the trick."

Max snapped around. "Oh, God, you're a lifesaver. Dump my brother, sweetheart. Marry me instead. You can bring me coffee every morning."

"Tempting proposition," Jenny said drily. "But I'm afraid I must decline."

He gave her a sleepy smile that had all three women freezing.

Tasha was the first to inhale. "Wow," she breathed on her exhale.

He turned his head to look at her. "You say something?"

"Um, I did." She dug in the sack she'd carried in and pulled out the cylindrical box of Quaker Oats. "Want some nice, hearty oatmeal?"

"Hell, no." He shuddered. "Have you ever *eaten* that stuff? It's got the consistency of paste, and I'm not exactly a wallpaper kinda guy, which is about the only thing it would be good for."

"Then why on earth did Jake say—?"

"I think I might be able to answer that." Harper indicated the three cupboards she'd opened in search of a mug. Handing Jenny the one she'd pulled from the last cupboard, she looked at Max. "It's amazing you've got that body given what I just saw in these."

He straightened and for the first time looked a little self-conscious. Then interested. "You like my body?"

"A lot more than I like what you have in your cupboards."

His thick, black brows lowered over densely lashed eyes, and he blew out a disgusted breath. "Why is everyone so damn interested in my diet?"

Because two of the three cupboards she'd opened had been packed with Cap'n Crunch and Froot Loops cereals, what her brother, Kai, called Toes food: Doritos, Fritos, Tostitos and Cheetos, both regular and hot, as well as two kinds of potato chips, a jar of Cheez Whiz, a big bag of frosted animal crackers, a couple—

Drawing a deep breath, she put a lid on her internal inventory. She and Tash and Jenny had already descended on him unannounced and rousted him out of bed, and he'd been pretty darn decent about it. Insulting his eating habits might be pushing her luck. So she merely said, "You've got a lot of junk food in your cupboards, including what looks like a year's worth of peanut butter cheese crackers."

"Hey, peanut butter is good for you."

"But a lot better if it comes without the trans fat-filled crackers. Why do you eat like that?"

"Dunno." His big shoulders hunched. "I just always have."

Oh. Crap. Meaning his parents likely had never made much effort to feed him properly. And here she was treading all over the fact and making him feel bad for something he'd probably had indoctrinated in him from the cradle. She waved a dismissive hand. "And it's not important—or at least not why we're here," she forced herself to say cheerfully. "Hello, Mohammad." She indicated herself and her friends. "Meet your mountains."

He looked at her as if she was speaking Swahili— which she could if she wanted to. "What?"

"Jake's been lording it over us that he's seen your

house and we haven't," Jenny jumped in. "So we need a tour. It's your God-given duty to cut your brother's bragging rights off at the knees."

"Ah. It is." Clearly starting to mellow, thanks to the coffee he'd drained from the mug Jenny had handed him, Max nodded. "Got it. You're right. And it will be my pleasure, as well."

"*That's* the charmer we all know and love."

His mouth ticked up in a wry, one-sided smile. "Look around while I go put on some clothes."

"Please," Harper murmured under her breath as she watched the bunch and flex of the muscles under his skin as he strode from the kitchen, "don't bother on our account."

"Amen, sister," Tasha agreed with a snort of surprised laughter as the three of them moved into the living room. But since Harper had been there before, she ignored the architecture and furnishings in favor of checking out the little things. Max didn't have a wealth of personal items lying around, so when she came across a sheet of paper on a side table next to the big leather chair, she drifted over for a closer look. As her friends rhapsodized over the fireplace she'd admired on her prior visit, she craned her head to read it.

It was a driver's license renewal reminder and, curious to see how old Max was, she looked for the birth date.

"Oh."

"Got all the information you need?" Max's deep voice spoke over her shoulder, and she felt it reverberate all the way down her spine. By the minty fresh scent wafting her way, she deduced he had taken the time to brush his teeth.

Working hard not to jolt, she slowly straightened and gave him her most charming smile. "You have a birthday coming up. How old will you be?"

"What? You somehow missed that?"

"I did. You were too fast for me to read beyond the month and day. So…forty?"

"Cute. Thirty-four. How 'bout you? Twenty-six?"

"Aw, you sweet talker, you. I'm thirty."

Jenny and Tasha came over to claim Max for their tour then, and Harper trailed in their wake, mulling over an idea as she eyeballed Max's butt and listened to the conversations with half an ear.

It seemed like mere minutes later that they were saying their goodbyes and climbing in the car. As she clicked her seat belt on, the idea she'd been kicking around solidified.

"I'm going to throw Max a surprise birthday party," she said. "You think he'll mind if I do it in his house?"

CHAPTER THIRTEEN

THE WEATHER GREW worse over the weekend and turned into a full-out squall, with whipping wind and rain on Sunday. Monday was better; the sun had been out more often than behind the intermittent cloud cover, but every now and then rain blew in out of nowhere.

The Cedar Village boys clearly didn't care. They got to use the inn's roped-off swimming area, with its free-floating dock and a low springy diving board, and were just happy to be there.

Max was happy to watch Harper. Clad in the black-and-white bathing suit she'd worn the night he'd run across her in the hot tub, she sat on the side of the float that she'd rowed Owen to with the rest of the boys swimming in her wake like—in her words—a big bunch of ducklings. Now, lazily fluttering her long, toned legs in the crystal water, she encouraged the boys to do the biggest cannonballs they could.

When Malcolm did his from the spring board, bouncing twice on the end before going high and tucking into a tight ball, the splash was so huge it drenched Harper from the top of her head to where her feet and shins disappeared into the canal. Her hair first flattened, then sprang up into tight, soaked ringlets—and to a man, they all stared at her in openmouthed horror and held their breath, awaiting the explosion. Because what guy hadn't been exposed to the seamy underbelly of a woman whose do they'd destroyed?

Women took their hair damn seriously.

Malcolm, who had resurfaced, treaded water. He engaged Harper in an ask-me-if-I-give-a-shit stare down, just daring her to dress him down. But his wide, brown shoulders inched up toward his ears.

Harper blinked saltwater from her eyes, squeegeed about a pint of it from the ringlets framing her face, then wiped away the rivulets trickling down her cheeks. She met the teen's 'tude with a cool-eyed once-over of her own. "That's it? That the best you've got?"

The boys' laughter was perhaps disproportionate to the actual humor of her words, but Max totally got it. A lot of these kids came from truly dysfunctional homes and weren't accustomed to receiving the benefit of the doubt—or, hell, even a rational response half the time to their so-called transgressions. So they laughed just a little too long and loud in relief. And given permission to make the biggest splash they could, they threw themselves into attempting to outdo each other. Even Owen, the not-so-great swimmer whom Harper had outfitted with a lifebelt, leaped off the dock and tucked himself into a ball around his flotation device, hugging bony knees to his narrow chest. His splash wasn't the biggest, but the smile on his face when his lifebelt bobbed him back to the surface said it might as well have been.

The boys grew sillier. And louder, their shouts and laughter magnified by the body of water surrounding them. They were happy and unself-conscious.

Until the three girls showed up.

They swam out to the float, and one by one hauled themselves up onto it. They had the look of sisters, all blonde, blue-eyed and pretty, ranging from around ten to maybe sixteen. Max couldn't have said exactly what it was—the white straight teeth, the pricey-looking, well-made bathing suits?—but there was an air of privilege about them that suggested they probably came from money. And the minute they began pulling themselves out of the water, the boys quieted.

For all the attention the oldest girl gave them, they might have been transparent. The middle girl, whom Max pegged for about fourteen, sent the boys covert glances but took her cue from her big sister. The youngest shot them an enormous, all-inclusive smile.

"Hey," she said, friendly as a puppy. "I'm Joely. These are my sisters Meeghan—" she indicated the middle sister "—and Brittany."

The boys returned her greeting and introduced themselves, but the disdain coming off the older sister made them subdued. Max feared that would soon be replaced by attitude, which he could already see brewing on Harry's face. The fifteen-year-old's sessions in anger management had barely ended, and Max feared that in a real life situation, he might not be able to recall all the coping mechanisms he'd learned to help deal with it. And if that happened, if the kid had an outburst, it would likely be the end of Jenny letting the Village use the inn's facilities. He looked at Harper, hoping to hell she had an idea for saving the outing, because he was coming up blank.

But he'd barely met her own concerned gaze when little Joely, with her megawatt smile, said, "Hey! Can you guys do this?" And she performed a handstand on the edge of the float that culminated in her flipping feet-first into the water.

Like Harper and her cannonballs, it got the teens'

competitive juices flowing, and with the same speed
that things had gotten deadly quiet, suddenly everyone
was talking trash and catcalling. Soon they were trying
to outdo each other. Jeremy, who tied with Malcolm for
the most athletic of the boys, held his handstand, then
lifted one hand a few inches off the decking, replanted
it and lifted the other, before straightening both arms
to flip himself into the canal.

The tide had been steadily going out, and the water
grew shallower, which soon put an end to tricks from
the float. Instead, the kids started horsing around in the
water, and the next thing Max knew, Joely was up on
Malcolm's shoulders and Owen was on Jeremy's and
the two were doing their best to push each other from
their perch and into the water.

"Oh, boy," he muttered, thinking he should probably call a halt to it before it spiraled out of control and
someone got hurt.

But Harper laughed, grabbed him by the wrist, and
started splashing toward the kids. "Let's show them how
it's done." She'd only gone a few steps, however, before
she stopped and turned to him. "Why am I walking
when I can be riding?" she demanded and smiled up at
him, all burnished skin and white teeth in the sunlight.
"Give me a hand up."

He ducked beneath the water and tapped her legs to
move them farther apart. They were smooth against his
hands and smoother still when he situated himself between them and came up out of the water with her on
his shoulders.

She whooped and clutched at his head. Water lapped
his waist and, wrapping his hands around her thighs, he
waded toward the kids in deeper water.

Owen knocked Joely off Malcolm's shoulders as they approached, and Max reached down to haul her to her feet, concerned again about stopping this. The girl merely laughed, however, as Malcolm plucked her up and swung her back up onto his shoulders.

"We're on their team," Harper declared and grinned at the little blonde. "We girls gotta stick together."

For sheer brilliance, Joely's return smile put the sun, which had finally quit playing hide-and-seek to come out in earnest, to shame.

"You're goin' *down,* Ms. Summerville!" Owen crowed. "Me and Jeremy, we're unstoppable! Plus, that means that we got Harry and Edward on our team."

"Ha! Prepare to drink brine!" she replied. "Because we've got both brawn—" she gave Max's shoulder a pat and Joely followed suit on Malcolm's "—*and* brains." With a modest twirl of her hand, she indicated herself and the little girl.

"'Scuse me?" Max squeezed the firm thighs beneath his hands. "*You're* the brains and I'm the brawn?"

She gripped a handful of his hair to tilt his head back and leaned over to grin upside down in his face. One of her breasts flattened against his skull. "I know! Perfect, right?"

Hell, yeah. She could bill herself any way her little heart desired. He was just happy to have her legs draped around his neck and her smile directed his way. Tearing his gaze away, he quirked his brows at the boys. "Let the games begin."

"And may the odds be ever in your favor!" Owen grinned at the laugh *The Hunger Games* line got him.

The next thirty minutes were among the top five best half hours of his life. There was just something about hot sun, cold saltwater, mostly blue skies and laughing kids.

And Harper. Because, face it, a large part of his enjoyment stemmed from her. She had a real knack for fun, for making the people around her feel as if they were a part of something special. And that was in *addition* to having his hands on her sleek legs, feeling her weight shift and her skin rub against his as she hand wrestled their opponents. That and hearing her laugh, loudly and from the belly, not only when she won a round but when she got knocked from his shoulders into the water...well, it made for a damn good time. Especially when she squeezed those thighs around his head.

It made him wish he could swivel it a hundred and eighty degrees like Linda Blair in that old classic movie, *The Exorcist*. Okay, she had done an actual three-sixty. Sue him if he had a few stops along the way in mind.

Which was *not* a smart thing to be contemplating, surrounded as he was by all these kids. Because pretty soon they'd have to vacate the cold water, and the fact that he was half-hard probably wasn't what he wanted the boys—and sure as hell not that sweet little girl, who had informed them she was eleven-and-a-half years old—to see.

"Joely!" snapped big sister Brittany from the shore where she and the other one—Meeghan—had moved to lie on beach towels a while ago. She eyed the younger girl sourly over the towel she was in the midst of folding. "C'mon. We're going back to the inn."

"Go on without me," Joely called. "Tell Mom I'll be in in a while."

"No." Brittany's voice brooked no resistance. "You come with us *now*."

Joely sighed and gave one of Malcolm's dreads a tug. Reaching up, he plucked her off his shoulders, then set her gently on her feet in the water. Left with no excuse to keep Harper on his own, with a regretful slide of his hands down her smooth legs, Max squatted so she could climb off, as well.

The little blonde looked up at Malcolm, then around at the rest of them. "Playing with you guys is the most fun I've had all week," she said with a sweet smile. Rushing over, she gave Harper a fierce hug. Then she turned and waded slowly toward the beach.

Malcolm watched her until she joined her sisters. "That's one seriously fly little dudette."

"No shit," Owen agreed, and Jeremy added, "You ask me, she got all the personality in that family."

"You know what, guys?" Harper waded up to the boys. "I am so proud of you. You all were great today, and you can bet I'm passing that along to Jenny."

"Who's Jenny?" Edward asked.

"She runs this inn." Harper quirked a brow. "In other words, the woman who says if you get to come back again or not."

"And you're gonna tell her we were great?"

"I am. I'm going to tell her that you were super great. Times *infinity* great."

"*Ex*cellent." Edward nodded. "Then we're proud of you, too."

LATER THAT DAY, Harper organized a volleyball game, finished up a tide pool exploration she'd held for a group of kids and headed up to her cabin to make some private calls. Her first was to Max's place of employment.

She'd never been so aware of a man as when she'd

sat on his shoulders and felt the hot grip of his hands on her thighs, the shift of solid muscles beneath her legs, her butt. At one point, he'd turned his head just as she'd tightened the grip of her legs around his neck, and rough stubble had scraped her inner thigh. She was more accustomed to smooth-shaven men—Max included, at least when he was in uniform. But there was just something very sexy about that coarse rasp of prickly hair against soft skin.

"Razor Bay Sheriff's Office," a voice said in her ear as her call was answered.

She gave her head a shake and wrested it back to the matter at hand. "Hi, is this Ms. Alverez?"

"Yes, it is."

"You probably don't know me, but I'm Harper Summerville, the activities—"

"I do know who you are," the woman interrupted. "This is Razor Bay, honey—everyone knows, or at least knows about, everyone else. And call me Amy. What can I do for you?"

"Direct me to the person who schedules personnel days off, please?"

"That would be me." Harper could almost hear the other woman's shrug over the airwaves. "This isn't exactly a metropolitan branch of the sheriff's department. So, at the risk of repeating myself, what can I do for you?"

"Schedule a day, or at least an evening off for Max Bradshaw." She gave the dispatcher the date.

A beat of silence went by, then… "Excuse me? Max *always* works his birthday."

No. That was just plain wrong. But she shook off the instinctual displeasure that stabbed her upon hearing it and merely said in a mild tone, "Not this year, hopefully. I'm planning a surprise party for him, and it'd be just too sad if the surprise was on me because he had to work. On his *birthday*."

"It totally would," Alverez agreed. "I'm changing it right now, because that's the coolest thing I've heard in a month of Sundays. Max is one of the good guys, and I swear it seems as if nobody ever does anything for him. And you don't have to worry that I'll spoil the surprise. I can come up with a logical reason for the switch." There was a tiny pause, then: "It just so happens that I have that night off, myself. Can my husband and I come, too?"

"Yes! That would be brilliant! And, please, if you know anyone else who'd like to attend, let me know. I'm just getting started on this, so I don't have any details for you yet. But I'll let you know as soon as I get organized."

Once they disconnected, she switched gears and gave the party's venue some thought. She'd really had it in mind to hold it at Max's place, but the truth was, it would be damn difficult to pull off. He was in law enforcement, for pity's sake; how likely was he to leave his place wide open while he worked long hours in a highly visible job? And even if he did, how would they get him back there again?

Okay, she could probably utilize Jake for that. Given the way the half brothers razzed each other, he'd no doubt be all over pulling the wool over his brother's eyes. But even if he managed it, the cat would be out of the bag the moment Max saw a bunch of cars parked in his yard. Hell, as a deputy he probably knew a lot of them by sight.

What they really needed was a location where a number of vehicles wouldn't seem out of place. Someplace like...

Oh. Harper snapped upright. "That just might work," she murmured. "It might actually be perfect, in fact." Glancing at her watch, she smiled. She had almost an hour and a half before her yoga class. She grabbed her keys and started for the door.

IT SEEMED LIKE mere minutes later that she was letting herself into the reception room fronting Mary-Margaret's office. She'd barely crossed the threshold, however, before she realized no one was around. About-facing, she headed down to the building where the kids spent a great deal of their indoor time. She'd been coming out here enough to understand that where the kids were, Mary-Margaret was likely to be found nearby.

When she reached the game room, she poked her head in and asked the boys inside if anyone had seen the director. Moments later, following their directions, she turned right where her corridor intersected another. Her gaze was on the open door of an office at the end of the hall when she heard a boy's mumble, then Max's deep voice, coming from within the room she'd just passed. She came to a halt, her heart inexplicably picking up its pace.

All right, so maybe there was no real mystery to the sudden *thud-thud-thud* against her rib cage. God knew she was seriously attracted to the big deputy. She took several slow steps backward.

And heard Max say in his brusque, matter-of-fact way, "You don't have a damn thing to apologize for, and you're sure as hell no baby. You lost your mom, kid. Of course you're gonna cry sometimes."

Peering through the barely cracked open door, all she could see of Max was his big hand rubbing slow circles on the seated teen's back. Nathan, an anger management kid who was having a tough go of his therapy, sat slumped over a wooden worktable, his head buried in the arms he'd crossed atop it. As she watched, the teen lifted his head. He turned it in Max's direction and through the gap between door and lintel, she saw wet silvery streaks of tears down his cheeks.

"I miss her so much," he said, and the crack in his voice raised tears to her own eyes.

"Hell, yeah." Max's hand lifted from the boy's back to give Nathan's hair a rough stroke from crown to nape, which he gave a squeeze before dropping his hand. "I bet you do. It's only been—what?—two months since she died?"

Voice stronger—and harder—the teen snapped, "Tell that to my old man. He thinks it's time I snapped out of it. Started actin' like a *man*."

Harper watched the boy's jaw jut out rebelliously. From the set of his shoulders, however, it was fairly clear he was braced for either condemnation or we-must-learn-to-get-along therapistlike advice.

"He's an idiot."

"Yeah, well, *you* try living with hi—" Cutting himself off, Nathan stared up at Max, and Harper wished she could see whatever he saw, but Max was behind the solid panel of the door. "What?"

"I know I probably shouldn't say that, because I'm pretty sure the counselors would have my head for dissing someone else's parent. But your dad is wrong if he thinks he can dictate the timetable for anyone's grieving process but his own."

"If he's even grieving at all," Nathan muttered.

There was a beat of silence, then Max said, "Were your folks divorced?"

The boy shook his head.

"Separated or fighting all the time?"

"No, man. I thought they were solid." He pushed back from the table and sat back. "That's why I'm so pissed at him. If they were okay, how can he just—I don't know—bounce back so damn fast?"

"I don't know your father, but I do know that everyone handles death differently. If your parents seemed solid, they likely were. Trust me, even if your folks were trying to hide it, you'd have known it if something was off. So maybe trying to move on is just the way he deals, and he thinks it will work for you, too. Or maybe he was raised to suck it up when it comes to emotions."

"Yeah." Nathan shifted forward. "My grandpa is a total hard-ass."

"So maybe you should ask your counselor to help you to talk to your dad about the way you feel about losing your mother."

Harper so wanted to jump in to tell the teen about the way she had felt when her father died. To share the gulf that had lain between her and her mother ever since his death.

But this wasn't about her, and not only would he likely be mortified to learn she knew he'd cried, but it wasn't as if she had a solution to impart. Much as she loved her mother, they were still worlds apart.

So, blowing out a soft breath, she tiptoed past the door once again and went to find Mary-Margaret.

But remembering the comment the director had made the day they met about how the boys related to Max because of his rough childhood, and the certainty in Max's voice just now when he'd told Nathan that kids recognized dysfunction within their family, she made a promise to herself.

First opportunity she got, she was totally asking Max to tell her more about himself.

CHAPTER FOURTEEN

DAYS LATER, WHILE telling Mary-Margaret about the discounts she'd negotiated for the Village with several more Razor Bay retailers, it occurred to Harper that her mother hadn't called to break the news that their grant application had been approved.

She couldn't believe she'd forgotten to follow up on it. During her first two visits to the compound after giving her mom the go-ahead, she'd fully expected to hear the news and share in the excitement. But that hadn't happened, and somehow, between one thing and another, it had drifted from her mind.

Clearly, Mary-Margaret had yet to hear. If she had, Harper was pretty darn sure every employee and volunteer at the Village would've spread the news by now.

Pulling her phone from her purse as soon as she entered the parking lot a short while later, she called the foundation.

Her mother's assistant put her on hold. Unlocking her car, she threw her purse on the passenger seat and was leaning against the car when Gina finally picked up. "Hey, darling. Sorry to keep you waiting."

Harper had been raised from the cradle to always, *always* be polite and diplomatic. And still she heard herself demand, "What the hell, Mom? You haven't told

Cedar Village yet that we approved their application? You said you'd call them the day after we talked!"

Silence throbbed in her ear long enough for her to reconsider her words and the inflection with which she'd spoken them. Then her mother's voice, several degrees cooler than it had been an instant ago, said, "Your Grandmama Summerville would spin in her grave to hear that tone in your voice, young lady."

"I'm sorry." Well, she was…and she wasn't. For a generously sized part of her didn't feel at all apologetic. *It* merely muttered rebelliously.

"I'm sorry, as well," Gina Summerville-Hardin said with a quiet graciousness that chafed Harper's conscience. "When you called that night I was in bed. I'm afraid it quite slipped my mind by morning."

Harper's well-taught manners clapped their flippers together like the trained seals they were, barking their longing to apologize yet again. *Your turn,* they yapped. *Tell her you're sorry that she's sorry. Abjectly distressed that you distressed her. Full of remorse regarding Grandmama's grave whirling.*

Yet beneath that impulse lurked Bad Harper, and she had to fight that bitch to a standstill to bite back the words crowding her throat. Bad Harper cared for neither her mother's nor Dead Grandmama's concerns. *She* wanted nothing more than to snap, "Hey, it's hardly as though I woke you from a sound sleep that night. Weren't you the one who told me you were reading? And since when have you forgotten a single thing to do with the foundation?"

She was disconcerted to realize that she didn't quite believe her mother was telling the truth. Still, what was she going to do, call the very dignified, very upstanding Gina Summerville-Hardin a *liar*?

"Hey, there," a deep voice suddenly drawled behind her, and Harper barely stifled a guilty start. She wasn't fast enough to prevent herself from instinctively hunching a shoulder against him to mutter hastily into the phone, "I have to go." Her heart slammed against the wall of her chest—more with guilt than the usual surge of lust she felt whenever she saw him.

"Is that Deputy Bradshaw?" her mother demanded, but Harper disconnected without replying. Sliding her phone into her purse, she turned to Max.

"Hey," she said so cheerfully it was all she could do not to wince. She could only hope that it didn't sound as falsely perky to him as it did to her. If the piercing inspection he subjected her to with those all-seeing eyes was anything to go by, however, that was probably a futile wish.

But when all else failed, deflect—that was her shiny new motto. And an idea she'd been turning over in her mind since seeing all the junk food in his cupboards suddenly solidified. "When's your next night off?" she asked.

"Wednesday." He stepped closer. Heat radiated from his body as he plucked one of her curls between his thumb and fingers and pulled it straight, his mouth quirking when he released it and it immediately sprang back into its original spiral. Then he raised his gaze to meet her eyes, his own dark and intense. "Why? You wanna go on a date?"

She blinked, startled. "Oh, God. I haven't been on one of those since—" She shook her head "I can't even remember when." If the warmth spreading through her veins was anything to go by, however, her body was all over the idea. "Still, I suppose that's what it would be—since I want to make you dinner."

He stilled for a second, then gave her a crooked little smile. "Yeah?"

"Yes. A *nutritional* dinner that will taste so good it'll knock your socks off and maybe change your world—or at least your way of eating. I'd have to cook it at your place, though—all I have in my cottage is a hot plate, fridgie and a micro. But I'd provide everything."

He shook his head. "I don't know what it is with everyone and my diet, but I'll tell you what. You bring the food. I'll buy the wine. Red or white?"

Yes! She eased out the breath she hadn't even realized she'd been holding. "Do you like fish?"

"I like cod, halibut and salmon. I'm sure there's others, but I've only had those three."

"Then make it a Pinot Grigio or a Riesling. Or if you prefer red, maybe a Pinot Noir."

"I prefer a good Bud."

Her brow wrinkled. "You smoke *marijuana?*" For all that her voice practically cracked on the word, she wouldn't have been shocked if she'd heard anyone else was smoking it. But *Max?* She was sure as hell stunned at the idea of him doing so. He was the ultimate Mr. Law and Order.

He let loose one of his rare laughs, a deep, loud boom of sheer enjoyment that wrapped around her along with the hard, hot-skinned arm he snaked out to circle her shoulders. Hauling her to his side, he gave her a bone-cracking hug.

Then he turned her loose and grinned down at her, all white flashing teeth and good humor. "I'm talking

Budweiser beer, honey. The department frowns on its upholders of the law smoking weed."

Heat climbed her cheeks. "I knew that."

He laughed again. "Uh-huh. You stick with that." He grazed her cheekbone with the pad of his thumb. "You're such a convincing liar."

"Funny guy." She stepped back. Made a production of checking her watch. "I have to run. I have a Kickerama for preschoolers scheduled in half an hour."

"What the hell is a Kickerama? No, wait." He looked at his own watch. "You'll have to tell me Wednesday night. I'm starting a shift soon, and want to grab a shower before I clock in." He stepped close again and looked down at her. "So, I'll see you then, right?"

"Absolutely. I have to check my schedule, but if anything interferes I'll talk to Jenny about getting someone to fill in for me. So, say, six o'clock?"

"Sounds good to me."

To her, as well. But recalling his silly, and specious, no-sex-until-marriage rule—and, okay, maybe to get a little of her own back for the dumb marijuana misunderstanding—she paused at the door to shoot him a look over her shoulder. "In the spirit of full disclosure, I should tell you that I'm not doing this strictly from the goodness of my heart."

His thick level brows arched. "No?"

"*Heck,* no. I have big plans for you."

"Yeah?" He stepped back into her space, his dark-eyed gaze skimming her gauzy blouse and cargo shorts as if it possessed X-ray vision. "Tell me."

"Well, you do understand that when a girl goes to all this trouble for a guy, she expects a little something in return, right?"

"A little something like, what? We're not talking engagement ring, are we? Because that's kind of a steep price for a good meal."

"No!" Okay, maybe that came out a bit strident. But just the idea of something so…permanent sparked tiny flares of panic. If her father's death had taught her nothing else, it had taught her that you stop moving, you die.

Then she got a grip, because really, like he was *serious?* Clearing her throat, she said lightly, "That is, you think? It's our first date, Bradshaw. Althoooough…" Dragging the word out, she blinked up at him in faux innocence. "It's gonna be a very *good* meal."

He snorted. "What are we talkin', then? You gonna make me sing for my supper?"

"Do you have a good voice?" she demanded as if that were an actual consideration, but didn't await an answer. "Actually, I have something in mind that I'm ninety-nine percent sure you are good at."

Max twirled a lazy hand as if to say, "So let's hear it, already."

"My apologies if I'm holding you up," she said loftily. "I didn't mean to turn this into such a production."

"And yet here I stand, still clueless as to what it is you want for this allegedly fine meal."

"Fine." She sighed. "If you're going to be all say-your-piece-and-get-out-of-my-way about it, I thought you'd be so overcome with gratitude after eating a delicious meal that's actually—and I know this is a radical concept—*good* for you that you'd…put out."

His big frame froze, and Harper saw the arrested look that leaped in his eyes before he slowly lowered his thickly lashed lids to block it from sight.

When in the next instant they rose again, his look

was hotter than hell. So blistering, in fact, that she almost took a step back.

But his sage nod and dry "Ah. *Screw* for my supper, then" nailed her in place.

"I wouldn't have put it quite so crudely," she murmured. "And of course you don't have to do anything that makes you uncomfortable." She allowed her gaze to slide down the black T-shirt that hugged his muscular shoulders and the hard curves of his biceps, skimmed his pectorals, then hung straight to the fly of his jeans.

When her gaze reached the latter, she sucked in a breath at the hard length pressing against the worn denim. Okay, clearly he wasn't *that* discomfited by the idea. She looked back into his eyes.

"And, as I said, it will be a *very* good meal." Then she waved a hand. "But I repeat myself. The bottom line is that come Wednesday night? We play it *my* way." She wanted him. He wanted her. It was past time they moved things to the next level.

Besides, that was a pretty dandy exit line. Shooting him a final sultry glance over her shoulder, she sauntered out the door.

WHAT ON EARTH were you thinking? she demanded the following Wednesday evening as she climbed Max's front porch and tapped the door with a sandal-clad foot, because her arms were full of groceries. Talk about putting pressure on both of them. *God, Harper. You couldn't just spring a seduction on him instead of setting up all kinds of crazy expectations?*

The door opened, and her heart, which had begun tripping with performance anxiety, quieted at Max's easy posture.

"Hey there," he said, as if he didn't expect anything at all. His shoulders were relaxed and his gaze steady as he smiled at her, reaching for the two sacks she hugged to her chest. "Let me take those." Big, competent hands reached out to relieve her of her burden, then he stepped back. "C'mon in. I've been looking forward to being wowed by your cooking all week."

"I've been looking forward to it, myself," she said as he ushered her into the kitchen. "I like to cook, but since I'm hardly ever home I rarely get the opportunity." She'd been exhausted after her last job, all the coming and going and living out of a suitcase finally catching up with her. Part of the appeal of taking the job at the inn had been that she would have more than two full months in one spot instead of the usual in and out in a week. She'd needed a break.

Max dumped her groceries on the plywood counter at the same time that Harper squared her shoulders defensively. It wasn't like she was settling down or anything. Once she caught her breath, she'd be more than ready to go back to her travels.

"What do we have here?" Max started pulling items out of the sacks. "Salmon, romaine, tomatoes, butter, lemon, balsamic vinegar." His brows drew together as he held up a produce bag of purple-veined green leaves. "What is this?"

"Swiss chard."

"Huh." He gave her an I'll-try-it look but the last thing Max could be called was a prevaricator, so his doubt about actually liking it came through loud and clear.

She patted his forearm. She'd intended it as a there-there gesture, but the heat saturating her palm and crisp hair tickling it made her abort that mission. She pulled her hand back. Good God. *Down, girl.*

She cleared her throat. "I think you'll like it," she assured him. "But don't worry. I brought some fresh peas as well, just in case."

"At least I know what those are," he said with a self-deprecating shrug and an off-kilter little half smile. Circling the plywood counter, he hauled a stool up to it to perch a hip against its seat and braced one foot on its crossbar, the other against the floor. "I gotta watch and see how you do this. You want a glass of wine?"

"That would be lovely."

He flashed her a smile so full-blooded she blinked. "What?" she demanded.

"'Lovely.'" He shook his head. "I love the way you talk." He plucked a wine bottle off the end of the counter and presented it to her. "This okay? Mary Bean at the General Store recommended it."

Her hands full of ingredients, Harper leaned in to read the label. "Oh, that's a nice one."

"Good. She sold me some wineglasses as well, so you don't have to drink it out of a Wile E. Coyote jelly jar." Leaning over the counter, he retrieved a corkscrew from the work surface beneath it, then sat back and went to work on opening the bottle.

Harper watched his hands, large, rough-skinned and competent. They were a bit nicked up and wouldn't have looked out of place on a carpenter, which come to think of it, considering all the work he'd done on his house, he was. She had the impression he could do just about anything. His hands were übermasculine, yet deft as a sommelier's as he dealt with the cork.

He looked up suddenly and caught her staring. An

unexpected white noise suffused Harper's mind, making it go momentarily blank—an occurrence so rare she couldn't even remember the last time she was at a loss for words. But as she fell into his level yet heated gaze, her mind was one big void.

Then she remembered the conversation she'd been wanting to have with him. "The day I interviewed for a volunteer position at the Village, Mary-Margaret raved about how good with the boys you are."

He gave her a pleased look. "Yeah?" The cork pulled out with a little pop.

"Oh, yes. She thinks you're the best." Harper inspected the glasses he'd brought to see if they should be washed before they used them, since men rarely thought of the niceties. They looked fine, and, passing two to him, she added, "She mentioned that you totally get them because you had a rough childhood yourself—and they respond to that."

His hands stilled for a moment, then he set one of the goblets aside and poured wine in the other. He handed it to her without a word.

Okay, not real encouraging. She took a sip for courage, studied his blank expression...and plowed on. "Would you be willing to tell me a little about that?"

HELL, NO!

Okay, probably not the thing to say out loud, but... shit. Max faked concentration on getting the cork back into the wine bottle to give himself a minute.

Christ on a stick. Everyone and their brother in this burg knew his story, and he really liked that Harper regarded him through eyes untainted by his old garbage. But here she was, looking so pretty and crisp in slim white pants and an ultra feminine little white top splashed with blue and purple watercolor-like flowers, asking to hear all about it. Her sincerity shone like a flipping beacon from her gold-shot olive-green eyes.

And, dammit, as much as he'd rather simply admire the smooth upper slopes of her gorgeous breasts rising above the top's squared neckline, he just couldn't say no to those eyes. He blew out a breath. "My dad dumped my mother and me for Jake's mom when I was just a toddler."

The blade of the knife she held poised over several green onions froze midchop as she gazed at him, all sympathy. "Aw, Max, I'm sorry. That had to be tough, having a father only on alternate weekends and holidays."

He couldn't prevent the cynical laugh that escaped. "There were no weekends or holidays. Once he left us for the second Mrs. Bradshaw, we didn't exist. I grew up watching him being a dad to Jake, but he looked right through me."

"The bastard!"

Her prompt outrage on his behalf warmed him. He knew it shouldn't. Hell, he'd come to terms with his father's dysfunction years ago. Still, her support was… nice. He liked it.

"I'm glad you at least had your mom."

This time he swallowed his snort, but the warmth faded. "Sure," he agreed neutrally. "At least I had her."

She paused in the chopping she'd resumed to study him. "What aren't you telling me?"

"Nothing—" But he couldn't lie to that straightforward don't-kid-a-kidder gaze. "Mom was…bitter."

Harper's eyes narrowed. "How bitter?"

"Pretty damn," he admitted. "I don't think a day went by that she didn't remind me of what Jake and his mother had stolen from us." Was it hot in here all of a sudden? "Hand me one of those beers I brought, wouldja?"

She grabbed a Bud out of the little dorm-sized fridge, twisted off the cap and passed the bottle across the bare-bones plywood counter. "Wow. It's a wonder you and Jake are as close as you are."

"Yeah, well, that's new. We hated each other's guts growing up. And that was my fault."

"Sounds more to me that it was your father's."

"Oh, Charlie's fathering skills sucked, no doubt about it." Then he corrected himself. "Well, not entirely, I guess. Up until he left Jake and his mom for the third Mrs. Bradshaw, they only sucked with me. He looked like he was a really good dad to Jake. And it wasn't the old man who bullied him." *Jesus, dude, shut up!* What was she, a fucking truth serum? She hadn't demanded every single detail; what the hell was he doing providing them anyway?

"Max Bradshaw, did you pick on your little brother?"

His shoulders crept up. "Yeah."

"How old were you?"

"When I started? I dunno, maybe eleven?"

"So you were a little kid."

"I was old enough. And nobody knew better what it felt like to have a father who no longer considered himself your dad. I knew exactly how crappy Jake felt and I was happy about it!"

"And this surprises you?" she asked gently, wiping her hands on a towel and reaching to graze her fingertips across his knuckles. Until he felt her touch he hadn't realized he'd curled his hands into fists on the temporary countertop. "After spending all those years seeing your father being 'a really good dad' to your little brother while he pretended you were invisible?"

He pulled his gaze from where her fingers rubbed his to meet those warm eyes. "It was wrong."

"Yes." She straightened, her fingers sliding away. "But you know what was a lot worse? A father who was all or nothing with both his sons. A mother who wouldn't let you forget an injustice she should have been shielding you from." She shot him a crooked smile. "And you can't tell me Jake didn't get his licks in."

For the first time since she'd started this conversation, he felt a smile tug up his lips. "No, can't tell you that. Jake wasn't shy about fighting back. Guy's got a mean right hook—and a knack for drawing blood with words."

"So it wasn't as one-sided as you'd have me believe. And maybe things really do happen for a reason. Because, just look at how good it's made you with troubled kids. You always seem to know exactly what to say to them."

He'd never considered it in that light and found the idea oddly comforting. Feeling somehow lighter, he squared his shoulders, tipped his bottle up and took a long, satisfying swallow of his beer. Then he settled deeper into his stool and watched Harper cook him a nutritious meal.

He couldn't recall anyone ever going to so much trouble just for him, and it really got to him. Who would have thought that she and Jake being so concerned about him eating right would mean so much?

The balsamic-and-butter-tossed Swiss chard turned

out to be really tasty. He'd been prepared to eat enough of it to be polite, but he actually went back for seconds. The whole meal was great, from the baked salmon to the wine-poached pears. Apparently, good for you didn't have to mean tasting like cardboard.

After dinner, he insisted on washing the dishes. Harper dried, and when the last one was put away, he took her by the hand and led her to the living room. They'd barely gone ten steps beyond the plywood breakfast bar, however, when he swung her around to face him. "So, about me putting out for my dinner," he murmured. Sliding his fingers along her jaw, he tilted her face up to his, her soft skin a sensory banquet beneath his fingertips. And lowered his head to kiss her.

He'd intended to keep things light, maybe even playful, which, okay, was kind of a stretch for him. But there was just something so damn combustible about their chemistry when mouth touched mouth. Harper's lush lips softened and parted beneath his, and she promptly pressed her body against him, winding her shapely arms around his neck and holding him close. The next thing he knew, he had her pressed up against the living room wall, his fingers plunged into her glossy curls to tilt her head to the position he desired as he slanted his mouth wider over hers and challenged her tongue to a duel.

God, she tasted good, and, groaning, he leaned into her harder. Her hands slid up to grip his head, her fingernails scraping through his hair, scratching against his scalp.

Breathing heavily, he pulled back and stared down at her. Her eyes were heavy-lidded, her lips parted, ruddy and swollen from the force of his kiss. With a rough sound, he bent his head to kiss her again, hard and fast, then dipped his knees to press an openmouthed kiss on the underside of her jaw. He sucked the soft skin there between his lips, then pressed additional hot, suctioning kisses down the length of her throat, leaving a path of tiny red stains that faded almost before he left the next one. He was pretty sure she wouldn't be thrilled with marks she'd have to explain or wear a turtleneck to conceal.

Reaching the base of her square neckline, he pressed a kiss to the creamy brown slopes of the breasts he'd been admiring all evening where they rose above a narrow edge of pleating. A gritty sound climbed his throat at the pliant give beneath his lips and the soft, needy moan that Harper made.

"Let's move this to my bedroom." His voice was hoarse, and he reached to pull her hands out of his hair—just as his cell phone sounded its *Law And Order* theme song ringtone.

"Shit!"

"Noooo," she moaned.

Straightening, he dropped his forehead to hers. "I'm sorry," he said. "I have to get that. It's work."

She sighed, then nodded, and Max went to go answer his call.

For the first time since coming home to Razor Bay, he was sorry—really, really sorry—that he'd joined the damn sheriff's department.

CHAPTER FIFTEEN

"Happy birthday, bro."

"Thanks." Trying to act cool, as if birthday wishes from a guy he'd battled with for too many years didn't tickle him on a deep-down, more-masculine-shade-than-pink level, Max pushed open his screen door and stepped out onto the porch, closing the front door behind him. "You didn't have to come get me—I could've met you at The Anchor."

"It's your birthday, dude. Everyone deserves extra good treatment on their big day."

He'd neither grown up in a household that ascribed to that idea, nor had he ever taken the day off as if his birth were something special to be celebrated. But he could sure get used to both those things in a red-hot hurry. He liked the way it made him feel.

A lot. "Let me just lock up, then I'm ready to go."

"Yes!" Jake jerked in a victory fist. "At *last* someone besides me who thinks their house oughtta be secure before they just waltz away, one-horse town or not."

Max grinned at his brother's New Yorker sensibility. "Razor Bay isn't exactly a hotbed of crime," he said. "But I've gone out on enough calls for the places that have been broken into. And I don't ever want to feel the way those folks did."

"Wouldja tell that to Jenny? Because she treats me as if I'm a big-city idiot whenever I try to say anything."

"As opposed to the regular idiot the rest of us think you are?"

Jake's fist shot out in a quick, hard jab to his arm. He immediately shook out his hand. "Damn, you're like hitting a brick shit house—it hurts me a helluva lot more than it hurts you."

"Well, it *is* my birthday."

His brother grinned. "True. And you look very spiff. I see you took my advice."

He glanced down at his club clothes. "That the birthday kid has to dress like someone's going to drag him to a hot restaurant at any minute? Yep." He checked out Jake's duds. "You look all right, yourself."

Jake made a rude noise and struck a pose, modeling his own sharp outfit. "I look a damn sight better than 'all right,' bro."

Inside The Anchor ten minutes later, Jake stopped him as he started to stride past the bar. "Have a look at the brew list," his brother commanded, jerking his chin up at the overhead blackboards. "You gotta try at least one beer that's not a Budweiser on your birthday."

Willing to give it a shot, he looked up, studied the boards, then admitted, "I have no idea what to choose."

"Hey, barkeep!" Jake yelled. "I'll take a Fat Tire in the bottle—and what brew besides Bud can you recommend with a nice cat piss bottom note? It's my brother's birthday, and I wanna give him a special treat. But we can't wander too far away from his preferred taste."

The patrons were pretty much equally divided between cheering or booing Jake's Budweiser trash talk. And Max was taken aback at the number of people who shouted out cheerful Happy Birthdays to him, half of them nodding at his clothes and adding, "Lookin' good, Deputy!"

Laughing, Elise, the bartender, waited for the hubbub to die down before promising to send over something he'd enjoy.

It didn't take long for the waitress to deliver their beers to the booth they'd snagged. After dealing out coasters, she set a longneck bottle in front of him along with a pint-style beer glass. "Elise said to tell ya you oughtta be supporting your local breweries instead of sending all your beer allowance to other states."

"We have a local brewery? I mean, I know they're all over the state, but *local* local?"

"Hell, yeah. Silver City right in Silverdale."

"How could I not know that?"

"Because you don't drink anything but Bud, and you go to places where you can dance instead of to breweries," Jake said, picking up his bottle of Fat Tire.

The waitress lifted Max's bottle and poured it into the glass. "This is Ridgetop Red, an ale she thinks you'll like. It took Gold in the *altbier* class at the North American Brewer's Association."

Nudging the glass on its coaster closer to him, she looked at him expectantly. He realized she wasn't walking away until he tasted it, and took a sip.

The flavor flowed smooth and rich over his tongue and down his throat, and he lowered the glass. "Damn," he said. "That's good."

"Yes!" Jake crowed, and the waitress nodded.

"Damn straight." She gave him a "good boy" pat on the shoulder, collected the money Jake passed her and smiled her thanks when he told her to keep the change.

A second later she was dashing off to answer the hail of a patron down by the dartboard.

Max was relaxed, laughing at an Austin story his brother was relating and getting ready to flag the waitress down to order another Ridgetop Red when the cell phone he'd set on the table rang. He didn't even look at it.

Jake gave him a funny look. "Aren't you going to get that?"

"Nah. If it's important they'll leave a message." Not feeling the least bit tempted to be his usual responsible self, he shrugged. Hell, the last time he'd let the phone interrupt a good time, it had kept him from getting lucky with Harper. So, no. He wasn't answering. "And if they do that, then I'll decide if I actually want to listen to it or not."

Jake reached over and snatched the phone off the tabletop, hitting the talk button. "Max Bradshaw's phone."

Max stared at him. "What the hell, Jake!"

His brother shrugged. "Hey, I thought it might be important." He held the cell out to him. "It's a kid named Nathan from the Village."

"What are you, my fricking social secretary?" Max muttered under his breath, but reached for the phone. Nathan had been pretty upset the last time he'd talked to him, and there was no way he could turn his back on the kid if he needed him. He brought the phone to his ear. "Hey, Nathan."

"I'm sorry to bug you, man," the teen said, "but d'ya think you could come out here? Something's happened, and I really need to talk to you."

He felt surprisingly disappointed at the thought of cutting his birthday celebration short but blew out a breath and nodded, even though Nathan couldn't see him. "Okay. It's going to be a while, though. I'm away from my car, so I have to go home first to get it, but—"

"I'll take you," Jake said.

"Hang on." He covered the mouthpiece and looked at his brother. "You don't have to do that."

"You just going out to the Village?"

"Yeah, but—"

"You live in the opposite direction. I can take you and hang around while you talk to the kid, and maybe we can continue this when you're done. If not, I'll call Jenny to pick me up, leave you my car and collect it at your place in the morning."

"Okay. Thanks." Liking the idea of maybe picking this up again, he uncurled his hand from around the speaker. "I'll be right out."

"Dude. Thanks. I'll be in the activity room."

He repeated that to Jake as they headed out. "Odd place to meet. The activity room's hardly ever empty."

"Maybe that means whatever the kid's problem is, it's not too serious," Jake suggested.

"I hope not, both for his sake and mine. It would be nice to resolve this quickly."

"Amen to that, Deputy D." Jake grinned at him. "Here's to getting back to drinking good beer ASAP."

Since nothing was very far from anything else in Razor Bay, in what seemed like no time they were striding down the hallway to the activity room. "Whoa. Door's shut," Max said over his shoulder to Jake, unable to mask his concern. "I don't think I've ever seen that before." Turning the knob, he pushed it open.

"Surprise!"

Max's heart seized like a blown engine at the roar

from a couple of dozen throats. It shocked him so much, in fact, that he had an awful feeling he might have pulled his gun if he'd been wearing it.

He rarely had PTSD-type symptoms anymore, but occasionally he had to fight the shoot first, talk later instinct that was prevalent in war. As it was, he froze for a second, gaping at all the people yelling and laughing on the other side of the door.

"Deputy Dawg was so into his b'day being *his* day, he damn near didn't answer the phone," Jake said with a laugh to the group at large, nudging Max forward into the room.

That's when the word *surprise* finally unjumbled in his mind. Sank in and made sense. Holy fucking shit. This was a surprise birthday party.

For him.

Warmth and an emotion that felt almost like—no, who was he fooling, that *was*—happiness replaced his confusion, and he turned to his brother. "You arranged this?"

"No. Harper did."

His heart smacked up against the wall of his chest, and he barely heard Jake's "My and Nathan's job was to get you here" as he located her standing next to Mary-Margaret by the windows. She smiled at him and mouthed, *Happy birthday.*

With a single purpose in mind, he headed straight for her.

The boys mobbed him before he made it halfway across the room and dragged him over to a table in the corner laden with cold cuts and bread, fruit and veggie platters, potato salad and bowls of chips, crackers and dips.

"Dude, lookit all the food!"

"Did you see this *cake?* 'Happy Birthday, Deputy Dawg!' How epic is that?"

Very—and undoubtedly Jake's contribution.

"There's soft drinks in the coolers, too. Mary-Margaret said we couldn't have any until you got here. But you're here now, so I guess that means we can dig in, right?"

"Surprised ya, huh?"

The last was Nathan, and Max hooked the inner bend of his elbow around the boy's nape and hauled him close. He scrubbed his knuckles against Nathan's scalp in a rough noogie. "I'll say," he said, turning him loose. "I 'bout had a heart attack, I was so surprised."

They all laughed, and Nathan ducked his head, clearly pleased.

Max grinned at them, touched deep inside at their delight in pointing out all the details of his party to him. But he had a purpose burning bright, and he said, "Go grab yourselves that pop. I need to thank Harper for planning all this."

He walked right up to where she stood talking to… someone, snaked an arm around her waist, yanked her flush against him, plunged the fingers of his free hand into the back of her hair and bent her back over his arm in one smooth move. Sealing his mouth over her little squeak of surprise, he laid a kiss on her.

Only the knowledge that he was in a room full of impressionable boys—all of whom were currently cheering and catcalling in the background—kept the kiss chaste, his lips safely, or at least mostly, closed. Her hands had grabbed his shoulders, and, cracking an eye open, he saw that hers, so close they were slightly blurry, were wide open. He grinned against her soft, soft lips and hauled her back upright. Then slowly, reluctantly, he lifted his head away with a tiny, final sip at the sweetness of her mouth.

"Thank you," he said, smoothing back a curl that had flopped over her eye. "Nobody has ever done anything like this for me, and it's the coolest thing ever."

Color washed the apples of her cheekbones, but she said calmly in her blues singer contralto voice that never failed to lift the fine hairs on his body, "You're welcome. It was a kick to put together."

"Happy birthday, Max," a feminine voice said next to them, and he pulled his gaze from Harper's to see the woman she'd been talking to was Amy Alverez, the sheriff's department dispatcher.

"Hey!" he said in surprise. "I didn't see you there."

"No foolin'," she murmured and laughed.

"Wait a minute." He narrowed his eyes at her. "Jim didn't need the extra hours?"

"Oh, he's always happy for them. But I was Harper's first call to make sure you had the day off."

Amy's husband strolled up, popping a bite of spinach-dip-covered cracker in his mouth. He chewed, swallowed and thrust out a hand. "Happy birthday, Max."

Jenny danced up on the heels of their shake. "Bet we'll be seeing that kiss on the Razor Bay Blog as Best Response to a Surprise Party Ever! Jake captured the money shot on his trusty camera." She gave Max one of her ubiquitous hugs, and for once he didn't feel all stiff and clueless as he returned it. "Happy Birthday, almost Brother-in-Law!"

Austin barreled over, came to a halt in front of him

so abruptly it rocked the kid up onto his toes, then gave him a punch to the arm. "From me, too, almost Uncle—Oh, wait!" He grinned. "You're already my uncle! But happy birthday. This is pretty epic, huh? Dad and Jenny and me gotcha—"

Jake, who had strolled up in the boy's wake, sealed his hand over his son's mouth. "Something you'll see for yourself later," he said over Austin's head.

"Whoa. All this and I get a present, too? Kid's right. This is epic." And a little overwhelming.

But, God, in such a great way.

He was amazed at how many people had turned out for him and spent the next half hour making sure he greeted and talked to everyone. He watched the boys at the Village covertly watch Austin and his friend Nolan and girlfriend, Bailey—and vice versa. When several of the Village kids converged on the refreshment table at the same time as his nephew and his friends, he started over.

"You've played baseball with him?" he heard Austin say. "That's buck, dude. I've been to a Mariners game with him, and he's come to a lot of my games. But we've never played ball together."

"Yeah, but he's your uncle—so that's even better," Owen said, and Max realized they were talking about him. As though he were some hotshot sports star or something.

"You shoulda seen the most awesome baseball game ever," Owen continued enthusiastically. "See, Harper knows shit-all about the game, and she tried to keep Nathan from second base by guarding him like a basketball player. And Max, he—"

No two ways about it, he thought later after he'd visited and laughed with every single person who'd come out just for him, had photos taken by Jake with all the boys, both individually and as a group, chowed down everything on the overloaded paper plate that Tasha had dished up for him, blown out candles and eaten a piece of chocolate cake with cream cheese frosting, then opened not one, not two, but a whole boatload of presents both large and small. This was simply:

The.

Best.

Day.

Ever.

"THANKS FOR AGREEING to drive me home, Harper."

She glanced over at the sound of Max's voice. His back was to her, and she watched him put away chairs, even though she'd told him that this was his day and he wasn't supposed to help. "Of course. It's not a problem. I'm happy to do it."

"And I have to thank you again for the party."

"You're welcome again," she said, silently willing him to look at her.

"This was great, really great," he said in a low voice.

It always clutched at something deep inside of her, the way he was so unabashedly grateful for any little thing anyone did for him. It was hard wrapping her mind around how sterile his childhood must have been, but she sure appreciated the miracle of how well he'd turned out in spite of it.

"And it's not even over yet," she said lightly. The trash bag that she'd been tossing used napkins, plates, cups and torn wrapping paper and ribbon into sagged in her hands as she admired the shift of muscles in his back when he lifted a stack of folding chairs five deep onto the shelf that held them.

He stilled, his hands still braced on the outer edges of the chairs, then slowly craned his head to look at her over a big shoulder. He must have read something in her eyes, because his own commenced a slow smolder. "That a fact?"

"It is. Giving you a ride home was meant to be, since you need to take me back to your place in order to get your present from me."

With a final pat for the shelved chairs, he turned to face her. "You don't think this party and all the work you put into it is enough? You decided you needed to buy me something, too?"

"Not exactly." For nearly the first time since he'd walked into the room to the cries of "Surprise!" she allowed her gaze to roam to her heart's content from the top of his dark hair to the soles of his dress shoes, scoping out every hard plane and rounded muscle in between. "It's more of a…service."

"Yeah?" He took a step nearer.

"Mmm-hmm."

"You gonna wash my car for the next month?"

"Nope."

"Make me nutritious meals, maybe?"

She shook her head, then laughed. "Well, possibly. But that's not it."

He took another step in her direction. "Swiffer my floors?"

"I don't do floors or windows."

"Make my bed?"

"You're getting warmer."

His long legs ate up another giant step. "How much warmer?"

"Well, if you must ruin the surprise—"

"And I find I must," he agreed, crossing muscular arms across his chest.

"I thought I'd help you wreck it instead."

Electricity seemed to spark as they considered each other. The moment played out until finally Max, with a visible effort, tore his gaze away to glance once around the room. "Looks good to me. Let's go."

She rattled the trash bag in her hands. "There's just a few more things that need to be thrown in here."

With blinding speed, he snatched up every last piece of party detritus, tossed them in the bag, snugged up the plastic drawstrings and slung the bag over his shoulder, clearly prepared to throw it in the Dumpster on his way to her car. The hand he wrapped around her own was hard and hot, but that was nothing compared to the heat in his eyes as he stared down at her. *That* damn near left singe marks.

"Like I said, let's go."

CHAPTER SIXTEEN

HARPER PULLED UP in front of Max's house and had barely shut down the engine before he had the passenger door open and was outside circling the hood with long-legged strides. She'd witnessed his almost catlike grace before. Yet maybe because it wasn't all that common for a man of his size and muscularity to be so fluid, she was struck anew every time she saw it.

He yanked her door open. The guy was all broad shoulders and lean hips, his eyes burning down at her with a fierce intensity. A muscle jumped in his jaw. "I'd like to be all suave about this," he said in a low, gritty voice, "but I've wanted you from the minute I clapped eyes on you the day you came with Jenny to the baseball field. Suave is beyond me at the moment."

God, her heart was *pounding,* and for a second she simply stared up at him. No one had ever looked at her, talked to her like this, as if she were a slice of mochaccino cheesecake that he was ready to eat with his bare hands. Unbuckling her seat belt, she swung her legs out of the car and extended a hand to Max. She'd had a lifetime of smooth, urbane men. And compared to him? "Suave is boring."

The corner of his so very nicely shaped mouth ticked up, and he reached for her hand, helping her out of the car. "Yeah?"

"Most definitely."

"So, What's your stance on caveman tactics? Those work for you?" He stroked a thumb down her cheek.

"Pretty much—as long as it doesn't involve being dragged by my hair. I'm not into having my hair torn out by the roots."

He hustled her up the porch stairs and dug a house key out of his pocket. "I'll shoot for more finesse than that." Opening the door, he ushered her in.

Kicking it shut behind them, he crowded her against its solid panels. "You look really pretty today." Linking their fingers, he pressed her hands against the cool wood above her head. The position sent her skinny copper, silver and rose-gold bangles sliding down her left forearm almost to her elbow. "This dress rocks."

He stepped in close but not quite close enough to touch except at their hands and forearms, and the heat, the feel of even that much, made her blood burn. "And that's about the extent of my finesse."

His deep voice reverberated along her nerve endings, and she was focused on the sensation when he lowered his head and rocked his mouth over hers.

Like a man on a mission.

She moaned deep in her throat, grateful to finally feel his slightly chapped lips on hers again. Their last kiss had given her several restless nights of tossing and turning as she'd relived it over and over again, gnawing like a puppy on a chew toy at the thought of where it might have led if Max's summons to work hadn't brought it to such an abrupt end. But now, finally, he was back where he had been before they'd been so rudely interrupted. Kissing her again.

And, oh, God, what a kiss. She wouldn't be surprised

if her skin was smoking; Max was all hot lips, talented tongue and sharp teeth, and he knew exactly how to use them. He had mad skills, and it was clear he was very passionate about the way they were applied.

Never in her life, in fact, had Harper been kissed with so *much* passion, and she surged against his hold as she tried to get closer, closer.

He merely pressed their hands, their arms, tighter to the wall and nipped her bottom lip, tugging on it with his teeth. But then he moved in and bent his knees to press that hard body against her softer one. His chest was a hot wall flattening her breasts, his thighs a muscular cage imprisoning her hips. And between those thighs, the rigid length of his penis nudged her stomach.

She tried to lift onto her tiptoes, but he leaned harder against her. Letting her bottom lip slide through his teeth, he moved his mouth to her ear, lightly biting her lobe.

"Who's in charge here?" he demanded, and the assured as-if-we-need-to-ask rasp in his voice tightened her nipples into painful points.

You are.

No, no, no! That was just too politically incorrect for words. Forcing a coolness into her voice she was light-years from feeling, she willed her muscles to relax. "Seriously?"

"As a toxic spill, sweetheart." His warm breath hitting the whorls of her ear sent a chilly wash of goose bumps racing down her arms, her legs. Then he moved his mouth to the sensitive spot behind her ear and touched it with his tongue.

She shivered, and he said again in that twenty-grit voice, "Who's in charge, Harper?"

"Well, I suppooose that would be you," she acceded slowly with a manufactured reluctance she hoped would give the impression she hadn't just caved like a cheap suitcase. "It *is* your birthday, after all."

She felt his lips curl up against her skin. "That's right, baby, and you're my present. Isn't that what you said?"

"Well, not in those exact words."

"But that was the general message, yeah?" He didn't wait for her reply. "You're my prez, and I'm going to unwrap you. Real. Slow."

Her sex clenched deep between her legs. She had a feeling she could really get into this dominance thing.

Bending his knees deeper, he dragged his erection downward until it finally bumped the sensitive cleft at the juncture of her thighs. They both sucked in a sharp breath, and the feel of him sliding over that sweet spot, even through their clothes, set off a whole series of miniclenches.

With a rough sound, Max released her hands, plunged his into her curls and held her head tipped back as he kissed her with long, hot, thorough precision. His hips slowly oscillated, and his hard-on rubbing against her set up a firestorm of friction.

When he pulled back to stare down at her with hot eyes, his breath soughed in and out of his lungs. "I love your hair," he said. "Love the way it wraps around my fingers like something alive. I want to see it wrapped around my—" Cutting himself off, he shook his head.

But oh, boy. Her imagination had no problem taking it from there.

He kissed the side of her neck near her racer-backed sheath's scooped neckline. "This has been driving me crazy ever since I laid eyes on this dress," he said, his free hand sliding down the exposed rose-gold zipper that ran the length of her side from the deeply cut-in arm hole to the several-inches-above-her-knee hemline. He nipped her bare shoulder, then licked the small hurt he'd caused. "Two zipper heads, baby. Gives a guy twice the options."

Slowly, he stroked his hand in a return journey up the long zipper. As his fingers slid over her hip, they stretched to fondle her butt, the pads of his fingertips pressing into its resilient fullness. His thumb provided the same service to the side of her breast on his way past that.

"Where to start?" he growled. "Down from the top?" Grasping the zipper tab between his finger and thumb, he slowly lowered it a miserly couple of dozen teeth, then pulled it back up. Unzipped it and zipped it. With each pass, his palm brushed her breast's outer fullness, and the heel of his hand grazed her nipple, which promptly puckered up even tighter than it already was.

A small, needy sound escaped her throat, and he pressed his erection harder against her.

"You like that?" But he removed his hand. "There's still that up-from-the-bottom option to consider." He reached down to grasp the other zipper tab and pulled it up, one inch, two, turning the five-inch slit she'd created earlier into a seven-inch one. His hand snaked beneath the opening to wrap around the back of her thigh and tugged her leg up as far as the narrow opening would allow.

Which wasn't nearly far enough. Harper's panties had been steadily dampening beneath his red-hot attentions; now suddenly they were mortifyingly wet. "Max, please."

His callused fingertips rasped over her skin as he slid his hand out from under her skirt. He reached to lower the top zipper a fraction of an inch at a time. "What do you want me to do, Harper?"

"Tear off the damn wrappings, already!" she said between her teeth.

Pushing back, he laughed. "Well, since you asked so nicely," he said, still grinning.

And yanked the zipper down.

IT RAN INTO the still-raised bottom tab.

"Shit." Max had been on a roll until he forgot about zipping the side slit closed so he could unfasten the upper zipper in one fell swoop. Harper's dress sagged open, but between its racer-back top, which meant the dress had to be pulled off over her head, and the spot where the bottom of her dress was still connected, it only afforded him a stingy view of the pretty taupe-and-black bra and panty set beneath it—and only a slightly less stingy portion of her even prettier skin.

"Suave, indeed," he muttered, squatting cautiously around his raging hard-on to rectify his mistake.

Above him, Harper chortled, making his hands still at their task. He looked up at her.

She still leaned against the door, fingers splayed against the panels on either side of her hips. Her goldy-green eyes were slumberous as she returned his look, and her full lips, rosy from his kisses, quirked up in a slight smile. "You know what, Max?" she said when his eyes met hers. "I really like you. You are such a straight-forward *real* guy."

His heart smacked up against his sternum with such force he was surprised she couldn't hear it go *Bam!*

like that TV chef guy. "Yeah? I really like you, too."
He swallowed a snort—but just barely. Because, really.
Understate much?

Without looking away, he fixed the zipper issue, and
her dress sagged open farther. He trailed a hand up her
bare leg as he rose, stepping into her space the second he regained his full height. Grasping her thigh, he
hooked it over his hip.

And suddenly he was back where he'd left off, his
dick firmly nestled against the heated nest between her
legs. "Would it be too straightforward to tell you I'd really, really like to get you naked?"

"Well, I don't know. I'm standing here in a dress
that's half-off. You're fully dressed. It seems a little one-
sided to me. You plan on getting naked, too?"

"Absolutely."

She reached for the top button on his shirt and slid
it free of its buttonhole. "Then I'm all over the idea."

"*Ex*cellent."

Her lips curled up at the corners. "You're a man of
few words, aren't you, Bradshaw?"

"Yep." He bent his head to kiss the side of her neck
as she made fast work of the rest of his buttons. "I can
think of a better use for my mouth than talking."

His shirtfront separated, the two sides falling free,
and Harper's hands slid beneath the material. Stroking
them up his chest and over his shoulders, she pushed at
the fabric and the shirt fell down his arms.

Then she bent her head and placed a kiss over his
heart.

He sucked in a breath, but before he could start strip-
ping her, she reached a finger to his nipple.

"You *do* have a nipple ring," she breathed, gingerly

touching the small loop half hidden beneath the fan
of hair on his chest. "I thought I saw one that day you
played basketball on the skin team at the Village. But
when we took the boys swimming at the inn I thought
it must have been my imagination. You didn't have one
then."

He shrugged. "I had it pierced when I first joined
the Marines—and during those years I wore it all the
time. These days it depends on my mood. I figured my
birthday was a good day for it." He studied her. "If you
hate it, I can take it out."

"I don't *hate* it. I just don't want to think too closely
about what it took to get it where it is now." She hunched
her shoulders as if protecting her own nipples.

She glanced up at him. "Still, I kind of appreciate
the unexpected mystery of it. I like the fact that a guy
as quiet as you has this secret thing going on beneath
his clothes.

"Sweetheart, right this minute I've got all kinds of
secrets going on beneath my duds."

"Oh, God, tell me you didn't pierce your...you
know!"

"My you know?" The cartoon lightbulb went off over
his head, and he stared at her, horrified. "My *dick?* Holy
shit, Harper—*no!*" He did a little hunching of his own.
"I think I just lost my hard-on."

She made a scoffing sound. "You so did not."

He rocked against her. "I easily coulda, though.
Never mention that again."

She arched an eyebrow at him, and he shook his head.
Who knew a woman could pack so much irony into one
eyebrow and a lopsided little smile?

He trailed the backs of his fingers down Harper's

bared side. "What do you say we peel you out of this dress?"

She raised her arms over her head, the bangles jingling as they dropped down her arm, and he pulled the khaki dress off over her head. The neckline tugged her curls straight, but they sprang back a little wilder than before as soon as the dress cleared it.

With the garment still clutched in his fist, he took a step back to get the full effect of Harper in her bra and skimpy panties. And his breath left his lungs.

"God," he murmured when he finally remembered to inhale. He rubbed at his chest. "Look at you."

She was so damn beautiful, with her warm, burnished skin, her clear eyes and healthy curls. Her breasts, round and ripe as peaches, rose out of the black-embroidered taupe bra, her waist dipped in before flaring into womanly hips. And, oh, God. Stepping up, he slipped his hands under her matching panties over the full curve of her ass, spreading his fingers to clasp the lushness of it. "You must know you're gorgeous."

She flashed him that wide, white-toothed, flash-of-pink-gums smile that was so bighearted it narrowed her eyes into crescents. "You think so?"

"Oh, yeah."

"I think you're gorgeous, too." She scratched her nails through his chest hair, gave his adorned nipple a whisk of her thumb and a cautious tug of his ring that had his cock ready to rumble. Then she ran a hand down his abs, following the stripe of hair that disappeared beneath his slacks. She reached for his waistband. "Aren't we fortunate to be such pretty people?"

Having no idea what to say to that since he was nowhere in her league looks-wise, Max swept her up before she could unfasten his pants. She yelped and clutched his neck.

"Let's take this to my bedroom," he said roughly.

"Ooh." She wiggled her butt. "Good idea."

He looked down at her. "You have no idea all the things I want to do to you, do you?" he demanded in a low voice. If she did, she might be gone so fast he wouldn't see her through the trail of dust she left in her wake.

Her eyes went heavy-lidded, and she tightened her hold around his neck. "Maybe not. But I do know I can hardly wait to find out."

He bit out a short, succinct word and took the stairs two at a time up to his room, hoping like hell he could hold it together long enough to do even a fraction of the things he'd fantasized doing.

Carrying her to the bed, he bent a knee into the pillow top and laid her on the mattress. Following her down to lie atop her, he pushed up to take his weight off her chest and spread his thighs on either side of hers. Then he buried his hands back in all those clingy curls. And kissed her again.

IT COULD HAVE been the very first time as far as Harper was concerned. She went up in flames as if the fire between them had never been banked.

God, he was such a good kisser, and he was so hot and hard and smelled so good, and she wanted, wanted, *wanted* him like crazy. Massaging the length of his spine, her hands eventually hit the waistband of his slacks, and she wiggled her fingers beneath it to the first knuckle, then the second, her fingertips dipping into the dimples just above the firm rise of his ass.

Like a magpie after something sparkly, she reached for his butt.

Ripping his mouth free, Max inched lower. She made a little sound of protest when her fingertips slid out of his pants.

But his mouth on her throat was bliss incarnate, and she angled her jaw to give him more access as he kissed his way down it. Then he was pressing openmouthed kisses to her collarbone, her chest. His hands reached behind her to unfasten her bra, and as it fell free she wrestled it off and tossed it aside. It landed on the floor, and Max bit off a curse. She pushed up on both elbows to look down at him.

"You've got the prettiest tits," he murmured, cupping one. A flush tinted his cheekbones. "Breasts, I mean."

"I don't care what you call them," she said. "In all honesty…guy words kind of turn me on. But I'm more interested in touching you. In you touching me."

"I can do that." He caught her nipple between thumb and finger and pinched. She sucked in a breath as a hot thrill zinged straight to ground zero and set off more of that clenching thing.

Max glanced up from observing his handiwork to study her. "Guy words, huh? You like it when men talk dirty?"

"I don't know, no one ever has to me. But I'm thinking…possibly." She shrugged helplessly. "I might, anyhow."

"I want to fuck you so bad."

Ca-lench!

"Want to fuck you slow and deep—" he inserted a muscled thigh between hers "—until I feel you coming all over my cock."

"Oh. My. Gawd."

He dipped his head, pulled her nipple into his hot mouth and used his tongue to press it against his palate. And sucked. Releasing it with a pop barely an instant later, he looked up at her, all hot dark eyes. "Yeah," he growled. "I'm thinking you like dirty talk."

"Maybe." Was that her voice, all breathless? "Maybe not."

He snorted.

"Okay, smart-ass. What makes *you* think so?"

He brushed a few curls out of her face and gave her a slight smile. "Oh, I don't know—the fact your panties are wet?"

Oh, God, it was true. She'd locked her thighs around his like a horny Chihuahua, her hips subtly rocking her mound against its hardness. She forced herself to still, even though it damn near killed her.

He pushed back and pulled her bikinis down her legs, dropping them over the side of the bed. Gliding his fingers into the slippery heat between her legs, he lowered his mouth back to her nipples, doing things that felt so wicked she couldn't catch her breath. And in between the use of his tongue, his teeth and his fingers on what seemed like every erogenous zone she possessed, he talked dirty to her.

Really dirty, telling her all the ways he was going to make her come.

By the time he reached for his own waistband, she was nearly mindless with desire for *one* of those ways to push her over this raw edge of need he had her straddling. But she fumbled semi-upright to help.

When her fingers brushed the back of his hands as

he unfastened his fly, however, he turned a look on her that was almost feral. "Let me do it."

"Isn't this supposed to be reciprocal? Because I've been doing all of the taking and none of the giving."

"You can reciprocate next time," he said. "It's been a while for me, and if you help me now I'm afraid it'll be over before we get to the good stuff."

She flopped onto her side, propping her head in her hand. "We don't want that."

His laugh was strained. "No, we don't." He pushed his slacks down his thighs and kicked them away. It left him in a pair of gray boxers with a navy waistband, and he began pushing those down as well, but paused to look at her.

"You planning on watching?"

"Heck, yeah! I might not be able to lend a hand, but there's no way I'm not getting a look at the goods."

"As you wish, Buttercup." He shoved the boxers down.

"Whoa." She sat up. Stared. Licked her lips. And helplessly repeated, "Whoa."

Buck naked, Max somehow appeared larger, not diminished in the least by the lack of clothing. She studied him so avidly, she was surprised her ardent perusal didn't leave scorch marks in its wake as she ogled his wide shoulders and hard, lean abs, his big hands, bigger feet and long, hard legs.

"Hoo," she breathed softly. Because that wasn't the only thing long and hard on the man. His sex stood proud, extended and thick.

She squeezed her thighs together. "I want that. I want...you."

A flush rose in his cheeks. A muscle ticked in his

jaw. Then he turned away to pull a handful of condoms from the drawer of his nightstand. Tossing all but one onto the stand's top, he flopped onto his back to efficiently roll on the protection.

"You've done this before, I see." *Well, duh.* Of course he had. She hadn't a doubt in the world he was light-years ahead of her, experience-wise.

He dove atop her. "Not recently, I haven't." He stroked a hand down her hip. "I keep interrupting your pleasure. Let me just build you back up."

"You're kidding me, right?" She stared at him. "Enough foreplay—I want you inside me. *Now.*"

He snaked his hand beneath her thigh and tugged her leg up. "I can do that. Oh, man, can I do that."

She hissed in a breath as she felt his erection slap against her lower stomach. She reached between them to wrap her hand around all that covered rigidity.

Max froze at the first touch of her palm, of her fingers wrapping around him. "I wasn't kidding when I told you it's been a while," he said hoarsely. "I'm on the ragged edge here."

"Which is exactly why I'm not doing what I really want to do."

"What's that?"

"To squeeeeeze you through my hand from tip to root."

His penis pulsed, and she smiled at the knowledge that she could make him as crazy with a few words as he did her. She couldn't stop herself entirely from stroking him…and even through latex it was incredible the way his skin shifted over pure hardness.

"You haven't let me do much of anything else— I am putting you in me." She made an adjustment beneath him that brought them sex to sex and gently rubbed him up and down the slippery wetness between her legs, almost choking on the breath she sucked in as the head of his penis bumped over the inflexible little pearl of her clitoris.

"Then you'd better do it now, before I explode and leave you in the dust."

She lined him up, but Max took over from there, easing all that rigidity inside her. "Tight," he said through his teeth. "So damn *tight*." He pulled back a little, then thrust forward again.

The stretch to accommodate him pinched for an instant, then suddenly everything worked the way it was supposed to. Shuddering out a breath, she wrapped her legs around him.

And immediately felt him bump against what could only be her G-spot. "Omigawd!" She raised her hips for more.

He pulled almost all the way out of her, and she whimpered at the feel of sensitive tissues dragging against the retreating source of all that pleasure. Then he pumped back in with less gentleness than the time before.

"Max?"

He pulled out, surged back in.

"Oh, God, *Max*? I'm not going to last, I'm so, so, so—"

"Close?" Rearing up on his knees, he pressed her legs back against her chest and fell over her, catching the backs of her knees in the bend of his elbows before planting his hands on either side of her shoulders. It tilted her to an angle that made her even more sensitive as he slowly, tortuously, pulled out and thrust in.

"You don't have to hang on, baby," he said and pulled out and slowly sank as far as a man could go once more.

Hitting that spot with each reentry.

"There's been too much teasing for that." He contorted himself to suck her nipple in his mouth, and she clenched hard around his sex. He swore, releasing her breast, and his hips began to piston in and out of her, picking up more speed and force with every propulsion. "Neither of us is gonna— Christ." Gritting his teeth, he slammed his eyes shut.

The next instant they were open, if heavy-lidded, as he looked down at her and licked his lips. "We've gotta get you yours, baby—fast. Because, Houston, we're about to have lift off." Balancing on one arm, he reached between them and slid his thumb into the wet slit between her legs. It slid over her clitoris and retreated.

Then came back to lightly circle. "I'd planned to take my time licking this. Sucking it."

"Omi—" Her climax hit her in hard, fast contractions. "Omigawd, *Max?*" Then her ability to speak deserted her, and the only sound she could produce was a moan that kept growing higher and higher in pitch as she convulsed and convulsed and convulsed some more around him. Sinking her nails into his strong, damp back, she hung on.

"Oh, fuck," she vaguely heard him whisper, then he thrust deep one last time and held there. "That's it, that'sit, that'sit. God, you feel so damn *good* coming all over me." Then his voice degenerated into a long, raw groan, and his eyes went blind as he ground against her.

An instant later he collapsed on her like a felled tree. Two hundred plus pounds of dead weight likely would have driven her right through the mattress, but the back of her thighs prevented him from dropping that hard.

"Sorry," he mumbled and helped her straighten out her legs. Then he lowered himself a little more cautiously atop her. "Thank you," he mumbled into her hair.

"Are you kidding?" She felt as if she were glowing from the inside out. "Thank *you*. That was the Best. Sex. Ever."

He lifted his head up and gave her a sleepy smile. "Nah. That was just the warm-up. Give me a few to recuperate, and I'll show you the best sex ever."

He did a face-plant back into her hair. "Promise."

CHAPTER SEVENTEEN

I'M GONNA MARRY this woman.

Max was propped up on one elbow, watching Harper sleep next to him when the thought drifted unbidden through his head. He jerked upright.

She startled, one sleep-blurred eye cracking open. "Wha—?" she mumbled.

Soothingly, he stroked her shoulder where the sheet had slipped down. When her eyelid slid closed once again, he gently covered her, then pushed back to lean against the headboard. Christ. His damn heartbeat was *tripping*.

"Whoa, dude," he whispered, staring at a glimmer of diffused moonlight filtering through the thin cloud cover outside the open window. "Get ahead of yourself much?"

But his gaze was drawn back to her all sprawled out on her stomach, one drawn-up knee poking the side of his leg, her crazy cool hair spiraling all over the place.

And he admitted to himself that, okay, sure, what he felt with Harper—especially now that they'd had sex—was larger than anything he'd felt with anyone else. Ever. But he sure as hell hesitated to call it *love*. He was probably just grateful because of the sex thing. Damn, how long had it been, anyhow?

Way too long, he was thinking, if he had to work

this hard to remember the last time. Which only went to prove his point.

Still, didn't that explanation seem just a little too pat?

"Dawg," he muttered. "*No.* Sex three—count 'em, *three*—times. *Grateful.* You really need to say more?" With a shrug, he slid back down the mattress. No sense getting himself all bent out of shape.

Like a heat-seeking missile, Harper immediately gravitated to him and he gathered her in, letting her situate herself as she would, but easing that wandering knee of hers a safer distance from the jewels. He wrapped an arm around her, and his hand found its natural resting place on the full curve of her hip. Holding her felt too good to be worrying over vagrant thoughts and what-ifs. And, hell, he had to work tomorrow, he needed some shut-eye.

He could always hash out the details, if he absolutely felt the need, some other time.

"Mom," Harper said urgently into her cell phone in Max's backyard the following morning, "this has gone on way too long. I know you have issues with the way I run my life, but will you *please* inform Cedar Village that they've been approved? To *not* do so is just plain—"

Max stuck his head out the back door. "Breakfast's ready," he said, and she disconnected from the answering machine she'd been talking to.

The good humor in his eyes dimmed a little as he looked at her. "Everything all right?"

Giving him a strained smile, she said, "Yes, of course, fine." She wasn't sure why she was lying, though. There was no reason she couldn't tell him the truth without telling him the *complete* truth. And she could see by his sudden stillness and the narrowing of his thick, dark lashes over even darker eyes, that he wasn't buying the platitude, anyhow.

"No, that's not true." She made a helpless gesture with the phone in her hand. "It's my mom."

He stepped out onto the small back porch, his concern instant and genuine. "She sick or something?"

"No, no, nothing like that." She climbed the stairs and stepped past him into the mudroom, then turned to face him. "I just hate the way she hates the way I live my life."

He nodded his understanding. "I get that. You've heard my story, so you know my mom has issues with my choices, too."

Feeling her jaw drop, she snapped it shut. But no way could she also stop herself from saying indignantly, "It's not bad enough that she encouraged you to be angry all your childhood, she has a problem with you being a responsible, upstanding citizen doing an important job, *too?*"

He gave her one of those off-kilter half smiles that were more golden than anyone else's full-out grin and slung an arm around her shoulders, hauling her against his side. He squeezed her in a warm, hard, much too brief hug before turning her loose. His hand moved to grip the back of his neck as he gazed down at her.

"Nah," he said. "My job's never been her problem. Her big issue is me being friends with Jake." His shoulders rose and fell in a whataya-gonna-do shrug.

Then he made an impatient gesture. "But I've told you about that. Tell me about *your* mom's issues. Were you close at one time?"

"We were. We *are*." She grimaced at her overemphatic tone. "Okay, maybe that came out a little too defensive."

"Maybe just a tad." Max rubbed his hand over her hair in the same rough caress she'd seen him use occasionally on the boys at the Village. If they were anything like her, she'd bet they got all sorts of comfort from the gesture.

Then he reached for her hand, linking their fingers. "C'mon in and have some breakfast. Everything's better on a full stomach."

He ushered her through the kitchen and over to the little table on the other side of the counter. He'd set it for two, complete with paper towel placemats and a fistful of slightly scraggly flowers in that Wile E. Coyote jelly jar glass he'd mentioned the other night.

And her heart melted around the edges.

Releasing her hand, he thumped out a chair for her. "Sit. I'll grab the food. You want OJ? Coffee? Or I've got some cocoa—I could make you a poor man's mocha."

God, the best sex of her life aside, how could anyone not really, really like this guy? "I'll try that last one." She raised her voice slightly to project to where he was bent over the stove on the other side of the counter. "What's on the menu?"

"I made an omelet with—you'll like this—some honest-to-God veggies. And I bought some Canadian bacon at Costco in Silverdale, which is not only tasty but waaaay leaner than bacon."

"Oh, my God. You paid attention to my nutrition lessons?"

"You bet." The oven door closed, and he came around the counter, flashing her one of those gorgeous almost-smiles. He set the platters on the table in front of her.

"Well, except maybe for when it comes to the potatoes. I used a little olive oil but added a big pat of butter. You'll just have to muscle through it, though, because hash browns aren't hash browns without butter." He went back into the kitchen.

"I never said you had to monitor every bite you put in your mouth," she informed his muscular back. "The trick is to shoot for eating the good-for-you stuff more often that not." She laughed. "Besides, *any* change you make is a huge improvement over your old diet."

"Smart-ass." He set a steaming mug, redolent of both coffee and chocolate, in front of her and took the seat across the table. "Try that," he ordered, tipping his chin at the mug, and reached for the omelet plate. After dishing them up with eggs and the Canadian bacon rounds, he passed her the hash browns platter.

They dug in, and for a few moments it was quiet except for the click of cutlery, her murmured appreciation, first for Max's homemade mocha, then for his breakfast at large, and his request for the pepper. When the edge was taken off their hunger, he looked at her across the table. "So, you were a daddy's girl, huh?"

She felt a little start of surprise. "I was. How did you know?"

"You mentioned it at Jenny's barbecue."

"And you remembered?" Her smile was no doubt as dazzled as she felt by the knowledge that he'd paid such close attention. "I thought you thought I was a ditz that night."

"Nah. I thought you were a well-educated rich girl."

"Oh. Well." She flashed him her version of his lop-sided smile. "I kind of was. My parents weren't *rich* rich, but I certainly never wanted for anything."

"And that's sure as hell not a bad thing. It's just that I've never quite known how to talk to the silver-spoon girls. So I maybe came off as a little rigid."

She laughed. "God, you tickle me."

He looked at her as if unsure whether or not she was mocking him, and she just wanted to crawl onto his lap and wrap him in her arms. She had to content herself instead with merely leaning over the table toward him.

"I'm not making fun of you," she earnestly assured him. "I simply adore your honesty. You don't play games—if people don't immediately know where they stand with you, they do shortly thereafter. It's nice. Re-freshing, even."

He gave her a wry, one-sided smile. "That's me. Re-freshing. So, you like blunt talk?"

"It turns out that I do. Very much."

"I want to get naked with you again."

She laughed, but beneath the table where he couldn't see, she squeezed her thighs together. "I'd like that, as well. But I promised Jenny I'd come in today to work on the Razor Bay Days stuff."

"Damn."

She indicated the uniform he'd donned. "It looks like you're ready for work yourself."

"I am. But I'm motivated—I can give you a down-and-dirty good time real fast."

She shook her head but couldn't suppress a grin. "Will you give me a rain check?"

"Hell, yeah." Then his eyes went more serious as he looked at her over his coffee cup. "Tell me about your mama woes while we finish up breakfast."

She took a bite of her potatoes, chewed, swallowed,

then set her fork down. "Mom hates that I travel so much."

He nodded. "I remember you saying that you and your dad liked all the moving around, while your mom and brother didn't."

For a moment, she simply stared at him. She couldn't recall one other person who'd ever paid as much attention to the things she said as Max did.

Then she gave her head a little shake. "Yes, well. As we established, I was a daddy's girl. And my father always had this saying—you stop moving, you die. It drove my mother crazy—she thought that was a stupid excuse for never settling down. But the thing is, Max? He finally did give up all the traveling, mostly for her. I was several years out of college, working a job in Stockholm at the time, but my folks and my brother moved back to the Carolinas, where Mom and Dad started up a business. And ten months later? He was dead."

Max put down his own fork. "You can't believe it had anything to do with his saying."

"Intellectually, I know that would be superstitious nonsense and, worse, probably silly, to boot. But emotionally?" She nodded. "Yeah. I think he was onto something."

"Jesus, Harper."

"What can I say? Emotional truths don't have to adhere to any rules of logic. Besides, it's more than just my dad dying. I *like* traveling, love seeing new places and meeting new people. But my mom refuses to extend me the courtesy of acknowledging that perhaps I actually do know my own mind."

"How about you? Do you blame her for your father's death?"

"What?" Shock at the idea zipped like an electrical current along her nerve endings. "Of course not! Why would you even say such a thing?"

He gave her a level look, patently unconcerned with her indignation. "You just said that emotionally you believe in your dad's 'You stop moving, you die' motto. According to you, your mother made him stop moving." He raised a hand. "Seems like a reasonable question to me."

"There's nothing reasonable about thinking my mother's to blame!"

"Then doesn't it correlate that sometimes things just happen and there's nothing reasonable either about believing somebody dies just because they stop traveling?"

She studied him mutinously for a moment, then heaved a big sigh as if *that* would help her get back on track. "I don't know. You've got me all confused."

"And you've gotta get to work—I know." He reached across the table to run a gentle fingertip over the fists she hadn't even realized she'd balled upon the tabletop. "Just…give it some thought, okay?"

She didn't know why she suddenly felt like crying, but she did. Preventing herself from doing so by sheer willpower, she gave a jerky nod of agreement. "I've gotta go."

"Can you finish your breakfast first?"

She shook her head. "I'm not hungry any…" She swallowed a lump in her throat. "I'm quite full."

"Okay." He rose to his feet and watched as she collected her purse, then walked her out to her car. He opened the driver's door for her but stopped her before she could climb inside. Cupping her nape, he bent his knees to bring himself closer to her height, then dipped his head. He gently kissed her with lips that married softly seeking to seductive suction.

With the very first touch of his mouth, she felt some of her tension melt away. There was just something about the feel, the taste, of this man.

Just something about *him*. He touched her, and she felt wrapped in warmth. In comfort.

For a moment, after he finally raised his head and stepped back, he studied her solemnly. Hooking a knuckle beneath her chin, he rubbed his thumb over her bottom lip. "I made you sad, and I'm sorry for that. It wasn't my intention."

"I know. Sometimes, I just really miss my dad." And Lord, it was true…but not the whole truth. What she felt was somehow more than simple grief.

The problem was, she couldn't even say to herself what that "more" might be, never mind try to find the words to explain it to Max. So she gave him a helpless shrug, got in the car and reached for the door handle to pull it closed.

With one of his hands on the roof of her rental and the other holding the outside handle to prevent her from closing it, he leaned down, his shoulders blocking out the morning sun just rising above the treetops in the woods behind his house. "Will I see you soon?"

"Yes."

"Good." Straightening away, he slapped the car roof. "I've got your word on that, right?"

"Yeah." She closed the door. And realized as she drove away that he truly did.

Her emotions might be all over the place at the moment, and she sure as heck needed to run her mother to ground and somehow convince her to get off the dime and follow through on informing Cedar Village of their grant status. But even with all of that, she'd had a major taste of Max's lovemaking last night. Being with him had been…incredible. Incredible in so many ways she couldn't put a name to them all. All she knew was that he'd made her feel things she had never felt before, sexually, emotionally and, well, every way there was.

And if her time here was finite, she planned on getting as much more of that everything as she could. Right up until the day she packed her tent and moved on.

LATER THAT WEEK Max stared at the screen on his work computer, but for once he was too distracted to see a word of the report he'd been typing up. Vaguely, he was aware that Sheriff Neward was holed up in his office, but that was hardly news. The man spent most of his time there these days and had begun talking more and more often about retiring.

In all honesty, Max thought the department would be better off if he did. Neward was a dinosaur who had pretty much quit doing his job. Plus, he was old school all the way, opposed to anything he considered newfangled. Hell, Max and Amy had had to talk themselves hoarse to convince him to *computerize* the department. They'd been years behind the rest of the state.

The question was, did *he* want to run for Neward's position when Neward did finally retire? He knew he'd be good at the job, but all the glad-handing it would take to get there wasn't exactly his strong suit.

But, man. He had a million ideas for improving the efficiency of this department.

The phone rang out at the dispatch/reception desk,

and he heard Amy pick it up. When she didn't buzz his line, he tried to go back to his report.

And failed. This time his thoughts went straight to Harper. They'd gotten together twice in the past three days. And Jesus, the sex had been so damn good. When he was inside her, when he held her and felt her holding him, it made him feel…whole.

Their conversations, unfortunately, were less satisfying. Hell, who was he kidding—meaningful conversation had basically become nonexistent. He couldn't think of one significant thing they'd discussed since the morning after his birthday.

He couldn't kid himself any longer. Something had been niggling at him for a while now. For all that he'd gotten her to talk a little about her family that morning, he still had the sense there was more that she wasn't saying.

For years he'd longed for a relationship that was solid—something along the lines of what his brother had with Jenny. He really wanted someone who'd feel free—no, anxious—to share the details of her life, her thoughts, with him.

He'd like to believe that's what he was building with Harper. He was crazy about her, but her jones for keeping on the move aside—which, c'mon, all on its own hardly boded well for her remaining in town—his cop instincts were screaming that parts of her story didn't add up.

He'd given her a lot of openings; she'd ignored them all, shying away from saying more than the little she'd already told him. Then there was her habit of disconnecting every damn time he walked in on her talking on the phone. And the girl didn't exactly have a poker face. She was definitely up to something.

Well, either that or had someone else, and *he* was the piece on the side.

He hated that idea, and God knew, he'd tried to ignore it, because any way he looked at it, it didn't strike him as Harper's style. But something was sure as shit off, and he just couldn't pretend otherwise any longer.

Which left him with only one recourse. He had to do some quiet digging.

It wasn't like he planned to run a full-scale background check on her or anything. But he could ask a few questions of the right people and see where that got him. Because if nothing else was true, he knew this much.

He needed to know what the hell he was dealing with.

CHAPTER EIGHTEEN

"HEY, IS THIS a race?"

Harper, who had suddenly sprinted ahead of Tasha on their trek down the beach, stopped next to the wind-and-salt-water-bleached log she'd scoped out earlier. Setting down the Styrofoam cooler she'd borrowed from the inn, she flashed Tasha an unrepentant smile.

"Sorry. I got a little excited. But, honestly, don't you think this is the most fabulous spot? Look, it even has an honest-to-gawd patch of sand." She waved at the rare-for-Razor Bay fine-grained strip of beach in the protected lee of the log, then snapped open her blanket and watched it drift down atop it. Sitting down, she stretched her legs out in front of her and crossed her ankles.

"You're right, it's really fantastic. And this was such a great idea." Tasha dropped her small cooler next to Harper's and looked out over the canal at the mountains. "I've lived here my entire life, but lately I hardly ever seem to get out long enough to enjoy the scenery." She toed off her Keds and plopped down on the blanket next to Harper.

"I know, right?" Resting back on her elbows, she looked at the strawberry blonde. "I was busy planning a bonfire for the guests at the inn when I suddenly thought *we* need one, as well. Sure, they're paying guests, but why should they have all the fun? And since

I haven't been to a bonfire since I got here, or okay, since I was—" mentally, she counted back "—good God, in college—"

"Holy crap, you two have long legs!" Jenny called as she and Jake approached. "I feel like a Corgi trying to keep up with a couple of greyhounds." She waved that aside to jump into the conversation she'd obviously overheard. "I'm not a native, but I have lived here since I was sixteen, so close enough, right?" She set her cooler with the others. "And unlike I-make-pizza-and-that's-all-I-do Riordan, I do get out and do a few fun local-recreation kinda things."

"Well, sure," Tasha agreed. "You have a teenager around."

"Yes, it definitely makes a difference." Settling next to Tasha, she looked around the secluded spot Harper had selected away from town. Then she grinned at them. "I gotta tell you, a no-kids-allowed/not-connected-to-work picnic is just what the doctor ordered."

"Sez you," Jake grumbled, squatting to drop a load of firewood on the pebbled beach between the women-occupied blanket and the high-tide line. "You frail, female types aren't the ones doing the heavy lifting for this non-work-related shindig."

"No, we left that to you," Harper said cheerfully. "We did the heavy thinking, recon and planning instead."

He sent her an easy smile over his shoulder. "Good one." Then he turned his entire body in their direction, a move that should have looked awkward to execute in a crouch yet somehow didn't. His hands hung loose and relaxed between his spread thighs in a pose that reminded her a lot of his brother. He gazed around him, taking in the cliffs that soared above this part of the beach and the line of trees that had tumbled down their banks over the years to stretch across the shore toward the water, down a bit from the spot where they'd congregated.

"You probably heard I grew up in Razor Bay but got the hell out of town the minute I could," he said. "I can't say I recall this exact spot, but it's a good one."

He brought a finger up to scratch at his temple. "I'm surprised I don't recognize it—I thought I knew all the good make-out spots." He wiggled his eyebrows at Jenny. "And that's a good-sized rock over there," he said, indicating a huge boulder jutting up out of the pebble and shell beach. "Bet we'd have all kinds of privacy to get busy in on the other side of that baby."

She rolled her eyes but gave him a slow, sexy, get-back-to-me-later-on-that curl of her lips.

"Don't mind me." Heaving a big sigh, Tasha let her head droop theatrically on the long stalk of her neck. "The fifth wheel will just sit here poking at the fire and eating too many s'mores while you couples disappear into the bushes and behind rocks to have all the fun."

Jake opened his mouth, but she raised her head enough to give him a look. "Trust me, sport. You don't even wanna go there."

Harper spotted Max striding down the beach toward them, balancing a sizable bundle of wood on each shoulder, and it was as if someone hit the mute button on her friends' conversation. Suddenly the only sound she heard was her heart beating like a bongo. *Holy Mary, mother of—*

Since Max's birthday they'd gotten together several more times, and she kept expecting the newness, the edgy excitement he made her feel, to wear off. Or at least to dim a little. Instead, she kept getting sucked in deeper, into that rampant sexuality, into his *life*.

And this despite her best efforts to hold him at arm's length from her own. She'd love to be insouciant about the affair they seemed to be having, to simply enjoy it while it lasted. At the same time, it didn't seem quite right to be so intimate on a sexual level when she refused to say anything the least bit intimate on a personal one for fear she'd give away who she really was and why she was here in the first place.

She was tired of having secrets and truly wanted to share all of herself with him. And not just with Max, but with Tasha and Jenny and Jake, who'd befriended her, as well. Then there was everyone at Cedar Village. This had gotten way out of control. She was giving her mother one final call, and if she didn't promptly come through, she'd inform Mary-Margaret herself that the grant had been approved.

Then she'd get busy explaining herself to everyone. But until then she really ought to at least take a big step back from the sexual relationship with Max.

She swallowed a snort. Right. She'd *initiated* a great deal of it. And every time she made a genuine attempt to stay away from him, he simply slid like smoke past all her barriers. She'd had a lot of opportunities to hold herself aloof. Yet Max seemed to be carving out a place for himself in her life—and might even have been carving a more long-lasting place in her heart.

At least for however long she remained in Razor Bay.

The thought made her very nervous. Because if anyone was settled in his life, it was Max. And she was so not.

She had to tell him the truth. To hell with her mother!

"Well, lookie here," Jake said drily as the man in question strode up and crouched to unload his wood next to Jake's. "If it isn't the overachiever."

Max snorted. "Says the guy who went to Columbia University while I went into the Marines to keep from ending up an angry, bitter loser."

"Aw." Jake grinned. "You're just saying that to make me feel better about only bringing one load of wood."

"Well...*yeah*." He turned to Harper. Flexed an impressive bicep, turning his fist forward and back to make it jump. "So, we manly men did all the heavy lifting—"

"You don't wanna go there, bro," Jake warned. "She's got a real good comeback for that."

Max dropped his hand to his side. "Tried it already, huh?"

"Yeah, and trust me, it didn't fly."

"Okay." Max's dark-eyed gaze made a leisurely trip up and down Harper's body.

It took all she had not to wriggle in place. She raised her eyebrows and hoped to heaven that she came across coolly amused and not like a toddler in need of a bathroom.

Or a woman thinking about her next orgasm.

The genuinely amused look he returned made her fear she'd fallen short of her goal. But all he said was, "What's for dinner?"

"I picked up some fried chicken and potato salad from the Sunset café."

"I brought a marinated veggie salad, s'more fixins and wine," Tasha said.

"And I've got corn on the cob," Jenny added. "Which I pre-buttered and salt-and-peppered and wrapped in foil. All you need to do is toss it on this little rack that

I leave up to you big, strong men to figure out how to put over the fire. I've also got grapes and some sliced watermelon and tossed in a couple of beers for you and Jake." She slid him a sly smile. "He tells me you're a new fan of Ridgetop Red."

"That I am." Max wasn't the least embarrassed to admit as much. Hell, prove him wrong, and he didn't mind owning up to it. But neither did he see a reason to beat the subject into the ground, so having done the owning, he moved on. "That's some great menu." He patted the back of his hand to his chin. Gave the women a little smile. "Am I drooling?"

"And if you were, how would that be different from any other day?" demanded Jake, who had come over to help him scrounge for the bigger beach rocks to form a fire pit.

"Hey!" Max used a couple of stiffened fingers to punch his brother in the sternum, and the next thing he knew Jake had him in a headlock. They wrestled on the ground for a moment, and it was like a blast from the past.

With one big difference. This time they weren't genuinely attempting to beat the shit out of each other.

Jenny came to stand over them, legs akimbo and her small fists propped on her hips. "If you boys are quite finished getting your clothes all gritty, we need a fire built," she said, then handed them each a beer when they promptly rolled apart, grinned at each other and started slapping sand, bits of shell and small pebbles from their jeans and T-shirts.

Jake's clothes, of course, were ten times classier than his, and Max indicated them with a jerk of his chin. "Who the hell wears a silk T-shirt to a beach party?"

"Hel-lo!" Jenny said. "Have you *met* your brother? He thinks silk T-shirts are appropriate for all occasions."

"Damn straight," Jake agreed. But in a patent bid to change the subject, he said to her, "So, have you told your posse our news?"

That got their attention. "What news?" Tasha demanded and was echoed by Harper.

"We're getting married," Jenny said.

Tasha blew a raspberry. "That's not news. He gave you a ring almost three months ago."

"We're getting married January seventeenth."

"You picked a *date?*" Tasha demanded, and the women did that female thing of squealing their enthusiasm. "When did you decide this?"

"It doesn't give you a lot of time," Harper added.

"Are you kidding me?" Max demanded. "That's almost four months from now."

They turned identical why-are-you-talking-moron looks on him, and he put his hands up in self-defense. "What?"

"Churches and reception halls tend to be booked a full year in advance when it comes to weddings," Tash explained kindly—if a bit as though she were speaking to a four-year-old. "And bakeries like notice for the wedding cake months in advance."

"That's fuckin' nuts."

She laughed. "That's the wedding industry, baby."

"We circumvented a lot of the problems by deciding to keep the wedding small and hold it at the Pierces' place."

Harper blinked. "Who are the Pierces?"

"Austin's grandparents and my former in-laws," Jake said. "They died last year within six months of each other, and after Emmett passed Austin moved in with Jenny."

"I lived with them from the time Austin was about four," Jenny said. "He's my little brother in every way but blood."

"And she's taken real good care of him." Jake turned a look full of love on his fiancée.

"Wait," Harper said. "I think I know the house you're talking about. That beautiful sage-and-cream Craftsman up on the bluff?"

Jake nodded. "It's been empty since Emmett's death, but we've decided to move back into it after the wedding."

"Austin is so thrilled the three of us will finally be living together," Jenny said. "The house is legally his, but I don't think that part's even registered."

"He's not the only one who can hardly wait to have us all together," Jake said drily, wrapping an arm around the petite brunette. "I'm tired of the living-in-two-houses thing myself."

"Not to burst your bubble," Tasha said. "But you do realize that most of the town will expect to be invited to your wedding, right?"

"That's why we're having a big reception at the inn. As long as we throw a big enough party, I doubt anyone will feel the pinch of not attending the wedding."

"Will you be able to accommodate everyone?" Harper asked. "Or did I totally miss the fact that you have a banquet room?"

"We don't," Jenny replied cheerfully. "But we x-ed out that weekend on the inn calendar, and we plan on using the entire first floor. We haven't figured out exactly how yet, but we'll make it work." She turned to Tasha. "You'll be my maid of honor, of course."

"But of course," Tasha said regally. Then her entire face lit up, and she hauled Jenny in for a fierce, quick hug. "This is sooo wonderful!" She turned the little brunette loose. "And we *are* going to get me a kick-ass dress, not one of those frou-frou monstrosities."

"Yes, we are." Jenny turned to Harper. "I want you to be my bridesmaid."

"Oh." Harper's expression radiated delight. In the next instant, however, the pleasure dimmed. "But I'll be gone by then."

A shard of pain cut through Max's chest at her talk of leaving. He realized he hadn't given it any real thought, but before he could ask himself what the hell he thought would happen when her gig at the inn was up, Jenny was pinning Harper in place with a stern look.

"Then you'll simply have to come back for the weekend, won't you?" she said. "You heard Jake—you're part of my posse now, one of my girls. I know we haven't known each other very long, sweetie, but I *feel* as if I've known you forever."

Tasha nodded her agreement. "Me, too."

Jenny essayed a gesture that said *there you have it.* "That's not something you get with just anyone."

"No, it's not," Harper agreed. "And I'd be so honored to be part of your big day. I'll x out the weekend on my calendar, as well."

"Alrighty then." Slapping her hands together as if checking another chore off her list, Jenny turned her back on everyone to fuss with her cooler. "Let's get that fire going. I don't know about the rest of you, but I'm starving."

"She's gonna cry," Jake murmured. "The woman's a sentimental fool."

"Am not!" she said, knuckling a tear away.

"Well, I am," Harper said, clambering to her feet and hauling Jenny in for a hug.

A few minutes later, as the women got busy pulling out food and plates and all the other stuff they considered essential for putting together a meal, Max and Jake finished roughing in a fire pit with a circle of stones, then laid the wood. Jake squatted to light it, but paused to look over his shoulder at Max.

"I asked Austin to be my best man," he said in a low voice. "But I'd sure like it if you'd be my groomsman." He gave him a sly smile. "I know how much you like to dress up, and this is your opportunity to rock a tux."

The fact that Jake wanted him to be part of his wedding gave Max an odd, warm feeling in his chest. But he merely said roughly, "I'm in."

"We're also going to figure out a place in the inn to set up dancing and—"

"Jake," he interrupted, "I'm in." Looking down at his brother, he smiled, feeling really good. "You had me at the tux, bro."

"YOU SURE CAN plan a party," Max said as he helped Harper haul her picnic paraphernalia into her tiny cabin. "First my birthday party and now this. That was one hella good picnic and bonfire."

"It was really great, wasn't it? And I'm starting to think having it tonight was good timing on our part, too." She looked at the trees that were beginning to rustle in the freshening wind. "Look how fast those clouds are blowing across the moon. I wonder if a storm's coming in."

"Hmm," he said. He wasn't interested in the weather.

What *did* interest him clearly showed on his face because her lips suddenly quirked up, and she raised her eyebrows at him. "Yeah?"

"Oh, yeah." He thumped the Styrofoam cooler down on the floor and nudged it out of the way with the side of his foot. He was reaching for her even before he fully straightened. Snaking an arm around her waist, he yanked her to him with an enthusiasm that would have sent her bouncing right off him again if he hadn't hurriedly angled his arm up her back. As it was, it flattened her breasts against his chest, which was A-OK with him. Burying his nose in her hair, he pressed his mouth to that sensitive hollow behind her earlobe. "I've been wanting to do this all night."

She made a rude noise. "Stop the presses," she said with wry humor. "You always want to do this."

He touched the tip of his tongue to the pulse beating beneath her soft, scented skin. "You say that like it's a *bad* thing."

"Aw, nooo," she crooned and, wrapping her arms around his neck, walked him backward. It didn't take many steps before his back hit a wall.

Yeah, baby. I just love me an aggressive woman. But pleased as he was, he gave her the most demure expression he could drum up. "Be gentle with me."

A laugh sputtered out of her. "Oh, I will," she promised, leaning back to give him a good, long look. "Or I'd planned to, anyway. But, you know—" she took a half step back and grabbed a fistful of his T-shirt in each hand and worked it up his torso, baring the muscles of his abs, his pecs, which tightened beneath her appreciative gaze "—on second thought," she said as he raised his arms to facilitate the shirt's removal, "maybe I'll go all dominatrix on you instead." She stood on her toes to pull it off over his head, then tossed it aside. She splayed her fingers through his chest hair and looked him in the eye. "So, maybe you should be afraid. Be very afraid."

"Oh, I am," he assured her, reaching for the tiny buttons that ran from neckline to hem on her little red sundress.

She slapped his hands away. "It's my turn to be in charge."

"Hey." He held his hands away from his body in a classic, I'm-just-a-harmless-guy gesture. "You're the boss."

"Oooh." She wiggled. "I am, aren't I? This is going to be fun." Leaning in, she kissed the side of his throat.

She worked her way down his neck, leaving damp kisses in her wake. Reaching the hollow of his throat, she lapped at his pulse, which was racing like a treed cat's. As her teeth scraped over his clavicle, she worked her hands between them to start opening her own buttons.

Groaning, he reached for her.

"Hands at your sides, mister!"

"Daaaaamn," he breathed, tucking his chin to watch her mouth's possum-paced approach to his nipple.

Finally, her lips reached it, a lush cupid's bow pursed over the silver ring that glinted through his chest hair. She raised her gaze to watch him looking down at her. "Is this what you want?" she whispered and lowered her mouth.

He hissed his approval as warm suction pulled at the

sensitive nub. Her lips pulled back and he saw the ring clasped between her teeth.

She gave it a little tug, and all the breath left his lungs in a loud "Hah!" Then—

"All right, baby, that's it!" He reached down to lightly squeeze her cheeks between his thumb and forefinger, loosening her grip on the nipple ring. Sweeping her up, he tossed her over his shoulder. Within moments, he'd packed her up the loft ladder and was flipping her onto her back on her bed.

He was frantic to get inside of her, but as he looked down at her on the patchwork quilt, she gave him a big pleased-with-herself smile, and the bolt of tenderness that shot through him took his breath away.

Climbing onto the bed, he straddled her hips and reached to undo the buttons that she'd failed to unfasten near the hem of her sundress. Slowly, he peeled it open like a kid with his one and only gift on Christmas morning. Then he simply stared at her spread out beneath him in all that sleek skin and a delicate, scanty white bra and panties set.

"You are so beautiful," he murmured, sliding down to lie atop her. He lowered his head to kiss her.

Slowly. Tenderly.

And was rewarded by the near silent "Ohhhhhhhh-hhh." She sighed into his mouth.

He took his time, kissing her slow and deep and thoroughly before sliding down to distribute openmouthed kisses along the length of her throat and over her collarbones. He dragged his mouth down her chest and used the tip of his tongue to outline the full upper slopes of her breasts where they rose out of her demicups. Pushing up, he admired the tight thrust of her nipples through the so-sheer-it-barely-existed fabric before bending his head to lock his lips around one. He sucked, a triumphant satisfaction roaring through his veins as a high-pitched whine sounded in her throat.

Her back arched, pushing the fullness of her breast against his face, and he reached behind her to unfasten the back clasp. The bra's flimsy cups folded in on themselves, and he slid his hand beneath the cobweb fabric and over the bare skin of her right breast to tweak the diamond point of her nipple as he continued to worry the left with his mouth.

Moaning softly, she reached between them and cupped his cock through his jeans, and he hissed in a breath through his teeth.

"I want back in charge," she panted and pushed at his shoulders.

Obligingly, he rolled onto his back alongside her. Harper promptly climbed onto her knees and straddled him. She peeled her bra off and dropped it over the side of the bed, then scooted down and planted a kiss on his sternum before moving lower yet. She reached for his fly button.

Oh, shit, was she going to…?

"You said you wanted to see my hair wrapped around your—"

Oh, yeah, she was. She undid his fly, and he lifted his hips so she could push his jeans and boxers down his thighs. His cock sprang free, and he shoved up on his elbows to watch as she lowered her head over it. She shook her hair, and it danced over his hard-on, three or four curls wrapping around his dick like pornographic tentacles.

Wrapping her hand around his erection, she squeezed

his cock, sliding it through a tight grip exactly the way she'd told him she wanted to do the first time they'd made love. She glanced up at him.

Then opened those lush lips around him and sucked the head into her mouth.

His breath exploded from his lungs, and in sheer reflex his hips shot up with a sudden power that startled her hand free. The lack of brakes thrust him deep into her mouth to hit the back of her throat.

"Shit!" He'd had more control—and sure as hell more finesse—when Christi Tate gave him his first blow job the day after his sixteenth birthday. "I'm sorry, baby, I'm sorry."

He dropped his butt back on the bed, which pulled her lips, which had gone slack, back up to the head of his cock.

She coughed and glanced up at him.

He grimaced an apology, and she gave him a tiny it-happens smile in return. Then she closed her lips around him once more and gamely sank her mouth damn near to the base of his shaft again with a tight, membranous suction that made his eyes glaze. Plunging his fingers into her curls, he stared at her lips wrapped around his hard-on as she moved her head up and down. He tried to keep his hips still, but found them moving in counterpart.

Then all of a sudden he was way too close, and his hands tightened around her skull the next time her head rose, preventing her from taking him in again. "Off-off-off-off."

They were the hardest words he'd ever said. But he wasn't going there unless she flat-out told him that's the way she wanted to finish him.

She raised her head, licking her lips, and he groaned. He had to displace her to fumble at his Levi's, which had worked their way around his calves, and get his wallet out of his pocket. He passed it to her. "Condom."

She fished it out and rolled it down his length, then threw a leg back over his thighs like a biker chick mounting a Harley. He thumbed his dick into position and watched as she lowered herself over it, then as it sank into her inch by inch.

"Ohhhhh," she breathed, her eyes fluttering shut.

Then they opened up again, and she raised back up until he was almost unseated. And slapped back down.

"Jesus, Harper!" He gripped her lush ass and lifted her up again. Groaned as she dropped back down.

"It feels so *good*," she moaned. "You fill me so full, and I can feel you literally *dragging* against me when you pull out—*God!*" Her demonstration when she raised her hips again clearly put her on the ragged edge, and she looked down at him, all flushed cheeks, slumberous eyes and bee-stung lips. "I'm gonna come, Max. God, I'm so close and—"

He worked his thumb and forefinger between plump, slippery lips and pinched her clit.

She screamed and slammed down one last time, those hot interior muscles clamping around his cock like a lubricious Chinese finger puzzle.

And it was all she wrote. Without time to move so much as a centimeter, all that muscular milking along his dick made him erupt like a fire hose. All he could do was sink his fingers into the full firm cheeks of her ass, shoot his hips up off the mattress and groan his satisfaction as she ground against him in return.

Minutes or aeons later, they collapsed like soldiers

whose horses had been shot out from under them. And as Harper draped bonelessly atop him, her face pressed against his hot throat, he came to an uneasy realization.

The sex was out of this world, but, *damn,* it was the woman who got to him every time. Her humor, her heart, her…hell. Everything. And it was time to quit fooling himself.

He was knee-walking in love with the girl.

CHAPTER NINETEEN

"OH, FOR—!" HARPER felt like *throwing* something when she got her mother's answering machine. The last time she'd called it had been Gina's personal assistant, Kimberly, who had put her off with some lame excuse.

"This is the last message I intend to leave, Mom," she said with hard-won civility after the beep. "I'm through dancing to your tune. If I don't hear back from you by noon tomorrow, I'm informing Cedar Village myself."

A soft click indicated the phone on the other end had been picked up. "You will do nothing of the sort," her mother stated categorically.

"Seriously? You were *lurking?* Since when does Gina Summerville-Hardin resort to hiding behind her personal assistant and answering machines?"

Her mother ignored the question, clearly focused on getting her point across. "You will not inform Cedar Village," she reiterated. "We have a strict protocol for grant approval notification—"

"Which includes you notifying the receiver of the grant in a timely manner once I've given you the green light," she rebutted firmly. "*You're* the one who has blatantly, inexplicably ignored the foundation's protocol, Mother. Not I. And not only is it aggravating beyond belief, it's *cruel*. I'm…ashamed of you."

It was hard to wrap her mind around, but she was so

disappointed in her—her *mother*, for pity's sake, whom she loved—that it was all she could do to draw her next breath.

"Harper…"

"These people run an amazingly effective organization on a shoestring, and I doubt they can predict beyond a fiscal quarter or two at a time whether or not they'll be able to remain in business. I've seen the progress they've made with these boys, and I honest to God do not understand why you're messing with them this way. But it stops now, Gina." She had never in her life addressed her mother by her given name, but for this moment she simply couldn't acknowledge the familial connection. "Either you inform them that we're giving them that grant or I'll do it myself."

"Darling, listen—"

"No. I'm so angry with you I can barely see straight. If you have a problem with the way I live my life— which, frankly, at my age I should be well beyond having to account to you about—then take it up with *me*. Don't take it out on a struggling charity that's manned by decent people knocking themselves out six ways from Sunday to keep it alive."

"Please, Baby Girl. Let me expl—"

She sucked in a sharp breath and pretended she'd heard neither the plea, nor her mother's pet name for her. "I have no desire to see our relationship permanently torn apart, so I really need to hang up before I say something I can't take back. But for the love of God, Gina. Do the right thing."

She disconnected and stood breathing heavily as she stared blindly at the wall. Then, with the power of all her unhappiness and frustration fueling her aim, she flung her cell phone at the couch so hard it bounced straight back toward her.

Lunging for it, she caught the darn thing before it crashed to the floor, then collapsed onto the couch, clutching it against her churning stomach. "Shit," she whispered. "Shit, shit, *shit!*"

She and her mother had certainly had their disagreements in the past. Quite a number of them, actually. But this one felt different.

This felt dangerously as if it might be the finishing splinter. The one that planted that final wedge between them.

"HER LEGAL NAME is Harper Louisa Summerville-Hardin," said the brusque voice of Max's old marine buddy Kev Conley at the other end of his call. "But from everything I can tell, she only goes by Summerville. Not just for this current gig in your town, Max, but all the time. She seems to be an upright citizen— she's never been arrested or gotten into trouble of any kind that I can see. She's had a few speeding tickets, but those have been promptly paid."

Okay. That's good news. He picked up the paintbrush he'd been using to finish up the exterior trim when his phone had rung. Between one thing and another, he'd never quite gotten around to completing it when he'd stained the body of the house. Then he blew out a soft breath and asked the question that had really been gnawing at him. "Is she in a relationship?" *Saynosaynosay no.*

"Nope," Kev said, and Max sagged in relief. "It doesn't look like she's been what you'd call serious about anyone since college." Paper rustled through Max's receiver. "She travels a lot and has had a shitload of temporary jobs."

"I know about those."

"She also draws a salary from a charitable foundation called Sunday's Child. Several of her temp jobs seem to be related, in that they appear on the list of charities the foundation endows."

His brush skittered off the narrow edge of the window frame he'd been painting and slopped black paint across the warm neutral color called Smoked Oyster that he and Jake had picked out for the shingles. Setting the brush down, he wiped off the glob with a rag he'd dampened earlier and tossed on the ladder's shelf.

All the while trying to ignore the acid chewing holes in his gut. "Son of a bitch," he said—and it had nothing to do with the small mess he'd made. "That I didn't know."

"Does it mean something to you?"

"Yeah, although I'm not quite sure what yet. Cedar Village, a group home for troubled boys that I give time to here, applied for a grant from Sunday's Child."

"Huh. Guess you're gonna have to have a talk with the lady about why she's there."

"Yeah. I guess I am."

But he didn't rush off to do so the minute he said goodbye to Kev. Picking up the paintbrush again, he turned his attention back to the trim, determined not to let his mind wander down the path leading to all things Harper.

Unfortunately, that was easier said than done. Because, dammit, she'd been deceiving all of them since the minute she'd rolled into town. Not only him, but Jake and Jenny and Tasha and Mary-Margaret. Hell, why stop there? She'd lied to the entire fucking staff at the Village *and* the boys. He would have liked to have believed there was another explanation, but what else could you call it when she hadn't told a soul about her true purpose for being there?

Nothing else, that's what. Yeah, sure, maybe in the beginning, when they were all strangers, she'd had a valid reason for hiding her purpose for being here. But they weren't strangers now. Hell, no, not after she'd wormed her way into all their lives, apparently without compunction. The woman was a stone liar, and she'd been fucking him in more ways than her Oscar-worthy performances in bed.

He tried with superhuman will not to let it, yet still it triggered all those old insecurities he'd struggled with as a kid of not measuring up. Of not *mattering*.

No, dammit. Infuriated, he took his paintbrush into the kitchen where he threw it in a produce bag, wrapped it up tight, then put it in the fridge. He washed his hands and slapped them dry on the seat of his cargo shorts.

He wasn't a kid any longer, and he'd worked too damn hard to outgrow his troubled past to let her devalue him this way. He couldn't change the fact that she'd been lying to him all along, but he could sure as hell let her know he was onto her. Patting down his pockets, he located his keys in the right front one and fished them out as he headed for the door.

His head was filled with too much white noise to recall what Harper had said her schedule was today, but he wasn't exactly bowled over with surprise to find her rental parked in the lot and her cottage looking mighty damn deserted. She'd probably taken some group out to do something fun.

She was nothing, he thought bitterly, if not fun.

He found a spot in the shade to park his SUV, climbed out and strode over to check her place. As he'd thought, she wasn't there and he returned to the parking lot. Leaning a hip against the vehicle, he drummed his fingers on its finish as he glared into the woods and tried to empty his mind.

It didn't work worth a damn, and he hiked himself up onto the hood of his car. He'd give it another fifteen minutes, and if she hadn't shown up by then he'd go kill some time at The Anchor. He had an uncharacteristic yen to knock back a few—maybe even more than a few. But he was on duty tonight, so he'd content himself with nursing a single bottle.

But maybe he'd treat himself to a six-pack to drink when he got home.

He heard the sound of a door closing from around the front of Harper's cabin—or possibly the one closest to it—and slid off the hood. Inhaling and exhaling deep, controlled breaths, he attempted to shove down the anger that kept crowding out everything else. Dammit, he was a trained professional in the Kitsap County Sheriff's Department; he knew better than to let his emotions rule.

Yet they kept shoving their way to the forefront anyhow.

When he rounded the cottage and saw that Harper's front door was open, he stopped to get his shit together. The last thing he needed was to go all caveman on her ass. He had to be calm. Rolling his shoulders, he shook out his hands. Cracked his knuckles. Then, sucking in another breath, he held it deep in his lungs for a moment before slowly blowing it out.

"Be cool," he coached himself under his breath as he silently climbed the steps to the little porch across the front of her cabin. "Do not lose it, dude, whatever you do."

He spotted her as he approached the screen door; she had her back to him and was bent over the couch, pawing through a stack of folders.

Instead of going all icy and reticent as he would have done even a few short months ago, his blood began to boil through his veins, his heart to thunder in his chest.

This was a mistake; he had to get the hell out of here before he made a giant fool of himself. He stepped back.

And knocked his size thirteen shoe against one of the rocking chairs.

Straightening, she turned to squint through the screen. Then that smile of hers, the one that flashed pretty white teeth and a glimpse of pink gums and turned her eyes into upside down crescents, broke over her face. "Max! What a nice surprise—I didn't expect to see you."

How the hell could he feel two such disparate emotions at once? Her professed enthusiasm at seeing him made his heart warm even as it caused his temper to flare. He pulled open the screen door and stepped inside. "I had an unexpected surprise of my own a while ago."

"Did you?" She took a step toward him. "A good one?"

"Not so much."

"Aw, I'm sorry. What was it?"

"I got the results of the background check that I had run on you and it turns out—"

"Excuse me?" Her eyes went chilly behind suddenly narrowed lashes. "You ran a *check* on me?"

"I did. Wanna know what it said?"

"Since it's my background we're talking about, I probably know better than you what it said. And I must admit I'm still hung up on the fact that you abused your position in the sheriff's office to—"

"Oh." A bitter laugh escaped him. "You're good, turning it around on me like *I'm* the one to break the faith. But guess what, baby? I didn't use departmental resources. I had an old marine buddy who worked for a P.I. before he joined the few, the proud—"

"Why?" She took another step in his direction.

"Because my cop instincts said something was off with you—just wasn't a hundred percent right. Occasionally your behavior just made me suspicious."

"What?" She looked at him as if he were an escapee from an insane asylum, and his anger burned cold and righteous.

"You don't think so? Well, let's look at the facts." He ticked up a finger for the first point on his mental list. "Hanging up every damn phone conversation you were in the middle of whenever I walked into the room—"

"I was talking to my mother!" Rushing over, she gave him a stiff-armed shove, then made a sound like steam escaping a teakettle when it didn't even rock him back on his heels. "My *mother!*"

His logically laid out bullet points went up in smoke. "You were lying to everyone in town!"

"Because I've found, as did my father before me, that the charities I'm sent to evaluate behave differently with Harper Summerville-Hardin of the Sunday's Child Foundation than they do with plain old Harper Summerville, and it takes longer to figure out what's the genuine article and what's simply part of a big old dog-and-pony show set to impress. And I hung up every time you came into the room because I approved Cedar Village for the grant the night of the baseball game with the kids, and for some reason my mother has been dragging her feet with the notification and I didn't feel I could tell you until she gave me the go-ahead. *Or* argue with her about it with you in the room."

She drilled his chest with her finger. "But you know what? If you found my behavior so darn suspicious, why didn't you just ask me what the heck was going on? I probably would have broken the unwritten rule at Sunday's Child and told you."

"Probably," he said with cynical disbelief. "Or...not."

"You'll never know, will you?" A laugh that was short on humor and long on animosity escaped her. "In any event, you could have saved yourself the expense of your big investigation into my oh-so-suspicious background. I had it out with my mother just this morning. I told her I would inform Mary-Margaret—and you and Jake and Jenny and Tash and anyone *else* who's interested—if she didn't get off the dime and do so herself before noon tomorrow."

Suddenly, she stepped back. "But why am I explaining myself to you? In fact, *screw* you, Deputy Bradshaw. I wasn't breaking any laws or running a big scam. I was merely doing my job in the exact same manner that I've assessed every other potential grant applicant. I don't owe you an explanation."

He rubbed at the pain in his chest, but found it a whole lot deeper than a massage could reach. "No," he said with stiff formality. "I obviously never meant a damn thing to you, Ms. Summerville-Hardin, so I guess you don't owe me anything at all."

She leaned toward him. "You think…you honestly *believe*—?" Snapping upright, she thrust her arm out, a shaking finger pointing at the door. "Get out."

"Gladly. But before I go—" He jerked her to him and kissed her angrily before setting her loose and taking a big step back. He wiped the back of his hand across his lips, as if that could somehow eradicate her addictive taste. "Thanks for being such a good fuck buddy."

He regretted the cheap disrespect of his comment even as he stormed out the door. Winced when he heard her enraged "Pig!" because he knew he deserved it. But she'd ripped his still-beating heart right out of his chest.

So damned if he intended to go back and apologize.

CHAPTER TWENTY

"Pigpigpigpigpig!" Harper snatched one of the water socks she'd donned for her kayak tour from her foot—and for the second time that day she threw something.

As a stress reliever, flinging a little piece of rubber with less than an ounce of connected mesh fabric was a total bust. Even if it had hit Max's hard head instead of bouncing harmlessly off the doorjamb and tumbling to the floor, it wouldn't have done any damage. Stomping over, she bent to whisk it up and work it back onto her bare foot. She slammed the door to give herself *some* satisfaction. Angry, frustrated, trying hard not to scream, she slammed it a second time for good measure. Before turning back to the empty room.

He'd run a *background* check on her? She fumed as she began picking up the files she'd been working on when he'd arrived. Hearing him say it had been like taking a hit from a baseball bat. She'd thought he *liked* her—and not just for the sex. But he'd found her suspicious and had had his ex-P.I. buddy run a stinking check on her.

All right, maybe she wasn't exactly what she'd portrayed herself to be, but she'd planned on telling him! This was just so, so wrong.

And all her mother's fault. If only Gina had informed Mary-Margaret in a timely manner that Sunday's Child approved their grant application, *she* would have told Max herself by now.

"Crap," she whispered and slowly set the stack of files back on the couch. "Are you listening to yourself?" Okay, so she hadn't actually verbalized anything. But she'd been thinking pretty darn loudly.

And the gist of what she hadn't said was: it's everyone else's fault and none of mine.

Screw you, Deputy Bradshaw. I don't owe you an explanation.

Oh, God, had she really said that? She'd lied to him by omission and likely *had* acted suspicious as all get-out every time he'd caught her on the phone with her mom. God knows she'd felt torn enough between what she wanted to do—tell him—and what she'd been trained to do—keep her mouth shut—for that to be true. Then, of course, she'd slept with the guy and clearly—given his anger—had made him feel as if she cared about him, as well. Which, face it, she did, if this sick feeling crawling through her over the words they'd hurled at each other was anything to go by.

So, yeah. She really had told him that she didn't owe him anything because he hadn't taken her at face value. Her being so trustworthy and all.

Still, she hadn't done anything truly reprehensible. And she had every right to be mad at him for that fuck-buddy crack and sick at heart to be the subject of a background check, which struck her as something one ran on a criminal—not someone you liked enough to want to sleep with.

But…

She got a pang when she thought of what was behind his anger. Because she wasn't a stranger to him now—

she knew darn good and well that he'd been disregarded far too much as a kid. And Max was clearly hurt that she might have disregarded him, as well.

So, for all her big words, she did him owe an explanation.

She might as well get it over with. She'd planned to finalize the plans for Razor Bay Days this afternoon, but she didn't have a prayer of concentrating until she got the apology off her chest.

She located her purse beneath the folders she'd been putting together for the Labor Day weekend festivities and headed for the door.

HALF AN HOUR later, she conceded defeat. Max wasn't home, and she hadn't seen his SUV in the parking lot between Jake's and Jenny's places when she'd driven past on her way out of the inn grounds, so he obviously wasn't visiting with his brother. She didn't think he was on duty until this evening, but maybe she was mistaken about that.

God knew she hadn't racked up an impressive score regarding her other assumptions.

She could go home and try to accomplish something this afternoon—except she was in the same position that had driven her out in search of Max in the first place: feeling all antsy and edgy and incapable of buckling down. So she turned toward Cedar Village.

If her mother still hadn't contacted the director about the Village's grant approval, then she would do so herself. And since she owed Mary-Margaret an explanation regarding her real identity as well, and it felt like yet another ax hanging over her head, she might as well get out from under it now.

She realized as she drove into the Cedar Village parking lot that she'd secretly hoped to find Max's vehicle there. Too bad it was a wish doomed for disappointment. She did luck out, however, when she opened the admin building's door moments later and discovered she wouldn't have to hunt Mary-Margaret down to one of the many other buildings. Spying the older woman through her open office door, she crossed the reception area and leaned into the room. "Got a minute?"

"Harper!" Mary-Margaret gave her a big smile. "Of course I do—come in. Throw the stuff on the chair on the floor and have a seat."

She did as directed and sat facing the older woman across the desk.

"I got some wonderful news today," Mary-Margaret said. "We got the grant from Sunday's Child!"

"Good!" It was a huge load off, but unfortunately just one of many. "Listen, about that," she said, rising to her feet. "I need to tell you some—"

"Your mother informed me that you authorized it a few weeks ago, and she forbade you to tell anyone that you were a representative of Sunday's Child until she contacted us."

Harper abruptly sat back down. "She did? Please believe I wasn't trying to snow anyone."

"Of course you weren't! Mrs. Summerville-Hardin said that in the usual course of events, you're in and out of a prospective charity in a week. I'm so thrilled that you continued to volunteer here even after you approved the application. And that you've given us all those other fund-raising ideas on top of it."

"Oh, no, I *love* Cedar Village. Everyone here is doing such a phenomenal job with the boys. I'm just sorry it took my mother so long to let you know how happy we are to have you under the Sunday's Child umbrella. Usually—"

"You mustn't worry about it, dear. She explained a little of her reasoning for holding off—"

You certainly know more than I do, then.

"—and I can't fault her for it."

She'd give a bundle to know what spin Gina had put on the situation. She was rather stunned that her mother had gotten so chummy. While her calls to break the news generally tended to be warm, she always maintained a professional reserve.

Still, that was hardly the important thing here. *That* would be the fact that her mother had finally come through.

"That said, however," the director continued, "I must admit I'm taking my first real breath in months." She laughed a little, shaking her head. "Who am I kidding? In years."

By the time Harper left, she felt more settled. Perhaps she could get a little work done when she got home after all.

As she drove past The Anchor on her way back to the inn, however, she spotted Max's SUV parked on the street in front of the bar. Heart starting to race, she whipped into the lot.

She had to pause inside the bar's door a moment later to let her eyes adjust. When she could see a little more clearly, she looked around.

And didn't see him.

Damn. The medical center was next door—perhaps he'd had an appointment there. Because he wasn't in any of the few booths or at the tables or the bar.

But apparently her eyes weren't as up to speed as she'd assumed because a movement down near the end of the room caught her eye, and she spotted Max taking aim at the dartboard just beyond the first group of tables she'd looked at. He looked exactly the way he had the day they'd met: all big and stern and humorless. And her heart did the same thing it had then: pounded out a *holy-crap-holy-crap-holy-crap* rhythm.

She wove between tables in the half-empty room, making her way down to his end of the bar, taking her gaze off him only long enough to avoid stumbling over the chairs in her way. She watched as he let a dart fly.

Then he took a step back, and she saw the woman he'd been blocking. She was tiny. Blonde. Stacked. And she smiled up at Max as she leaned into him, pressing one of her lush breasts against his bare forearm.

As if she'd strode straight into an invisible force field, Harper stopped dead. Oh, God. *This* wasn't a scenario she'd considered. And she didn't have the first idea how to address it.

Oh, hell, yes, she did. By getting the heck out of here before he saw her!

But just as his movement had drawn her eyes, her abrupt halt must have drawn his. For he suddenly turned his head and pinned her in place with a cool, noncommittal gaze. As if she were a stranger.

One he didn't like very much.

Something inside her splintered. All at once she was angry and hurt all over again. Only this time she wasn't going to lose it, she told herself firmly. *This* time—she ratcheted up her chin and forced herself to meet his cool gaze straight on—she was going to hold on to her dignity no matter what.

In truth she would have cut and run in a nanosecond. But that was before he'd have been aware of it.

Quietly sucking in a breath, she said evenly, "I don't want to interrupt your game. But I wonder if I might talk to you?"

"Knock yourself out."

Her back stiffened, but she managed to keep her voice calm and collected. "Very well. When I said I didn't owe you anything earlier? I was upset—and wrong. I do owe you an explanation, and when you have a moment to hear me out, I'd be happy to tell you anything you'd like to know." She waited, searching his dark eyes, but his lack of expression didn't miraculously change with her concession.

"Maybe later," the blonde said, hanging from Max's brawny arm, one of her breasts once again squished against his forearm. The cleavage the position exposed all but spilled out of her low-cut top. "We *are* kinda busy."

When Max didn't say anything, she nodded. "Of course." With a minute hitch of her shoulder, Harper turned on her heel and walked away.

She probably should have felt some kind of relief as she left the bar. She'd been spared having to come up with the words to explain her reasons for keeping him in the dark. But she wasn't relieved at all. Part of her just wanted to yank the bleached blonde away from him and snatch the bimbo bald.

But mostly, she felt even more heartsick than she had when he'd stormed out of her cottage earlier.

"I THOUGHT SHE'D *never* leave."

As if someone had suddenly popped the balloon he'd

been trapped in, Max's paralysis broke, and he looked at
Rachel, the woman who'd attached herself to him earlier when he'd grabbed the darts and started taking out
his anger with Harper on the bar's board.

The blonde gave him a saucy grin and held out a
dart. "You were two for three on hitting the bull's-eye.
Here's the deal breaker, big boy, the one that separates
the men from the boys."

He accepted the dart, but his mind wasn't on making his shot. It was on Harper.

Dammit, why did she have to come in here and be all
reasonable and gracious? For a moment, after he'd gotten his breath back from looking over to see her stroll-
ing his way, he'd been pleased as punch that she'd seen
him with another woman. Hell, before she'd shown up,
he'd even thought that maybe he could take Rachel back
to her place and use her to scrub the woman he really
wanted out of his head.

But when Harper's gaze had gone to Rachel's over-
ripe tit pressed against his arm, he'd only wanted to
yank free. To move Rachel back several steps. And he'd
known in that instant that sex with the little blonde was
never gonna happen.

Even then, however, he'd stood there like a fucking
coat rack, unable to say a word. It was like when he was
a kid and his ma would go on about all the injustices in
their lives. Half the time he'd just wanted to tell her to
shut *up,* already. To let it *go.* But his vocal cords would
just freeze themselves solid.

Jesus, Bradshaw. He gave his shoulders a little shake.
You haven't been that dumb kid for years.

He threw the dart without taking the time to line up
his shot, and it hit the small pie area near the triple ring.

"Huh," he said. "Guess I'm still playing with the boys." He took a step away from Rachel. "I've gotta go."

Ignoring her protests, he headed across the room, picking up his pace as he neared the door. By the time he pushed out into the sunshine he was damn near jogging.

He looked for Harper's rental on the street but saw no sign of it. So he strode around the side of the building to The Anchor's parking lot.

It wasn't there, either.

"Shit." Pulling his keys from his pocket, he went back to the street where he'd parked his vehicle. He supposed he could call her, but he didn't want to do that. He'd go see if she'd gone home.

Five minutes later he was happy to find her car in the lot behind her cottage and pulled his own alongside it. When he climbed her stairs a moment later and saw her in practically the same position she'd been in the last time he was here, he exhaled the breath he hadn't even realized he'd been holding. "Déjà vu."

She glanced over her shoulder, then slowly straightened, pivoting to face him.

He nodded at the screen door. "Can I come in?"

"Yes. Of course. Please do." Sliding her hands into her capri pockets, she watched as he opened the door and stepped inside. "Can I get you something to drink?"

"No. I just want that explanation you said you'd give me."

Her shoulders hunched up for a moment, perhaps due to the cold roughness of his voice. They promptly leveled out, however, and if he hadn't been trained to pay attention to body language, he might have fooled himself into believing she was coolly unaffected.

God knew her level gaze looked perfectly composed

when it met his. "I'm going to grab myself a glass of wine," she said and waved a hand at the few pieces of furniture. "Please. Make yourself comfortable."

Trying not to mourn the formality from a woman who was rarely formal, he dropped down on the couch. He'd no sooner done so than he had to raise his right cheek to fish a folder out from under his butt. He set it atop several similar files stacked on the cushion next to him.

She came back with a goblet of red wine and sat on the coffee table in front of him. It was the last place he expected her to sit, and he spread his knees to keep from touching her in the close quarters. Then he stilled, mentally kicking himself for his own tell.

But if she noticed, it didn't show. She took a sip of her wine, then lowered the glass, pressing its bowl between her breasts. "When I couldn't find you earlier," she said in a low voice, "I went out to the Village to talk to Mary-Margaret. My mother finally called to tell her they'd gotten the grant."

He crossed his arms across his chest. "That's nice."

"And not what you're interested in hearing."

"No, it really is nice." He dropped his arms—then, not knowing what to do with his hands, gripped his thighs. "No one deserves financial help more than they do."

"I agree. But I also know that's not what you came here to talk about." She took another sip, then set her wine aside and blew out a breath. And met his gaze.

He nearly jerked at the electricity that jolted through him when those big eyes locked on his. He'd managed not to react when she'd done the same thing in the bar, but the longer they were in the same room together, the harder it was to rein in his emotions.

"I didn't expect to get so caught up in everyone's lives when I came here," she said in her husky contralto. "Not yours or Jenny's or Jake's or Tasha's, either. Most of the charities I'm sent to assess are in urban areas, and I'm there for a week, tops. I enjoy the people I meet, but it's a much shallower connection than I've found with you all."

She glanced away for a second, then looked back at him. "I wasn't prepared for you on so many levels," she said. "Remember when we met at that park on Jake Bradshaw Photo Day?"

He nodded tersely. Christ, yeah. In repose, she'd looked so coolly somber and had held herself like a princess. He'd immediately wanted her but had been struck dumb in her presence.

"I've always been a pretty tactile person," she said. "My dad used to tease me that I communicate more through touch than most people do with words. You probably don't remember me patting your arm—"

"I remember," he said gruffly. As if he'd forgotten a single moment with this woman.

"Well, when I touched you that day—" she licked her lips " —it was like putting my hand on a stove burner I thought was turned off but was actually cranked on high." She shook her head. "No—it was more like coming into contact with a live wire. I felt that touch down to my toes." She pinned him in place with solemn eyes. "I still do."

He shifted.

"I have feelings for you," she said. "I'm not sure that I'm ready to define them, but they're very real. Frankly,

though, Max? I've followed the same protocol for the
position I hold at Sunday's Child since I took over when
my father died. It was put in place when my parents
started the foundation—and it's worked just fine up
until I came to Razor Bay. So while I like to think that
if I'd known you and I were going to have such a connection I'd have done things differently, I honestly don't
know whether I would have or not. The thing is, it's the
way my dad liked it."

"And you were Daddy's girl."

"Yes." She reached out to touch his hard wrist bones.
Then her hand dropped away, and her back straightened as she looked him in the eye. "But if you believe
nothing else, believe this. I had no agenda when I slept
with you."

"I know." He blew out a breath. "Hell, I knew it even
when I made that crack about us being fuck buddies,
and I'm sorry for that. It was rude and crude, and I'm
not proud that I only said it to make you feel as lousy
as I was feeling."

"It's all right."

"No. It's not."

"You're right. It really isn't." Her eyes flashed. "That
was a *horrid* thing to say."

"My only excuse is that I felt blindsided and played.
But I shouldn't have been so quick to assume the worst.
You've done things for me no one else has ever done.
Even more than showing me how to eat better and going
to a lot of trouble to plan my birthday party, because of
you I feel like I'm much more a part of the community
than I ever was before. So maybe—" He hesitated but
then exhaled a gusty breath and plunged in. "Maybe

we should see where this thing between us takes us. Go on a date even."

He straightened away from the couch. Damn. Until the suggestion came out of his mouth, it hadn't occurred to him that while the two of them had done a lot of stuff with the Cedar Village boys and had burned up the sheets, they'd never been on a simple date together.

"I'd like that. But I need to tell you something else."

Shit. "Tell me it's not that you're married." But, no. Kev had definitely said she wasn't in a serious relationship. He gave his head a little shake. He wasn't thinking straight.

"No." She laughed a little. "But that stop-moving-and-die thing I told you about? I know it's superstitious as all get-out—yet I believe it. So the idea of *not* traveling on a regular basis? I think it's the main reason that every time I think of having something deeper with you, I panic a little."

He frowned. "Why panic?"

"Because you're clearly settled in Razor Bay. And I'm —" She gave him a helpless look. "Max, I'm basically the definition of a rolling stone."

"We're not talking about getting married," he said with a wry smile. "So why don't we just see where this goes." But a wisp of unease twisted through him.

Because a woman with a yen to always be on the move?

Well, that was pretty much the antithesis of the white picket fence/someone to put him first relationship he'd always longed to find.

CHAPTER TWENTY-ONE

BELLA T'S PIZZERIA was such a madhouse Harper was surprised when Tasha not only spotted her, but actually interrupted her frenetic yet somehow graceful ballet between the order counter and her brick ovens to dash over.

"Hey, girl," the strawberry blonde said. "It's going to be another five minutes before your order is ready."

She nodded. "They told me it would be twenty minutes when I called it in. I thought if I got here early I could just hang out." She stepped out of the way of a harried mother who was trying to keep her place in the order line and at the same time corral two rambunctious boys who kept dashing away. "I didn't realize it'd be so crazy busy."

"First night of Labor Day weekend *and* Razor Bay Days, babe." Tasha shrugged. "It's gonna get crazier."

Spotting the Cedar Village boy whom Max had recommended for an after-school job bussing tables, she asked, "How's Jeremy working out?"

"Great, actually. He's a big, good-looking kid and I was half afraid he'd spend most of his time flirting with the teenage girls. But much as they'd like it if he did, he pretty much keeps his head down and gets the job done."

"I'm glad to hear it." She hesitated, then said, "Listen, I want to apologize again—"

"Harper. Honey. Give it a rest," Tasha said. "You apologized. I accepted." She shot her a wry smile. "It's not like you came to town to steal corporate secrets. Or the recipe for my top-secret pizza sauce."

"You and Jenny are certainly more forgiving than Max originally was."

"Well...yeah." She laughed. "Jenny and I aren't doing the horizontal cha-cha with you. Rules skew when you throw wild monkey sex into the equation."

"No fooling. I found that out the hard way."

"Oh, here's your order. Thanks, Tiff." Tasha took the two-foot-tall stack of pizza boxes from her helper and checked it against the original order. "Tiffany put this on the inn's tab so it looks like you're good to go." She turned back to Harper. "Come on, I'll carry it out to your car for you."

"You're up to your eyeballs in work. You don't have to carry my order!"

"I want to—it gives me an excuse to step outside for a breath of fresh air. Hey, did I tell you I got a renter for my apartment?"

"No. I know you were worried about the loss of rent." Reaching the pizzeria's front door, she held it open for her friend. "That must be a giant relief."

"It is. And Will, the guy you met the day he gave notice, actually came up with his replacement."

"Handy."

"No fooling. It's some guy named Luke...uh—" She blinked. "Huh. I have no idea what his last name is. I plugged the numbers and dates into a standard contract and had Will fill out the rest. He even mailed it for me." She shrugged. "Oh, well. I'll find out when it comes back. Anyway, how bad could he be—he's Will's college roommate. Apparently, he just left a government job and has some relatives he wants to catch up with in the area."

"And if he's anything like Will—" Harper let her voice trail off, but thinking back to the one time she'd met Tasha's current renter she could only remember that he was a quiet man with forgettable features. So forgettable, she doubted she could describe him accurately if she had to.

"Exactly." Tasha grinned. "If the new guy's *anything* like Will, he'll be the perfect substitute. And it's only a ninety-day lease."

"Are you okay with that?"

"Longer would be better, of course, but this gets me through the end of the year, and mid-November through the first full week of January is the pizzeria's slowest time. When things start to lag I'll have time to start spreading the word for the upcoming year." She unloaded the pizzas into the trunk Harper popped for her, efficiently rearranged them for transport, then closed the lid. Giving it a final pat, Tasha straightened and turned to her. "So, you and Max are good now?"

"We are. Once we got over our original mad on with each other, we straightened things out pretty quickly. He's even helping me at the Give a Parent a Break movie event at the inn tonight."

"Are you serious? How on earth did you talk him into that?"

Harper shot her friend a cocky smile. "You are looking at a girl with advanced social skills, luv. Ad-vanced. Social. Skills."

"I guess so, if you talked him into babysitting a room full of screaming kids."

"Oh, no. I've got all sorts of activities planned to keep these kids entertained. Trust me. There will be no screaming tonight."

MAX HAD TO raise his voice to be heard over the little girls racing by trailing screams in their wake that could strip brass off the door hinges. "How the hell did I let you talk me into this?"

"I have advanced social sk—excuse me a moment." Stepping back, she brought a whistle he hadn't noticed hanging from a lanyard around her neck to her lips. And blew. The sound bounced off the walls and brought every kid in the joint to a standstill to stare at her.

"Who wants pizza?" she asked, and when shrill shrieks of excitement promptly filled the air, she blew the whistle again, chopping yells off midscreech. "Look around you, boys and girls," she said, twirling her hands to indicate the suite they were using for the evening. Her voice was soft and low, making the noise level drop even further as the dozen or so kids leaned forward to hear. "We're using our indoor voices tonight. Becaaaause—?"

"We're indoors," several of the younger children, who hadn't yet developed a need to act cool, responded.

"That's right! So, line up and we'll get some food. No pushing, boys," she added for the benefit of two pre-teens who had started to do just that.

They gave her sheepish smiles and fell in line, and Max shook his head. She did have amazing social skills, and it clearly wasn't age dependent.

They'd eaten, played a couple of games and were maybe ten minutes into a Pixar flick that appealed to all ages when his cell rang. Seeing that it was work, he whispered a quick, "I'll be back," and stepped into the bedroom portion of the room and closed the door. "Hey, Amy, what's up?"

"I just had a call from a man asking for your number. He said it was about your father."

Max's heart gave a thump so hard he was surprised no one yelled at him from the other room to keep it down. For a second his mind went blank.

She said into the pool of silence, "I told him I'd get in touch with you—and if you wanted to talk to him, you'd call back."

"Thanks, Amy. What's his name?"

"Uh, that's the thing, Max," she said. "He said his name is Luke…Bradshaw."

"Christ."

"That was kinda my response, as well. You have an uncle or some cousins you don't know about?"

"As far as I know, Charlie was an only child. Like me—and Jake." A bark of unamused laughter escaped him. "But that says it right there, doesn't it? For all I know, the two of us could have enough half siblings to make our own baseball team." He rummaged through the drawer of the desk and pulled out a sheet of the inn letterhead and a pen. "I take it you got his number?"

"Yeah. You ready to copy?"

"I am."

Amy dictated it to him, then said, "And apparently the first name is spelled *L-U-C*." Her voice turned ironic. "Must be from a more hoopdy-do-dah town than the Bay."

He thanked her for the call and disconnected. For a moment he simply stared down at the black ink phone number—and more importantly, *name*—on the cream stationery. Then he gave his head a sharp shake to get his brain cells moving again. He punched the numbers into his phone and hit Call.

It was answered on the first ring.

"This is Bradshaw," said a voice almost as deep as his own.

"What a coincidence," he replied. "So is this."

There was a second of silence. Then: "Are you Deputy Max Bradshaw?"

"Yes."

"Good. I was hoping to hear from you."

He decided he might as well get to the point. "My dispatcher said you were calling about Charlie Bradshaw. What's your relationship?"

"He's my father."

"Jesus." He had no business being surprised, given Charlie's history. But…Jesus. Scrubbing his fingers over the pang in his heart, he blew out a breath. "Are you it, then? Or are there *more* half siblings?"

"I'm an only child. At least that's what I thought."

"So what number wife was your mom?"

"Third. Third and—" He cleared his throat. "Look, could we meet? I don't know if you know about Jake Bradshaw, but—"

"Yeah, I do. Where you calling from?"

"I've got a room at the Oxford Suites in a town called Silverdale."

"That's about fifteen minutes from here." Max issued succinct directions to Razor Bay. "When you get here, go to The Anchor—it's a bar on Eagle Road, which is the street behind Harbor in what passes for our downtown. I'll hunt Jake down and we'll be over."

Surprise colored the other man's voice. "He's in Razor Bay, too? I called *National Explorer* magazine's headquarters, but they wouldn't tell me how to contact him."

"Yeah. He lives here now."

"Okay. I'll meet you at The Anchor."

"How will I know you?" It shouldn't feel odd not to know what this supposed half brother looked like, since until five minutes ago he hadn't even known the guy existed. Yet somehow it did.

"I'm six-two, have black hair and I'm wearing a red-and-black running shirt."

Feeling slightly dazed, Max returned to the living room of the suite and picked his way over lounging kids—one of whom was sound asleep—until he was in Harper's line of sight. Catching her eye, he jerked his chin.

She rose off the couch and came to meet him. He pulled her out into the corridor.

"I've gotta go." He hesitated, then said. "I just got a call from a guy claiming to be another half brother." He scrubbed his temples with his fingers. Gave her a baffled look. "Another Bradshaw. I didn't have a clue, Harper. Well, I guess there were a couple of half-assed rumors back when my dad left town. People said he was with a woman and a boy, but no one knew if he was Charlie's." He shrugged. "And, hell, I was in *grade* school, so what did I know?"

"Oh, my gosh, Max!" She rubbed his arm. "Are you okay?"

"I honest to God don't know. I mean, I am. But I'm kind of overwhelmed, ya know?"

"Of course you are."

"I'm going to track down Jake and go meet this guy at The Anchor. Jesus." He rubbed his hand over his head. "I wonder how many more half siblings I have out there. As history proves, my father wasn't exactly in-it-for-the-long-haul material."

"Even if there are more out there, all you can do is take it a situation at a time. So, go find Jake and meet your new brother."

"*Half* brother."

Harper gave him a little smile. "That's exactly what you said about Jake when I first met you. But I haven't heard you refer to him as anything but brother lately."

It was true that he did think of Jake as a brother now. Still—

"I've known Jake most of my life. Maybe we didn't get along until this spring, but we at least have history. I've got nothing with this guy."

Her expression was soft. "What's his name?"

"Luc."

"Really? Tasha was just telling me she has a new short-term renter named Luc who's going to take Will's apartment when he leaves next week. In fact, he's in town to—" Maybe seeing he wasn't paying the strictest attention, she waved the interruption aside. "That's not important right now. Go break the news to Jake and the two of you meet Luc. Maybe you'll end up forging a relationship with him, too. But even if you don't, you must be curious."

He nodded. "Yeah. I am that." He bent to kiss her. "I'll see you later."

"Come to my place when you're done, or at least give me a call. I'm dying to hear how it goes."

"I will." He rubbed his thumb across her lower lip, then turned and left.

LUCKILY, JAKE WAS home, but when he opened his door, Max simply stood there for a minute.

"Well?" his brother demanded. "You got something on your mind, or did you just stop by to admire my manly beauty?"

He didn't even snort at the absurdity. "There's a guy in town says he's Charlie's son," he said flatly. "He wants to meet us."

Jake stilled. Then he hitched his shoulders in an elegant shrug. "I don't know why I'm surprised," he said. "Yet, somehow I am."

"Tell me about it. We're meeting him at The Anchor. Grab your wallet. You can buy."

Since Jake never did anything in a hurry, it was another fifteen minutes before they walked through The Anchor's door.

"Black hair, red-and-black shirt," Max muttered, looking around. "You see anyone besides the Latino guy who matches that description? Oh. Wait." He watched as Latino Guy looked straight at him and jerked his chin in acknowledgment. "Huh. Looks like he's our man. Didn't see that coming—I was looking for another you."

"Please," Jake murmured. "They threw away the mold after they made me."

The man slid out of the booth he'd been occupying as they crossed the bar. His skin was similar in shade to Harper's, except where hers was creamy, his was more golden-brown. The black hair he'd mentioned on the phone was cut very close to his head, perhaps to curb the curl, and the grooves bracketing his mouth looked as if they might evolve into dimples when he smiled.

Apparently, they'd have to wait for another day to find out, because New Bradshaw watched them as they walked up to the booth and didn't offer so much as a token smile when they arrived. He merely said, "Hey," and subjected them both to a quick study that reminded Max of every cop he'd ever worked with. "I'm Lucas— I go by Luc." He did, however, thrust out a long, lean hand.

Guy had a mean grip, too—Max had to admire that at least. He was reserving judgment about the rest until he got some measure of the man. "I'm Max. This is my brother Jake."

Luc indicated the booth with a tilt of his angular jaw. "Why don't we sit down."

They slid into the booth, Luc on one side and he and Jake on the other. They'd barely settled when the waitress showed up, tossed down a couple cardboard coasters and placed a Fat Tire in the bottle in front of Jake and a pilsner of Ridgetop Red in front of Max.

"Elise said she might as well save us all some time," the woman said, referring to the bartender. "You want me to run ya a tab?"

"Yeah, that'd be good," Jake said. "Thanks, Sally."

When she walked away, the three men simply looked at one another for a moment. Then Luc blew out a breath.

"This is harder than I thought it would be," he said, taking a sip of his beer, then setting his schooner down. "I've been searching for you ever since Dad died and I found out I had brothers."

"Charlie died?" Max demanded. Looking inward for a moment, he tried to figure out how he felt about that. It only took a seconds to realize that he felt…nothing. Nothing at all. It had been too long and too damn much water under the bridge. He glanced at Jake out of the corner of his eye.

His brother must have been doing the same to him, because Max saw him essay the faintest of facial shrugs.

"Yes," Luc replied. "April eighteenth."

"How long did it take them to notify you?" Jake asked.

"How lon—?" New Bradshaw's dark brows came together, then he gave his head a faint shake and smoothed out his expression. "I was notified right away."

"Like right away, right away?" Max gave him a curious look. "How did you manage that?"

"Uh, I'm…his son?"

"So are we, bro." Jake gave him a level look. "And yet here it is almost six months since his death, and this is the first either of us has heard it."

Luc shook his head. "Look, I'm guessing he was no kind of father to you—"

Max snorted and Jake said, "Ya think?" under his breath.

"—but he was a good dad to me."

"He didn't leave you and your mom flat when he fell in love with some other woman?" Max asked.

"No!"

Jake raised a brow. "Didn't go from being the greatest dad in the world to ignoring your very existence?"

"No, Jesus." He slowly set down his beer. "He did that? To both of you?"

"Yes." Jake's voice was hard. "At least he had the decency to leave town when he did it to me—so I didn't have to watch my perfect-up-until-then father cut me out of his life at every turn. Max had to live in Razor Bay when Charlie left Max's mom for mine. He was a great dad to me while it lasted, but Max might as well have been invisible, so thoroughly did our so-called dad ignore and look right through him."

Something about Jake's statement felt like the real mess-with-my-brother-you-mess-with-*me* kind of defense they'd never shared as kids. It probably made him too juvenile for his jeans that he *loved* how squarely Jake was on his side, but you'd just have to excuse the hell outta him if it did. Because, face it, they'd found themselves at war for far too many years. Feeling all warm and fuzzy, he bumped his shoulder against his brother's.

"Dammit, Max, you made me spill my beer." Jake set his bottle back on the coaster and blotted the drops around his mouth with the back of his hand. But he shot him a slight, lopsided smile.

Max raised a *see what I have to put up* with eyebrow at Luc. "He's always had a slight drinking problem." Then he got serious. "So, what you're saying is that Charlie stayed with your mom and raised you?"

"Yes."

"And never said a word about Jake or me?" Not that *that* was a big wedgie of surprise.

"I didn't know anything about you two until I started going through his stuff." Luc scrubbed his hands over his face, then dropped them to press against the scarred tabletop. "My mom died a couple of years ago," he said in a low voice to his whitening fingertips, "and it was just Dad and me. My work often took me away for long blocks of time, but he sure as hell had enough time to fill me in on the fact that I had a couple of half brothers." The dark eyes he raised to them were baffled. "He never said a word."

"Yeah, Jake and I know a little something about that." He looked the new Bradshaw half brother over. "You were in the picture when Charlie left Razor Bay with your mom. Or at least some kid was."

"That was me."

"I'm just trying to figure out the timeline. You look about my age. Did he adopt you or is he your father by blood?"

"Blood. I don't know how old you are—I'm thirty-five."

"I just turned thirty-four, so clearly Charlie didn't let any grass grow under his feet between your mother and mine."

"My folks always made their love affair sound like a star-crossed lovers' story. Mom got pregnant with me, but her dad, who was a very traditional Argentinean, butted in. He didn't tell my dad—Charlie—that she was expecting, but he did tell him that she didn't want to see him anymore. He told my mom the same thing—that Dad didn't want to see her. Dad married someone else—"

"A couple someones," Jake murmured.

"Then they bumped into each other when he was in San Clemente, where I grew up, on business. And that, they always said, was that." He killed off his beer. "But I can see it wasn't all that. Not for you guys." He knuckled a drop of beer off his lower lip. "Look, I grew up an only child, no cousins or anything. And when I found out I finally had some family, I wanted to meet them. But if my being here is just going to dredge up bad memories, I understand if you'd rather not get to know me." He swept his change off the table and lifted a hip to drop it into his front pocket. The dollar bills still on the table he pushed to the middle, then slid toward the end of the bench.

"Oh, sit down," Jake said. "Don't get your shorts all in a wad. 'Course we want to get to know you. Well, I do, at least. Max here tends to be resistant to change."

"Please," Max said. "I came and got *you* when I got his call, didn't I? Even though I knew you'd probably dick it up." He looked at Luc. Six months ago he likely would have questioned this guy's story. But from photos he'd seen of Charlie, he could see hints of their father in him. The full mouth was Charlie's and so was the shape of his jaw.

For a moment he heard his mother's strident voice in his head going on the way she used to do about some tramp and her little bastard running off with Charlie— then laughing bitterly and saying the only good part was how it had left that *other* tramp and her oh-so-precious brat in the same boat that Charlie had long ago left them. Her constant bitching had made him detest the unknown boy almost as much as he'd hated Jake in those days, and he waited now for the old rage to surface.

It didn't. Instead, Luc's word *family* resonated in his mind. Why should he cut himself off from exploring what was what with the guy? By blood at least, the newly discovered Bradshaw really *was* family—and it wasn't as if Max was overburdened with relatives. His and Jake's years-long rivalry had kept them from getting to know each other as real brothers until the past few months, and he actually felt a lick of anticipation at the idea of maybe forging some kind of relationship with Luc, as well. So he looked at him across the table.

"Jake's easy," he said. "Me, not so much. I can't say I'd be willing to give you a kidney anytime soon. On the other hand—" his shoulders hitched "—what the hell. I suppose I wouldn't mind getting to know you."

CHAPTER TWENTY-TWO

"Jenny thinks we're overdue for our Ladies' Night skinny-dip."

Harper wrenched her wandering attention back to Tasha. Part of her had been aware of Tash and Jenny kidding around with the kind of ease that could only come from a long, knows-everything-there-is-to-know-about-each-other friendship and had vaguely wondered what that must feel like. Mostly, however, she'd been thinking about the proposal she was contemplating running by Max. Belatedly, Tasha's words sorted themselves into a coherent sentence in her mind, and she gaped at both women. "Excuse me?"

Jenny grinned. "That got your attention," she said beneath the conversations and clatter of a crazy busy Saturday night at Bella T's. "We need to get Tasha away from here for a while. She's been working flat-out this weekend—hell, for most of the summer, really. And it feels like forever since we've gone skinny-dipping."

Tasha nodded. "Not since last year. We've let this entire summer slip by without going once." One of her waitresses came up with a question, and she stepped away for a minute.

Harper turned to Jenny. "You truly go skinny-dipping?"

"Sure."

"Buck *naked?*"

Jenny laughed. "That's kind of the definition." She studied her. "Haven't you ever been?"

"No."

"I've lost count of how many times Tash and I have gone. It started the first year I moved to Razor Bay." She smiled reminiscently. "We were sixteen and thought we were pretty daring."

"Let me assure you, as someone who's never once considered swimming without a suit, there's no 'thought' about it—you're positively daring." And wasn't it interesting how this subject tied in so neatly to her recent ruminations?

She'd been thinking a lot about roots lately. Which was rather funny, considering that as little as a week ago, she would have unequivocally sworn she was against them, at least for herself. Settling down equaled...well, not *dying* exactly—

Nerves zinged like an electrical shock up her spine, making her involuntarily startle. But, please. *Be honest with yourself, if no one else, girl. That's* precisely *what you equate it with*.

What she had always equated it with, especially since her father's death.

But even with such thoughts circling the periphery of her mind, it was exactly the sort of continuity and connection her new girlfriends enjoyed—this doing something with a friend year after year the way Jenny had outlined—that she had been thinking about with increasing curiosity.

And what it might feel like to stay in one place long enough to experience something like it.

"So, are you in?" demanded Tasha, who had sent

the waitress on her way and turned back to them. She looked directly at her.

Harper had participated in her share of daring adventures in far-flung places over the years. But they had always involved keeping her clothes on. "When were you thinking of going?"

"Tonight."

"Ah, gee, too bad. I've got flotilla duty tonight."

Jenny simply looked at her. "You already arranged and checked out all the boats to the guests scheduled to watch the fireworks, right?"

"Yes."

"Saw all those guests into the boats and on their way to the bay?"

"Yeeeees." Sensing a pitfall in admitting it, she dragged out the word. She'd done precisely that, of course. But she suspected a catch in saying so.

"Didn't Jed and Norm go along to supervise the actual transportation to and from the log boom?"

She nodded. "But you know I have to be at the dock to check all the boats back in and do a head count after the fireworks are over." Part of her was relieved she wouldn't be available to go skinny-dipping. But another, perhaps larger part, the one that adored being introduced to new adventures—and perhaps even more importantly, that adored these two women—was a bit disappointed.

"Then you're in luck, sweetie." Tasha gave her a knowing smile. "Because we plan to go while everyone's in town watching the show. We'll have you dressed in plenty of time to get those boats checked back in."

"Oh." She could actually feel the wry twist to her smile. "Busted."

Her friends laughed. "I plan on closing Bella's and walking out the door at nine on the dot," Tasha said. "Let's meet at the inn's boat dock at nine-thirty." She looked at Harper. "Wear your suit. Ever since Jenny started working at the inn, which was, oh, like the second she moved to town, we've always either swum out to the float or taken one of the boats out to it. You already know the boats are all taken tonight, but we won't strip off until we're there. It cuts way down on the risk of exposure."

"I like the sound of that."

"Buck up, baby—you're gonna love this." Jenny shot her a trust-me smile. "I'd put money on it."

An hour later, flanked by her friends, Harper found herself diving into the canal from the inn dock as the summer sky began to rapidly lose its grip on the late evening Pacific Northwest twilight. This wasn't like riding the shoulders of a hot-skinned male on an eighty-degree day where a dip in the shockingly cold water was refreshingly welcome. As they edged into September, the evenings had rapidly begun relinquishing the days' warmth, replacing it with an almost autumn nippiness, and every muscle in her body clenched when she hit the water. As she swam out to the anchored float, however, those same muscles began to acclimate. By the time she was within a few feet of it, she no longer felt chilled to the bone.

It wasn't yet fully dark, but she had learned over the course of the summer that even when the last of the light faded, which it would do mere moments from now, on a clear night like tonight the sky was more often a deep midnight-blue than black. Stars grew more brilliant as the sky grew darker, and the Milky Way washed a pale swath across the heavens. The moon was a meager sliver that had barely cleared the trees behind the inn. Yet even without its illumination, the mountains across the canal didn't disappear into the night sky. Instead, they sketched rugged silhouettes against it. Down on the water, however, all was stygian, even the few boats still anchored offshore visible only as murky shadows.

She reached the free-floating dock a few strokes ahead of Jenny and Tasha and swam around it to put its solid bulk between herself and the lighted grounds of The Brothers Inn a hundred feet away. Treading water, she unfastened the halter ties of her bathing suit and worked its wet fabric down her body, freeing her breasts, her stomach, guiding it over her hips and struggling to peel it away from her butt. When she'd finally slid it down her legs and over her feet, she tossed the garment on the float's deck. It hit with a soft, sodden slap.

As her friends' bathing suits, a bikini top and bottom from Jenny and Tasha's one-piece, followed her own onto the float, she kicked her legs.

And experienced the difference that the lack of a flimsy piece of material could make. "Oh."

Jenny's teeth flashed white in the night. "I know, right?"

"Oh, that's amazing." She smiled and kicked them a bit more vigorously. "I *like* it."

"Toldja."

For twenty minutes they played with the full-out zeal of slightly demented children, and Harper discovered the freedom of horsing around with friends. Jenny and Tasha were maniacs, and she soon learned it was dunk or be dunked. She did her best to emerge as the dunker more frequently than the dunkee, and while the results were mixed, it was wonderful fun. Bare butts momentarily flashed as the three of them dove beneath the canal's mirror-smooth surface in what was often the opening salvo in a sneak attack on whoever could be caught off guard.

Occasionally, one of them would climb onto the float and stand naked in the night for a thrilling moment before diving back into the cold shock of salty, buoyant canal water. Jenny's dark hair adhered sleekly to her skull, wrapped around her throat and clung like seaweed to her small breasts. Harper's and Tasha's shrank into wet, tight curls.

The three of them settled down when the first big ball of color exploded over the bay in extravagant sparks that started out green, then turned to orange, then white. Harper floated on her back, watching the show. She was dividing her time during a lull in the pyrotechnics between tracking a satellite's movement across the sky and trying to figure out if the slightly larger, ultra bright stars near the moon might actually be Venus and Jupiter when she became aware of the soft rhythmic lapping of oars in the water. She dropped her legs to tread water. "Hey," she said softly to the other two women, who were also floating peacefully. "Do you hear that? I think someone's coming."

"Whoa, mama," a masculine voice said. "Are my eyes deceiving me, or is that naked women?" The tone was hopeful, then sadly resigned when he added, "And me without my camera."

"Jake Bradshaw," his fiancée said sternly, "what the hell are you doing out here?"

"Sightseeing. There's too many damn boaters out to

see the fireworks, and we got tired of trying to maneuver around them. Decided to take a little tour instead."

Jenny must have spotted the second shadow that Harper had just noted in the rowboat slipping closer through the black water. "Is that Max with you?"

Harper could have told her it wasn't. Not only was he working tonight, but while the shadow looked very fit, it didn't have Max's breadth through the shoulders. She edged up to the dock, wondering if she could reach her suit without exposing herself—and if so, if she'd be able to wriggle into it in the water.

"Nope." Humor laced Jake's voice. He shipped his oars. "This would be Luc, the newly discovered other Bradshaw."

Great. A stranger. She felt more naked and vulnerable by the moment.

"They can't see anything," Tasha said in her ear.

Anchoring herself to the float with one hand, Harper turned toward the sound to find the other woman also clutching the dock next to her.

"I know it feels like they can, but trust me," Tash murmured. "Jenny and I have been doing this for years, and I doubt a spotlight would penetrate more than an inch or two beneath the surface of this water at night. They don't even have a flashlight."

She nodded her thanks. Hearing that made her feel a little less exposed.

So did Jenny's uncompromising, "Well, take your long-lost Bradshaw, turn your damn boat around and row on out of here. *Now*."

Jake leaned over the oars he'd pulled into the boat. His amusement was clear when he murmured, "Now, why would I want to do that, love?"

"Because if you don't," the little brunette said with a suspicious reasonableness that had him sitting back up, "I'll haul myself up on the float and give you—and your newly discovered brother—an eyeful."

"Time to go, Luc." Jake slid the oars back into the water, their rubber cuffs engaging the oarlocks with a muffled *thunk*. Dipping one oar deep, he hauled hard on it and whirled the boat a quarter turn so that the other man's back was to the women. His voice drifted to them as he put his back into rowing toward the boat dock. "See you at home, baby."

The other man laughed, and Tasha stiffened beside her.

Harper looked at her. "What it is? Are you okay?"

"Yes. Of course. It's just…for a minute there the new Bradshaw brother sounded exactly like—" Tasha gave her head a sharp shake. "No. Clearly my imagination's run amok." She hauled herself up onto the float and rapidly donned her bathing suit.

Then she picked up Harper's, shook it out and extended it toward her.

Harper hesitated.

"It's safe," Tasha said. "Even if they look back, the most they'll see is shadows."

Jenny materialized next to her and pulled herself onto the decking, so Harper did the same. Shivering in the chilling evening air as she worked the recalcitrant bathing suit up her body, she thought longingly of the towels Jenny had packed, which were back on the inn dock.

But she grinned at her friends. "What an amazing night," she said. "I'm so glad you included me. Last one to the hot tub has to fetch the wine from my place." As she dove into the water, the last thing she heard before the water closed over her head was her friends whooping their approval.

"I'VE ONLY GOT a few minutes." A frown gathering his brows over his nose, Max slid into the booth next to Jake and across from the newly arrived Bradshaw. The Anchor was packed to the rafters—and every damn person in it looked annoyingly happy.

Jake gave him a look. "Whoa, what's put a bug up your butt?"

"No bug." *Or not that big a one, at least.* "You called. I'm here. You didn't tell me cheerful was a requirement."

"O-kay. You still on duty or something, while everyone else is playing?"

"No. I just got off." But he'd been low-grade moody and a lot edgy for most of the day and wasn't feeling sociable, to say the least. Still, a guy didn't take out his crap mood on his half brothers—at least not more than he just had. He supposed he owed it to both of them to go through the motions and at least pretend to be friendly.

So he raised a brow. "Sorry if I seem distracted. But FYI, I have plans a helluva lot more satisfying than hanging with you two."

But for how much longer, Slick?

That was the question, wasn't it? Harper would be leaving town in—what?—two days, maybe three at the most? Not that they'd actually done anything as mature as discussing her timetable, but that was what he'd understood upfront. And he was trying real hard not to let the knowledge drag his mood down any lower than it already was. But, hell, it hardly took a genius to figure out what had given his irritability its chops in the first place.

When they weren't burning up the sheets, working their jobs or at the Village, he and Harper had managed to go out on a few dates. They'd mostly shared meals at a couple of Silverdale restaurants. But they'd talked about everything under the sun. Hell, he'd been downright chatty at times, even going so far as to tell her how differently he'd handle the department if *he* were sheriff. She made him laugh more than anyone he'd ever known.

A throat cleared across the narrow table, and, looking up, Max found Luc studying him. It disconcerted the hell out of him to look into a face with so much family resemblance when the guy was still a virtual stranger.

His new half brother slanted him a look. "Your plans happen to include one of those naked chicks Jake and I didn't quite get to see tonight?"

Max jerked his head back slightly in surprise. But he merely turned a look on Jake. "What the fuck, bro?"

"You can spare us ten minutes for a beer," his brother replied in a tone that brooked no argument and hailed Sally. Then he shrugged. "Luc and I got tired of all the people out on the water when we rowed out to see the fireworks, so I took him to check out the inn from the canal. You know how pretty it is all lit up at night."

He nodded, but thought grumpily, *Get on with it.*

As though Jake could read his mind, he did. "We came across Jenny, Tash and Harper skinny-dipping off the float."

"Which, nice as that inn is," Luc said drily, "was a helluva lot more interesting."

The waitress delivered a Ridgetop Red to the table

without first taking his order, courtesy, no doubt, of Elise, the bartender, who was still jonesing over his upgraded taste in beer.

"No shit?" he demanded after Sally ascertained the other Bradshaw boys had everything they needed and left to answer another patron's summons. "The three of them were Full Monty?" What red-blooded man's spirits wouldn't raise at the thought of naked women? "I would've paid to see that. Had to be one kick-ass peep show."

"Or it would've been, if we could have seen something besides shoulders," Luc said. "I've got excellent night vision, but that's some seriously dark water." Then he grinned. "You should have seen Jake, though, when his woman threatened to hop on the float and give me an eyeful if we didn't go away. He all but screamed like a girl and rowed us away so fast we probably carved a permanent wake."

Jake's arm shot across the table, his fist punching Luc in the shoulder. "Screamed like a girl, my ass." Then he laughed. "Okay, I've gotta admit that was pretty brilliant on her part. It didn't even occur to me to call her bluff. I only knew that I'd have to rip Luc's eyes out of his head and feed 'em to the fish if he saw her. And wouldn't that put a crimp in this little family reunion?"

"Uncle Sam taught me to be real good with all manner of weapons," Max said, deadpan. "So I could probably go you one better had the two of you actually seen Harper wearing nothing but her pretty skin." Then he gave Jake a faint smile. "Still, it's hard to beat a good eyeball ripping."

Luc examined him. "I've gotta say, man, it's a little

chilling that I'm not a hundred percent sure if you're bullshittin' us or not."

"He's BSing you," Jake said confidently.

"Or not," Max added.

A ruckus broke out at a table down by the dartboard, and Max leaned out to see what was going on. He blew out an irritated breath. "Oh, for cri'sake," he said, his mood spiraling downward once more. He slid out of the booth. "I've had it with Wade—it's past time he got a clue that Mindy is good and married to Curt. Jesus, it's been seven years—the woman's never coming back to him." He picked up his beer, knocked back half of it in one long chug, then dug some money out of his wallet and tossed it on the table. "I'll see you guys later. I'm hauling his sorry ass to jail."

"You're off duty," Jake said. "And this is Wade we're talking about. You really think it'll do any damn good?"

"I wish. If he had two brain cells to rub together, a night in lockup might drive the facts home—or at least make the man think." He hitched a shoulder. "Unfortunately, I'm not all that sure he has more than one. Otherwise he might have gotten a clue when she filed the restraining order against him."

"So why waste your time?"

"Because I'm hoping that having something concrete to concentrate on, if only for the length of time it takes me to book Wade for violating the terms of the no-contact order and get him settled in his cell, will help *me* work off this fucking mood before I try to catch up with Harper."

"Ah." Jake nodded. "Always a good plan, bro. *Always* a good plan."

CHAPTER TWENTY-THREE

HARPER'S GOOD MOOD carried over as she shared a bottle of Pouilly-Fuissé in the hot tub with Tasha and Jenny and continued when the inn's guests returned from the fireworks display. They, too, were cheery, and she exchanged lighthearted conversation with them as she checked in the boats and counted heads. As soon as she made sure everyone had been accounted for, she raced back to her cottage.

That's when she caught sight of herself in the bathroom mirror. It slammed a dent in her Saturday night.

"Holy crap." She watched her reflection as her hands rose in an attempt to tame a truly scary case of wildly frizzing curls, swallowing hard at the total lack of success.

But darn it, she was feeling too good to let it destroy her great night. So, she showered the salt water out of her hair and off her skin. She dried off, moisturized all over, then changed into her tank top and jammie bottoms. She had barely finished applying a defrizzer and was running a pick through her curls when a knock sounded on the door.

She all but skipped over to answer it, smiling hugely when she pulled the door open and saw Max standing there. He'd already opened the screen door, and she jumped him, twining her arms around his strong neck and wrapping her legs around his waist. "Hey there, big boy."

Big hands grasping her butt, he looked down at her. "Hey there, yourself," he said, the creases between his dark eyebrows smoothing out. "You seem to be in high spirits."

"I am! I am *ever* so happy! But what about you?" She ran her thumb over the now smooth skin between his brows. "You were frowning when I opened the door."

"Yeah, I've been in kind of a funk this evening. But seeing you makes me feel a whole lot better. Tell me what's got you so jacked."

"Oh, Max, I had the most interesting night." Tightening her thighs around him, she happily bounced her butt up and down.

"So I've heard."

She quit bouncing and blinked. "Excuse me?"

"Word has it you, Jenny and Tash were skinny-dipping off the inn's float."

"Are you bamming me—people know about that already?" She frowned at him. "I mean, I know this town is gossip central, but even for Razor Bay that got out at warp speed."

"It's not widely known." He kicked the door shut behind him and, with her still wrapped around him, crossed to drop into the chair by the couch. Rearranging several wayward curls, he said, "I had a quick beer with Jake and Luc."

"Ahhhh." She grinned and arranged her knees on either side of his hips. Then, praying Tasha hadn't been wrong, she said hopefully, "They couldn't see anything, you know."

His mouth crooked up in a little one-sided smile of

amusement. "That appeared to be Luc's general griev-
ance."

She'd had no real reason to doubt Tasha's assessment of the situation, yet she was relieved all the same
to have it verified. And for some reason, hearing it reinforced her confidence regarding the subject she'd been
wanting to bring up with Max. That in turn made her
feel friendly.

Very friendly.

She subtly gyrated on his lap.

"Yeah?" Those midnight eyebrows raising, he
gripped her hips as his penis stiffened, lifting her to
allow it a little space to straighten out beneath the fly
of his jeans. Once it had, he pressed her back down so
that the slippery seam of her satiny PJ bottoms aligned
along every long, hard inch of his sex.

She exhaled a shuddery breath, already way past the
need for foreplay. She was ready to dive straight into
the main event. Max was the only man she'd ever been
intimate with to make her feel this way. The only one
who, with the slightest touch, could make her want him
desperately. Her lips curving up, she subtly swiveled
her hips.

Flattening his hands against the round swell of her
butt to hold her in place, Max crunched up to plant a
short, fierce kiss on her mouth. Resuming his lounge,
he gazed at her through heavy-lidded eyes. "You look
like a cat who found the back way into the creamery,"
he said in a rough voice.

She put some purr into her *"Rrrr-ow,"* trying her
best to sound like a real feline.

She wouldn't have thought it possible, but the rigid
hard-on she was gently sliding back and forth against

grew even harder beneath her. Max's eyes glowed with dark fire behind his narrowed lashes as he studied her.

"Take your top off," he ordered.

The command in his voice made her clench deep inside. Crossing her hands at her waist, she grasped the tank top, tugged it out of the waistband of her PJ bottoms and peeled it inside out up her torso. Her elbows were jutted toward the ceiling, the top's fabric pulled over her face and obscuring her vision, when Max's mouth latched onto her nipple.

A desperate sound exploded from her throat, and he groaned in response. His lips released her, and he rose to his feet as she began to wrestle with her top in earnest.

"Easy," he murmured, laughter lacing his deep voice. "I've got you, but you're not hanging on in return, so you don't wanna lean back too much. I'd hate for both of us to end up on the floor." He strode across the room.

She finally got the stretchy chemise over her head and tossed it aside. She shot him a triumphant smile as she wrapped her arms back around his neck.

He stopped in his tracks. "Aw, man," he said and the vibration of his deep voice against her sternum seemed to resonate along her spine from the nape of her neck to her tailbone. "I love your smile. I just. Plain. Love it." Stamping his mouth over hers, he kissed her blind.

She kissed him back, writhing languorously against him.

When he finally raised his head, she stared in befuddlement into his eyes, loving the dense dark lashes that tangled together in the outer corners. It took her a moment to regain her power of speech. "Why did you stop?"

"Ladder," he said, and flipped her up over his shoulder in a fireman's lift. "Hang on."

She blinked, then clutched at his khaki shirt as he caught the rung of the ladder to the loft with one hand while the other splayed over the back of her thigh and began climbing. His warm, muscular forearm pressed the other thigh, securing her legs against his chest.

"Not exactly romantic, I know," he said as he stepped into her bedroom and set her on her feet away from the drop in the floor. "But it's hard to simultaneously sweep you off your feet and climb a ladder. And you know me, I'm all about safety."

She laughed and flung herself back into his arms.

He caught her with a growl and lowered them both onto her unmade bed, laying her on her back and rolling onto his side to face her. He pushed up onto one forearm, and as he reached past her his chest briefly brushed her breasts in their navy-and-pink bra. He clicked on the nightstand lamp, and a second later he was back on his side, his head propped in his hand.

"Maybe the light's not such a great idea." She kicked the messy bedding aside. "Because, my secret's out now. I'm kind of a slob."

"Yeah, I don't think this relationship has a prayer of surviving," he said drily. "Neatness is a priority for me, you know."

"That's a shame," she said. "Because our incompatibility means I probably shouldn't do this." Rolling onto her side as well, she mimicked his posture, then, reaching her free hand down, palmed his erection.

"Did I say priority?" he demanded. "Puzzling, I meant. I'm totally puzzled why anyone would give a damn about neatness." He rocked his hips, pressing into her hand. "Now, me, I've always been drawn to the slobs."

She snorted. "Of course you have. That was *precisely* my impression when I saw the military corners and bounce-a-quarter-on-the-tightness of the bed linens at your place." She shook her head. "Guys. You all will say anything to get your rocks off."

"But we always genuinely mean it in the moment."

Tickled as she was with his sense of humor, with his willingness to be silly, which she never in a gazillion years would have guessed he could be when they'd first met, she suddenly had a more urgent agenda. "Max?" she said softly.

He reached over and rearranged a curl that was dangling over her eye. "Yeah, baby?"

"Shut up and kiss me."

"I can do that," he breathed and rolled on top of her, pushing up on his forearms with the clear intention of sparing her his weight, an innate thoughtfulness she'd wager most people wouldn't realize came naturally to him. Lowering his head, he opened his lips over hers, then, with soft suction, slowly dragged them closed. Opened them and dragged them closed, sipping at her mouth in a gentle, lush rhythm that sent her fingers digging into the hard muscles of his arms and her breath stuttering softly through her lips.

Time disappeared, and she had no idea how much passed before she ran her hand up the placket of his crisp uniform shirt to the first fastened button. It felt as if she had barely begun undoing them when her knuckles brushed the waistband of his jeans. Efficiently, she worked the shirttails free and slipped the last two buttons from their buttonholes. She spread the plackets apart, pushing the shirt off his shoulders and halfway down his arms, semirestraining him.

Independent of her brain, her hands developed a life of their own as they moved to slowly explore his upper body. They traveled from the hot, satin-smooth skin that stretched over the defined ridges of his abdomen to the more roughly textured cloud of hair on his chest. She flicked a fingernail over the tiny nail head nipple buried in the latter and smiled against his lips when goose bumps washed down his arms and he shivered.

He raised his head. "You find me amusing?"

"Not at all. I'm just fascinated at how responsive your nipples are." She rubbed her thumb around his smooth, nickel-sized areola. "In my experience—" *which, okay, isn't massive* "—most men's aren't." She stroked her thumb across the unadorned nipple again. "Where's your ring?"

One massive shoulder hitched. "Either on my dresser or on the bathroom counter." Sliding half-off her, he reached out to rub his thumb against the point of her chin. It was such a platonic touch…yet one that tightened her nipples and made her press her thighs together against a renewed flood of sensation deep between her legs.

He stroked raspy fingertips down to the hollow of her throat, and from there lightly traced her collarbones, then zigzagged down her chest and climbed the rise of her left breast. Instead of paying attention to her achy nipple, however, his big-knuckled fingers moved to her diaphragm and from there to the stretchy elastic waistband of her pajama bottoms.

Abruptly, he pushed back to straddle her thighs. "Roll over."

Her heart hit solidly against the wall of her chest, and when he widened his thighs on either side of her, she did as he bid. She'd barely turned onto her stomach when he slid her PJ bottoms over her butt and down her legs. She felt him move down to her feet and then off the bed entirely. Hands she couldn't see tugged her lounge pants over her feet and discarded them.

His own pants rustled as he kicked them off and put on a condom, then he was back, his inner legs hard and warm against her outer thighs. His large hands spread over her cheeks, the pads of his fingers and palms scratchy against her smoother skin.

"I love your ass," he said in a rough voice.

She craned her head to grin at him over her shoulder. "You're the perfect guy, you know that? I've always considered my butt a little too big."

"Are you crazy? You have *this*—" his hands stroked the fullness they encompassed "—and you wanna be one of those skinny-ass women?"

"See what I'm saying? Per-fect."

His hands wrapped around her hips and tugged her up onto her knees. She pushed onto all fours, and Max leaned over her, his front pressing heat into her back.

"You're the perfect one," he murmured in her ear, the stubble on his chin catching on the curls near her temple. He bent his head and kissed the contour of her neck.

Her bones seemed to dissolve, and her upper body melted out from under him. Pressing her breasts into the sheet, she stretched her arms out, her fingers splayed against the pale yellow linens.

Her bottom was still raised, and Max reached between her legs. He sucked in a sharp breath. "Ah, sweetheart. You're so wet."

"I know. I'm so primed, Max. I want you. Now."

"God, you really are the perfect woman." And he slid into her, stretching her, filling her. He held himself deep for a moment, then began to move. Slowly retreating and sinking back in, he flattened the heels of his hands against the fullness of her cheeks, his fingers curled around her hips to hold her in place.

It only took a few strokes before she felt her climax begin to build. Pushing back against his steely sex with every thrust, she curled her fingers, gripping the sheets.

And heard herself whisper, "I love you, Max. God, I love you."

A rough sound, more an exploding groan than actual words, escaped him, and his hands tightened on her. He seemed to lose all control, his hips picking up speed until he was pounding, pounding, *pounding* into her.

She came in an explosive, fiery rush, her inner sheath clamping down around his invading hardness as if trying to wring an equally explosive climax from him.

If that was indeed the plan, it worked. Max pulsated inside her, her name a gritty rasp from deep in his throat.

He didn't collapse on her, but Harper felt the tension flow out of his body. The hands that had been gripping her hips so hard stroked them tenderly.

"I'm sorry," he said in a low voice. "Did I hurt you?"

"No, of course not. You made me feel... God. So wonderful. *Beautiful.*"

"You are wonderful. And beautiful beyond belief." He pulled out of her, and she rolled over onto her back.

And wondered why he didn't meet her gaze.

He dealt with the used condom, then came back to the bed. Sitting down next to her hip, he reached out to stroke her chest above the sheet she'd pulled up. Then he dropped his hand to the mattress. "Did you mean it? What you said? Or was that just sex talk?"

She *had* said she loved him in the heat of the moment. And yet...

Examining her feelings with ruthless candor, she realized that while they may have emerged in that context, they hadn't been heat-of-the-moment words. The knowledge caused something warm and fragile to unfurl in her chest.

She had always been a people person and got on well with practically everyone she met. God knows, her mother would have been the first to tell you she played well with others, which she likely would have meant less as a compliment than as a road map to Harper's rolling stone personality.

But there was playing and there was Max. And Max lit her up inside like no one else had ever done, *touched* her in places no other person had ever touched—and she didn't mean merely in a sexual way, although that was certainly a fact. But more important, he had a way of accessing emotions in her she hadn't even realized she possessed.

Compared to him, all the other friends she'd made over the years were mere acquaintances.

These thoughts ran through her head at the speed of light, but not quickly enough for Max, she was guessing, if the cool-eyed, give-nothing-away look on his face was anything to go by. Drawing a deep breath, she reached out to wrap her fingers around his hand, clenched now into a fist.

"No," she said. "It wasn't just sex talk. I'm not sure when it happened, but I love you."

A slow smile spread across his face. "Yeah?"

"Yeah." She felt unaccountably shy. But she looked him in the eye. "Definitely."

"That's good," he said. "Because the thing is?" He dragged his tongue across his bottom lip. "I love you, too."

Yes! Exaltation did the end zone dance in her heart, pumped its triumphant fist in the air. She grinned at him and gave the coverlet next to her hip a pat.

He settled his muscular butt on the mattress next to her hip, bent the leg closest to her on the rumpled spread and braced the foot of his other one against the floor. Hooking an elbow behind her neck, he hauled her off the pillow she'd propped against the headboard and laid a blistering kiss on her. When he finally cut her loose, he gave her that slight smile that always seemed to shine brighter than the toothiest grin as she flopped, breathless, back against her pillow. "Life is good," he murmured.

"It is," she agreed. "It really is. And I think now might be a good time to discuss something I've been wanting to talk to you about."

"Do I need to put on my jeans for this?"

She laughed. "Pants are optional."

"Okay." He stayed right where he was. "Shoot."

"I'd like to make Razor Bay my home base."

"That's great!" he said enthusiastically. But then his eyes narrowed, and he slowly straightened. "Define home base."

"You know that my job entails a lot of traveling," she said. "But I'd like to make this the place I come back to when the jobs are done. And if you're interested, then

I'd like to come back to you. Maybe…live…together when I'm in town?"

He merely looked at her for a moment. Then he gave a minute shake of his head. "No."

Her heart swooped toward her stomach. "What?"

"No." He rose off the bed, picked up his jeans and stepped into them without first locating his boxers. He looked at her with that give-nothing-away expression as he pulled on his shirt and started buttoning up. "Just once in my life, I want to come first in someone else's. So, no. I'm not going to be your place marker while you buzz all over the world." Fingers white with tension, he zipped up. "I want…more. More than it sounds like you're interested in."

Beneath his stony delivery there was an unmistakable thread of withdrawal, a pulling away from her and into himself that set off a zing of panic.

But she breathed through it and tried for reasonableness. "Max, I've put several years into this job, and I make a difference in people's lives. Can't we discuss it? Maybe come to a compromise?"

"That would be the mature thing to do." Eyes flinty, he swept up his shoes and socks. "But you know what, Harper? I'm feeling a little ripped off at the moment. So I think that's gonna have to wait."

And turning on his bare heel, he crossed the small room and swung down the ladder.

Seconds later, she heard the door bang shut.

CHAPTER TWENTY-FOUR

THE MOMENT MAX got home he walked straight to the cupboard where he kept the bottle of Jim Beam Sheriff Neward had given him Christmas before last. Hooking two fingers over the lip of a Wile E. Coyote glass, he carried it and the bourbon into the great room. He pulled a chair up to the unlit fireplace, contemplated turning it on, then said, "Fuck it," and set about lowering the level in the bottle as if it were an exam he had to ace.

He woke up in the chair the next morning with a killer crick in his neck, the Seven Dwarves hacking a path through his brain with their mine picks and the realization that his refusal last night to even consider Harper's proposal could very well mean giving her up entirely.

There was no way in hell he was prepared to do that.

Had he really told her that he loved her, then in the very next breath admitted he wanted to come first in her life? Not that there was anything wrong with that. Love—at least as he understood it—*should* mean automatically putting your loved one first. He truly believed that. But while he'd wanted to see the theory put in action by her, apparently he hadn't thought it applied to *him* to put her first, as well.

Not to mention that whole fifties-era give-up-your-job-to-be-at-my-beck-and-call thing.

"Shit."

He crawled out of the chair and shuffled into the kitchen where he knocked back three aspirin, then brewed a pot of coffee. When it was ready, he planted his butt back in the chair in front of the fireplace and, with a cup in one hand and the coffee pot for nonstop refills within reach of his other, he mainlined caffeine until his brain finally began to function.

He killed off the rest of the pot, then climbed into the shower and stood under the screaming hot, pounding spray until the water ran cold. By the time he dried off and shaved, he'd figured out what he needed to do.

Fifteen minutes later he was knocking on Harper's door. Luck was on his side. She was not only at home, which he hadn't been sure she would be since he knew she had things scheduled for the inn's Razor Bay Days Sunday festivities, but her smile when she saw him was immediate and genuine. He took heart that maybe he hadn't screwed things up entirely.

"Hey," she said softly.

"Hi. Can I come in?"

"Of course." Opening the door wider, she stepped back, then closed it behind him when he followed her into the cottage. She looked up at him. "Would you like some coffee?"

He couldn't prevent his slight wince. "No. Thanks." He shoved his hands in his Levi's pockets. "Listen, I'm sorry about last night."

"It's okay." She cocked her head inquiringly. "I take it you're ready to discuss my proposal now?"

"Not exactly. But I think I might have an alternate solution."

Her face lit up. "You do?"

"Yeah. It's pretty simple, really." He ran a thumb down her cheek and smiled. "I love you. You love me. You also love your job. And that means you have to travel."

She nodded. "That's all true."

"So how about I quit the sheriff's department and travel with you?"

Her expression froze. "Wh-what?"

Okay, not exactly the reaction he'd hoped for, but he warned himself not to jump to conclusions. He hadn't left room for discussion last night, and he was determined not to repeat the same mistake this morning. "I'll quit—"

The choppy swipe of her hand cut him off. "I actually heard that—it just…didn't sink in properly. You'll give up *your* job?"

"Yes." Okay, the idea pinched a little. But Harper was a thousand times more important than any job.

"But you love it."

He shrugged. "I love you more." He reached out for her, but she scrambled out of range. His gut iced over. "Harper?"

"Oh, God, I can't let you do that." She executed a hand movement that was uncharacteristically jerky. "Max, I've seen the stress that my mom's unhappiness with Dad's traveling put on their marriage, and I won't do that to you. To us. You should stay in Razor Bay. Stay with the job you love. I'll come back to you. Every time. I swear that I will."

He felt something deep inside of him shut down. How often had he tried his damnedest to be enough for the people in his life? And how many times had he fallen short?

Every damn time, that's how many.

Well, some things never changed, apparently. God, he was tired. Just suddenly really exhausted.

"I can't do this anymore," he said to the floor. "I can't keep trying and failing." He looked at her for the first time since she'd thrown his offer back in his face.

And said goodbye in his head. "When your job is done—what, tomorrow, the day after?" He shook his head impatiently, because, really. Like he gave a good goddamn about the exact date. "Whenever it is, I think you should leave Razor Bay."

"What? Max, plea—" This time she was the one who reached out.

He sidestepped her touch. "I don't know what to do with a relationship where I'm relegated to the shelf like a kid's toy. But I do know I can't spend my life waiting for you to come back to play with me. So do us both a favor. Just leave Razor Bay." Even to his own ears, his voice sounded flat with finality. "And don't come back."

Then, needing to remove himself to somewhere— *anywhere*—that wasn't painfully within her proximity, he turned on his heel and, without a backward glance, walked out on the woman who'd lifted him to the greatest heights imaginable.

Only to send him crashing on his own back to earth.

FOR SEVERAL LONG moments Harper stared dumbly at the door that closed behind Max, too stunned to react. This was the second time in less than twelve hours that he'd walked out on her, and when her ability to think finally kicked in, she really wanted to be furious with him for it.

Because, really, could Max *be* any more dictatorial

or controlling? For a moment she managed to drum up a decent snit, her posture stiff with righteous anger.

"It's my *job,* dammit," she said to the door. "Not a series of pleasure trips where I bring my boyfriend along! And how long before you're bored to tears and change your mind again and want me home where you can keep me—what, barefoot and pregnant?—like a good little Stepford wife?"

Then she sagged so abruptly she had to feel her way to the couch to sit down. Hugging herself, she rocked back and forth, back and forth. "Oh, God, oh, God, oh, GodohGodohGod."

She could whip herself into a frenzy of indignation, but she knew in her heart that wasn't what Max wanted at all. It wasn't about having her under his thumb. Max was the best man she'd ever known. A whole lot better than he should be, considering his upbringing. Certainly the people who should have gone out of their way to make things special for him—if only on occasion— never had.

And he wanted her to leave town and never come back? She couldn't seem to draw in a deep enough breath to satisfy the basic need for air.

He'd offered to give up everything for her, and she'd panicked, just like she did whenever she thought about not traveling. The first was almost a guarantee that he'd end up resenting her. And the second? Well. *You quit moving, you die.* God knew, *that* was all but tattooed on her psyche.

As it turned out, she hadn't had the least idea what true panic felt like until she'd looked into his eyes… and watched the light that had burned there for her extinguish.

"But you know what?" she whispered, unwrapping her arms from around herself and straightening her spine. "He doesn't have to give up his life here. And you *don't* die."

Her father had never meant his saying literally, but somehow she had twisted it around until she'd convinced herself that it was the gospel truth. The real gospel, however, was that she could travel until the end of her days and never feel a fraction of the satisfaction she'd felt these past few months in Razor Bay. That came from being loved by Max and making friends like Tasha and Jenny and even Mary-Margaret, and got an assist from working at the inn and with the boys of Cedar Village.

Determination slowly edged her panic aside. She'd acted like an idiot and pushed Max past his limit. But he'd been a bit of an idiot himself. And damned if she planned to give him up without a fight just because he said so.

She wiggled her feet into her flip-flops and looked around for her purse. She had no idea where he had gone, but, by God, she would find him.

She was *not* losing him.

A knock sounded at the door just as she unearthed her purse from beneath the coffee table. Hope exploding, she raced for it and whipped it open. "Oh, thank God you came ba—" She stilled in shock. *"Mom?"*

Gina Summerville-Hardin, tall and elegant in flowing ivory silk that contrasted beautifully with her glowing, deeper-brown-than-Harper's complexion, smiled at her as if it weren't the least bit unusual that she should turn up on Harper's porch. "Hello, darling."

"What are you doing here?"

"You haven't been returning my calls, and I can't abide knowing you're angry with me. So I came to tell you face-to-face why I took so long informing Cedar Village about us giving them the grant." She smiled gently. "And I wanted to tell you a few things that I don't believe you understand about your father and me."

"Mom, truly, any other time, that would be lovely. But this isn't a good—"

"Please, Baby Girl," Gina said, and the stark need in her eyes stopped Harper. "Just give me ten minutes. Five, even."

"All right." She stepped back. "Come in. Can I get you something to drink?"

Gina passed her, trailing an elusive whiff of Clive Christian's 1872 perfume. She looked around, clearly taking in everything regarding her daughter's little cottage with one comprehensive glance.

Then her mother turned her attention back to her. "A glass of water would be nice."

"How did you get here, Mom?" Harper crossed to the little college dorm-sized refrigerator and took out the quart bottle she used to store chilled water. "Sea-Tac airport is nearly a hundred miles away."

"But like every other airport in the world, it rents cars that come equipped with a GPS."

"So, you drove?" She splashed some water into a glass and carried it back to her mother. *"Yourself?"*

"Darling, I set up households all over the world and broke them down again in order to move on to the next one. Why on earth would you think an hour and a half's drive would throw me in a tizzy?"

For the first time in a long time, Harper recalled more than just her mother urging her father to quit traveling.

She remembered Gina directing everyone's packing, remembered her making the moves *fun*. "You used to play music while we packed. And you'd dance from box to box." In another first, during the century it felt like since Max's departure, a small smile curled up the corners of her lips. "Daddy used to say you could really shake your thang."

Gina smiled reminiscently. "Your father used to say a lot of things. And despite what you seem to believe, we were madly happy together."

"But you were always trying to get him to quit moving."

"Oh, always, schmalways, Harper. I brought it up maybe every third move. And your father invariably sweet talked me out of my objections."

"But you guys fought!"

"You can't possibly believe married couples don't on occasion."

"Of course not—I'm not a child. But you have to admit that you and Daddy never fought about anything except that."

"That's not quite true, but since it was the only subject that truly got us all hot under the collar, I'll agree it's close enough. There were times when I was weary unto death of moving from country to country while virtually being an ex-pat from my own." She reached over and touched the back of Harper's hand. "But, darling, I loved your father much more than I ever disliked all the moving."

"Oh, God." A sudden rush of tears filled her eyes. "That's what Max said."

"Max?" Gina blinked. Then her posture, already impeccable, subtly straightened even more. "Max Brad-shaw? The deputy?"

"Yes. He offered to give up everything to travel with me, but I argued that he loved his job—which he does." She looked at her mother. "But he said exactly what you did—I love you more."

"So...you and the deputy?"

Harper's tears dried up. "Don't worry, Mother," she snapped. "He won't be joining the family. You'll be happy to know I panicked and drove him away."

Gina's delicate brows furrowed. "You're no longer a teenager, Harper Louisa—don't you think it's time you quit putting the worst spin on everything I do and say? *Happy* is never my first reaction when I hear my daughter is panicking. And why would you think the idea of him joining the family would worry me? Which I assume to actually mean *bother* me."

"Please. You're always talking about how I must meet so-and-so's doctor/engineer/CEO son."

"That's true," her mother agreed easily. "I long to see you settle down with someone who thinks you hung the moon." She smiled tenderly. "With a man who makes *you* want to hang it for him. My friends' sons are the only men I know in the correct age bracket. God knows your brother's friends are too young—and in more than mere age."

Harper snorted.

A little smile tugged the corner of Gina's lips. "Would you like to know what made me put off informing Cedar Village that we'd approved the grant?"

"Yes!" Because she'd never understood it. For all the differences she and her mother had had, she'd never known Gina to be anything but professional when it came to the foundation.

"Your voice changed whenever you mentioned Deputy Bradshaw's name."

Harper blinked. She gaped at her mother. "What?"

"Your voice changed. You savored the vowels in his name as if they were made of crème brûlée. And I wanted to give you more time with him."

"But I'd already agreed to stay in Razor Bay until next week."

"I didn't say it was well thought out." She shrugged one elegant shoulder. "In my zeal, your work ethic slipped my mind, and I worried you'd get wanderlust and take off for a new adventure. I messed up, Baby Girl. But I vow I did so with the best of intentions." She looked at Harper. "So you two had a fight?"

"I screwed up so bad," she said, then gave her mother a rueful look. "It must run in the family."

Ignoring the aside, Gina went straight to the heart of the matter. "What are you going to do about it?"

"I was about to hunt him down like a hound after a fox when you arrived."

"Go." Her mother waved her away. "Don't worry about me, I can entertain myself. Go make amends. And after you do, bring your young man back to introduce to your mama."

AFTER MAX LEFT Harper's cottage, he drove aimlessly through several of the little blink-and-you-miss-them towns outside of Razor Bay. Finally, thinking to distract himself with the boys, he headed for the Village.

That didn't work out quite the way he'd hoped. He simply hurt too much, was too distracted and just couldn't immerse himself in their doings the way he usually did. It didn't help that both Owen and Malcolm separately asked if he'd seen Harper.

Ground glass in his intestines couldn't have made him bleed more inside. It took every shred of willpower he possessed to answer levelly that Razor Bay Days plans at the inn were keeping her busy.

He was wrung dry by the time his group dispersed either to meet with a counselor or go to class. When the last boy disappeared through the doorway and the sounds out in the hallway began to die down, he bent forward in his chair to brace his elbows on his thighs. Dropping his head onto his fists, he dug his knuckles into his forehead where a headache throbbed.

God, what was he going to do? He couldn't wrap his mind around living day after day after day with the kind of pain he felt right now. And one thing was certain. He had to get the hell out of here. As long as his mind was stuck in the never-gonna-get-to-hold-Harper-again rut, he was no damn good to these kids.

Slowly, he dropped his hands and straightened up. Blowing out a breath, he shoved to his feet. He felt like he was eighty years old.

A slight disruption in the air alerted him he wasn't alone, and, hoping like hell it was Mary-Margaret or some other Cedar Village personnel and not one of the boys, he turned. He just couldn't deal with another kid at the moment.

Harper stood in the doorway.

She was the last person he expected to see, and it damn near brought him to his knees. It took every re-source at his disposal to not merely keep from buckling but to stand tall, as well. Slapping on his poker face, he met her olive-green-eyed gaze head-on. "What do you want?"

"I choose you," she said in a voice that trembled slightly.

"Dammit, Harper," he said. "Could we just not—" Her words sank in, and he shook his head to clear it, unsure he'd actually heard what he thought he'd heard. "What?"

"I put you first," she said more strongly, stepping into the room and reaching for the open door to close it behind her. "I want to be with you. Want to love and live with *you*."

His heart slammed up against his rib cage. "Are you messing with me?" God, if she was—if this was some sick joke, and she laughed and took it back after making him hope...

It would kill him.

"No." She came a step closer. "God, Max. *No*." Those long legs carried her another step nearer. "I love you." She slicked her tongue over her bottom lip. Looked at him earnestly. "*Love* you. So. Much. *God*. So, so much."

He held up his hand like a traffic cop as she started to take yet another step toward him. "Stay where you are. So, you want me to travel with you after all?"

"No, I—"

"You *are* fucking with my head." He speared his fingers into his hair and clutched his skull, pressing the heels of his hands against his temples. "I never pegged you as having a cruel streak."

"Just listen—I am *not* messing with you." Ignoring his demand to stay back, she stepped up to him and took his face in her hands. "I love you," she said. "Do you hear me?"

He nodded cautiously. Lowered his hands to his sides. But he couldn't bring himself to touch her, for fear he'd discover this was a dream that would pop like a bubble the instant he did.

"When you walked out on me," she said, "I realized I could travel until I was old and gray and never feel half as good as I do when I'm with you." She brushed the pad of her thumb over his lower lip. "Right here in Razor Bay."

"You were pretty adamant about how much you love your job."

"But as *you* said, I love you more. I panicked for a minute when you told me that, but I so understand what you were talking about now. Because I do love you more than any damn job. *So* much more. I can talk to Jenny about working at the inn during the busy season. Talk to Mary-Margaret about maybe working part-time here." She shrugged. "Or volunteering, if they can't afford another employee. I have a decent nest egg saved. I can afford to take a break if I want."

"Maybe—" his hands moved with a life of their own to slide around her hips "—we could put each other first and compromise like you suggested." He shuddered with the pleasure of feeling the warmth of her body through her clothing. "Maybe it doesn't have to be an either-or proposition."

Her eyes lit up. "You mean maybe travel a week a month or every other month, something like that?" She considered. "Assessing grant applicants generally only takes three to five days. The time I spent here was the exception." Then she shook her head. "But that's not important. I can go without ever doing that again and be happy, Max. As long as I have you."

He couldn't hold back a second longer; he lowered his head and rocked his mouth over hers. At the first taste of her, he felt as if he'd come home, and he took his time savoring her flavors and reassuring himself that she was really here in his arms, her own winding tightly around his neck as she kissed him back.

He eventually raised his head and gazed down at her. A slight smile tugged at the corner of his mouth. "Do you really think the foundation would be okay with you only being on the road one week a month?"

"Well, I don't know." The smile she flashed damn near blinded him. "We'll have to ask my mother." She rose onto her toes to press a quick there-and-gone kiss on his lips. Lowering her heels back onto her flip-flops, she grinned up at him. "Who happens to be at my place."

"Your *mother* is at your place? Here? In Razor Bay?"

"Yes."

"Oh, man. She's gonna hate me."

She patted his chest. "No, she's not. She's going to love you almost as much as I do."

He snorted. "Like hell. I'd lay odds she had someone a little more upscale than me in mind for her only daughter."

Harper laughed. "That's what I thought, too. But the reason she kept putting off telling Mary-Margaret that I'd approved the grant was to give me more time with you."

His brows furrowed. "How would she even know we were spending time together? Did you tell her?"

"No. In fact, we'd barely stopped circling each other at the time. But she said my voice changed whenever I talked about you."

A smile tugged at his lips. "Yeah?"

"Yes. She also said, and I quote—'All I want for you is a man who thinks you hang the moon.'"

Tension he hadn't realized had taken up residence in his shoulders released its grip. "That would be me."

"Yes, it would. She also wants me to feel the same for the man I love. And I do, Max." She nipped his lower lip. "I want to snatch that darn thing right out of the sky and hang it around your neck like an Olympic medal."

He wouldn't have thought it possible to go from the lowest point of his life to the happiest he'd ever been. But he had done exactly that. And it totally worked for him.

"Then I guess we both have our work cut out for us," he murmured, bending his knees to kiss her again. Moments later he lifted his head and smiled down at her.

"I can hardly wait."

EPILOGUE

LEAVING HER MOTHER browsing a few feet away in the towel department, Harper danced up to Max, who was trying to pretend he wasn't associated with what he called the frou-frou section. "Look," she said. "Aren't these perfect for your guest bathroom?"

"*Our* bathroom," he said, giving her a firm look. He kept insisting everything was theirs, even though she'd only moved in on Wednesday.

And she supposed she should start looking at it that way herself. "Okay, ours. Aren't they great?"

He gamely inspected the little guest towels she held out, then snapped his head up to pin her with a look of horror. "They have ribbons on them!"

"I know, aren't they gorgeous?" She stroked the rich stripes of colors appreciatively, even though she could see that they weren't, in his eyes. You would have thought she'd presented him with something bristling with lace and glitter. "They're not streaming ribbons," she said with a laugh. "It's two bands sewn across the ends. And just look at these colors—they'll go beautifully with the paint job."

"*Ribbons*, Harper. If my brothers see these, they'll take away my man card."

She kissed his chin, smiling against it at the feel of the slight stubble beneath her lips. Pulling back, she splayed her hand on the hard chest covering his heart. "Trust me, Max, we could deck you out in pink lace from head to toe and your man card would be safe."

Her mother came up to them. "With a woman living with you, darling, you're going to have to make some concessions to the feminine stuff." She patted his arm. "But I agree with my daughter. I bet your man card is solid platinum."

"Damn." He shook his head. "First candles and now this. The invasion of girly stuff is traumatizing."

His words said one thing, but his dark eyes were full of contentment, so Harper stroked his cheek and played along. "There, there," she murmured. "Just keep telling yourself at least you didn't have to go makeup shopping with me. And if you can hold on for five minutes while I pay for these, I'll buy you an ice cream."

He snorted and let Gina haul him over to the kitchen gadgets adjacent to the cash register.

As her purchase was rung up, she heard her mother say, "All the work you and Harper are putting into my farewell party? I have to tell you, Max, it touches me right to the depths of my soul." Then she laughed whole-heartedly, making Harper smile. "Well, as long as it's not because you're just so damn glad to get rid of me."

Max laughed. "Hell, I don't want you to go at all," he said as Harper accepted her change from the clerk. "If I had my way, you'd move here permanently."

He was perfectly serious. It had been love at first sight between Max and her mom. Gina had taken one look and clearly seen right through his sometimes coolly reserved facade, for she'd started mothering him as if he were an orphan she'd pulled in from the storm. Max ate it up like the ice cream she'd just promised him.

And why not? No one else had ever taken the time to do the job right.

Watching Gina with him was an eye-opener for Harper, as well. She'd grown so accustomed to viewing Gina in a certain light that, until this visit, it hadn't occurred to her the beliefs so firmly entrenched in her mind might not be the absolute truth.

Watching her with Max these past several days had jump-started all the good memories she'd relegated for far too long to a distant, dusty corner of her mind. She appreciated her mom again, and a small hollow space she hadn't acknowledged was suddenly filled.

She crossed over to Max and Gina and gave her mother a hug. "I'm going to miss you, too, Mom."

Gina's smile was brilliant as she reached out to hug her in return.

When they got back to Max's—*their*—place, her mom helped her arrange her girly stuff. Not long after they finished, their friends began to arrive for Gina's farewell party.

"Where's Tasha?" Harper asked Jenny a while later when everyone else had arrived and the strawberry blonde was nowhere to be found.

"Oh, sorry. She said to tell you she's got a problem at Bella's and not to wait dinner for her." Jenny gave her a little hip bump. "But you'd be wise to save her a plate. She gets cranky when she misses a meal."

The men went out to man the barbecue, but as the women gathered in the kitchen to organize the food, Harper heard the bathroom door close and Jake's voice say, "Max. *Dude.* You have ribbons on your towels. That's just wrong."

"Watch it, bud," Jenny called. "I'm looking at lace for the ones in our house."

The women laughed, and Rebecca, a regular at their get-togethers, smiled at Harper over the fruit salad she was assembling. "How's it feel to be retired?"

A little snort of laughter escaped Harper, and Rebecca raised her eyebrows inquisitively.

"She's coming back to the inn next summer," Jenny said.

"And working for me part-time as our official fund-raiser," Mary-Margaret added.

"Plus she's going to continue doing the usual assessments on grant applicants for the foundation—also on a part-time basis," her mother said and gave Harper a fond look. "I tried to get her to take over some of my administrative duties for Sunday's Child, as well. They have amazing computer programs these days that make that kind of long-distance participation possible. But my baby girl likes variety in her work."

Harper just grinned and shrugged a shoulder. She topped off everyone's wine. "What can I tell you—when Mama's right, she's right."

"Still, you might change your mind once you see how much time each of your jobs takes and find yourself with too much still on your hands. I'm really hoping you'll take over the foundation when I'm ready to retire."

"Mom, you're only fifty-four years old." She gave her a knowing, who-do-you-think-you're-kidding smile. "I don't envision you relinquishing the reins for a good long while."

"I might surprise you, darling."

"I'm sure you will, but I doubt it will be with an early retirement. In any event, Sunday's Child is in Winston-

Salem. And sophisticated programs or not, now that I've found a place to call home, unless you move here and set up shop, I'm never going to be interested in running it."

"Then perhaps I'll do precisely that," Gina said. "Especially if you give me grandbabies."

A startled laugh escaped her. "Max and I haven't even lived together a full week," she said. "I don't think we're quite ready for a ride on the Baby Train yet." She'd never even considered kids, for pity's sake. And yet…

At the thought of someday maybe holding a mini Max in her arms, something deep inside gave a visceral lurch that felt suspiciously like yearning. She just knew that he'd make the best father.

WHEN SHE AND MAX climbed the stairs to their bedroom after the last guest had departed, the idea resurfaced. She watched him shuck off his pants and pull the silky T-shirt Jake had given him for his birthday over his head. "Have you ever thought about having children?"

He stilled in the midst of folding his shirt and looked at her. "You pregnant, sweetheart?"

"What? No! My mom said something about grandchildren when we were in the kitchen earlier, and it made me realize I've never really thought about having kids."

He looked a little too noncommittal when he asked, "Does that mean you don't want any? Ever?"

"I have no idea. I honestly haven't given it any thought. But I don't think I'd rule it out, out of hand." She watched his shoulders relax. "You do want them, don't you?"

"Yeah. I'd like some someday." He studied her and slicked his tongue over his bottom lip. "You'd make really pretty babies." Then one corner of his mouth crooked up. "Still, we can probably put off the big discussion until we've been together, oh, say, a month or so." Then with a casualness that put her on alert, he said, "Along those same lines, this is sort of jumping the gun—but when I stopped by the department to pick up my check today, Sheriff Neward told me he plans to retire next June."

She turned from her rummage through her pajama drawer. "Will you run for his position?" She beamed at him. "You'd be *perfect!*"

"You think?"

"I don't merely think it—I *know* you would. You've told me quite a bit about the things you would do differently if the job were yours."

He looked pleased yet uncharacteristically uncertain, and suddenly she faltered. "Oh, God, Max. Is it me? Will *I* be a detriment to your bid for sheriff?"

"Huh?" He looked baffled for a heartbeat, then gaped at her. "Your *race,* you mean?" He suddenly laughed, a loud boom of sound that exploded up from the depths of his hard belly. "*Hell,* no. This is Washington State, baby—Liberal Central. I'd bet today's paycheck that, overall, the people here wouldn't even blink at the idea of a mixed-race relationship." He shook his head. "Damn, girl. You're the one who's opened up a shitload of friendships—or at least nodding acquaintanceships— for me with other people."

She blew a pithy sound of dissent. "Not true. People like and respect you all on your own."

He gave her tender smile. "They may have respected me, but, honey, damn few of them liked me until you came along."

He looked confident of his facts, but not displeased by them, so she let the subject drop. And she felt unashamedly happy as she changed into a pink tank top and pink polka-dotted black pajama bottoms. Max went into the adjoining bathroom. Water ran, then turned off, and his electric toothbrush buzzed.

Then he was back.

"Hey, what was going on with Tasha? She said she didn't feel so hot but she looked more, I don't know— off." He flopped onto the bed, propped his shoulders on a pillow against the headboard and folded his hands behind his head.

She looked up from rubbing lotion into her hands and feet where she sat across the end of the bed and shrugged. "It's possible her sugar levels crashed. Maybe that's what made her feel so sick. Jenny said she gets cranky when she's hungry."

"That doesn't explain her and Luc, though. I didn't think they'd even met, but it sure as hell looked like she was giving him an earful—a pissed-off earful—out in the yard after I thought she had left."

"I don't know any more than you about what's going on. She was late because of a problem at the pizzeria, so it's possible it hadn't been fixed after all and she was worried about it. But you're right, she wasn't her usual self. I heard her muttering something about Luc being a guy named Diego and not Luc at all."

For an instant she thought Max's gaze went watchful. When she looked closer, however, all she saw were warm bedroom eyes, not his cool cop's gaze. She shook her head. "I must have gotten it wrong, though, because that doesn't make sense." With a shrug, she rose and put the lotion back on the dresser.

"And it's not like we could do anything about it even if it did make sense—at least tonight." Max climbed off the bed and came up behind her to wrap her in his arms. "But I've known Luc for all of ten minutes in the greater scheme of things. So I'll look into it tomorrow to be sure he's on the up-and-up. It can wait until morning, though." Hunching, he rested his chin on her shoulder. "Come to bed."

"Well, I don't know," she said with faux reluctance. She tilted her head to rub her cheek against his. "It's really not all that late, and I'm kind of a night owl. Whatever shall we do until I get sleepy?"

"Trust me." The vibration of his deep voice made her feel as well as hear his words against the spot where her neck curved into her shoulder. Between that and the openmouthed kisses he started tormenting her with, she had to concentrate to make sense of his words when he said, "I have just the thing to help you sleep like a baby."

Feeling his erection against her butt, she smiled and said drily, "You're much too good to me."

"Oh, honey." He slid one tank top strap off her shoulder and laid a line of kisses from the curve of her neck out to the ball joint. Then he turned her in his arms and met her eyes. His burned with that light she'd temporarily despaired of seeing again, and warmth that had nothing to do with sex washed through her veins.

"You haven't seen anything yet," he said. "Because, baby? We're just getting started."

* * * * *

REQUEST YOUR FREE BOOKS!

2 FREE NOVELS
FROM THE ROMANCE COLLECTION
PLUS 2 FREE GIFTS!

YES! Please send me 2 FREE novels from the Romance Collection and my 2 FREE gifts (gifts are worth about $10). After receiving them, if I don't wish to receive any more books, I can return the shipping statement marked "cancel." If I don't cancel, I will receive 4 brand-new novels every month and be billed just $6.24 per book in the U.S. or $6.74 per book in Canada. That's a savings of at least 22% off the cover price. It's quite a bargain! Shipping and handling is just 50¢ per book in the U.S. and 75¢ per book in Canada.* I understand that accepting the 2 free books and gifts places me under no obligation to buy anything. I can always return a shipment and cancel at any time. Even if I never buy another book, the two free books and gifts are mine to keep forever.

194/394 MDN F4XY

Name   (PLEASE PRINT)

Address   Apt. #

City   State/Prov.   Zip/Postal Code

Signature (if under 18, a parent or guardian must sign)

Mail to the Harlequin® Reader Service:
IN U.S.A.: P.O. Box 1007, Buffalo, NY 14240-1867
IN CANADA: P.O. Box 609, Fort Erie, Ontario L2A 5X3

Want to try two free books from another line?
Call 1-800-873-8635 or visit www.ReaderService.com.

* Terms and prices subject to change without notice. Prices do not include applicable taxes. Sales tax applicable in N.Y. Canadian residents will be charged applicable taxes. Offer not valid in Quebec. This offer is limited to one order per household. Not valid for current subscribers to the Romance Collection or the Romance/Suspense Collection. All orders subject to credit approval. Credit or debit balances in a customer's account(s) may be offset by any other outstanding balance owed by or to the customer. Please allow 4 to 6 weeks for delivery. Offer available while quantities last.

Your Privacy—The Harlequin® Reader Service is committed to protecting your privacy. Our Privacy Policy is available online at www.ReaderService.com or upon request from the Harlequin Reader Service.

We make a portion of our mailing list available to reputable third parties that offer products we believe may interest you. If you prefer that we not exchange your name with third parties, or if you wish to clarify or modify your communication preferences, please visit us at www.ReaderService.com/consumerschoice or write to us at Harlequin Reader Service Preference Service, P.O. Box 9062, Buffalo, NY 14269. Include your complete name and address.

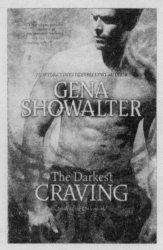

USA TODAY Bestselling Author

RaeAnne Thayne

Sometimes going back is the best way to start over

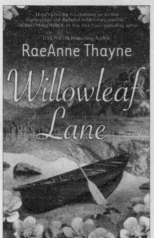

Candy shop owner Charlotte Caine knows temptation. To reboot her life, shed weight and gain perspective, she's passing up sweet enticements left and right. But willpower doesn't come so easily when hell-raiser Spencer Gregory comes back to Hope's Crossing, bringing with him memories of broken promises and teen angst. A retired pro baseball player on the mend from injury—and a damaging scandal—he's interested in his own brand of reinvention.

Holding on to past hurt is Charlotte's only protection against falling for the new and improved Spencer again. But if she takes the risk, will she find in him to be a hometown heartbreaker, or the hero she's always wanted?

Available wherever books are sold!

Be sure to connect with us at:

Harlequin.com/Newsletters

Facebook.com/HarlequinBooks

Twitter.com/HarlequinBooks

HARLEQUIN® HQN™

www.Harlequin.com

PHRT769

oct 0 7 2013

Susan Andersen

77691	THAT THING CALLED LOVE	___ $7.99 U.S.	___ $9.99 CAN.
77589	PLAYING DIRTY	___ $7.99 U.S.	___ $9.99 CAN.
77457	SKINTIGHT	___ $7.99 U.S.	___ $9.99 CAN.
77419	HOT & BOTHERED	___ $7.99 U.S.	___ $8.99 CAN.

(limited quantities available)

TOTAL AMOUNT	$ _____
POSTAGE & HANDLING	$ _____
($1.00 FOR 1 BOOK, 50¢ for each additional)	
APPLICABLE TAXES*	$ _____
TOTAL PAYABLE	$ _____

(check or money order—please do not send cash)

To order, complete this form and send it, along with a check or money order for the total above, payable to Harlequin HQN, to: **In the U.S.:** 3010 Walden Avenue, P.O. Box 9077, Buffalo, NY 14269-9077; **In Canada:** P.O. Box 636, Fort Erie, Ontario, L2A 5X3.

Name: _____
Address: _____ City: _____
State/Prov.: _____ Zip/Postal Code: _____
Account Number (if applicable): _____

075 CSAS

*New York residents remit applicable sales taxes.
*Canadian residents remit applicable GST and provincial taxes.

HARLEQUIN® HQN™
www.Harlequin.com

PHSA0613BL